Clark Hays
Kathleen McFall

The Cowboy

and

The Vampire

Rough Trails and Shallow Graves

Pumpjack Press
Portland, Oregon
Tap your creative reserves

This is the third book in *The Cowboy and the Vampire Collection*.

First Edition
First Printing, 2014
ISBN: 978-0-9838200-4-8
Library of Congress Control Number: 2014903089
Pumpjack Press
Cover design by Aaron Perkins; www.aaronperkins.com

Pumpjack Press
Portland, Oregon
www.pumpjackpress.com

Praise for *The Cowboy and the Vampire Collection*

"Riveting. Love and blood in the modern west. Meaningful conflicts, world-altering choices, existentialist underpinnings, but first and foremost a thriller." *Kirkus Reviews*

"This deliciously dark, witty novel will be a hit with fans of Anne Rice." *Booklist*

"A choice and very much recommended read, not to be missed." *Midwest Book Review*

"If you're looking for a combination of sex, blood and western romance, pour yourself a shot of the good stuff and settle in for a wickedly good read." *The Eastern Oregonian*

"A must read for fans of vampire fiction. It's one of the best in the genre that I have read this year." *A Chick Who Reads Book Blog*

"Rawhide romance with bloody fangs. While mashing up all the stereotypical plot elements of Paranormal Vampire and Contemporary Western Romance, *The Cowboy and the Vampire* delivers unremitting fun, and a damn good read." *Freshfiction*

"Sexy, dark, witty, and nothing less." *Erin Cole, author of Grave Echoes*

"A sizzling dark tale, and surprisingly funny … an enigmatic journey from Wyoming to New York to New Mexico where vampires snap at your heels and what stands between you and your enemy is your cowboy and his sheer will to survive. Oh, and his cow dog too." *For the Love of Reading Book Blog*

Also by Clark Hays and Kathleen McFall

The Cowboy and the Vampire: A Very Unusual Romance

The Cowboy and the Vampire: Blood and Whiskey

Also by Clark Hays

Red Winter

To
scientists, and other dreamers.

About the authors

Clark Hays was raised on a ranch in Montana and spent his formative years branding cows, riding horses and writing. His poetry, creative fiction and nonfiction have appeared in many journals, magazines and newspapers. Most recently, he was nominated for a Pushcart Prize for a short story appearing in Opium magazine.

Kathleen McFall was born and raised in the heart of Washington, D.C. She has worked as a journalist and has published hundreds of articles about natural resources, environmental issues, biomedical research, energy and health care. Previously, she was awarded a fellowship for fiction writing from Oregon Literary Arts.

The authors live in Portland, Oregon.

Connect with the authors
www.cowboyandvampire.com
www.facebook.com/cowboyandvampire
@cowboyvamp (Twitter)
@cowboyvampire (Instagram)

Prologue

Two months ago

"This guy Lenny is absolutely bat-shit crazy," the analyst said, pulling off his headphones.

"If you lived in, where was it again?" The second man rustled through the papers strewn across the desk, looking for the map. "If you lived in LonePine, Wyoming, don't you think you'd be a little on the unpredictable side too?"

The two Blaylock & Wolfe men sat in cubicles located on the first of three basement floors of a purposefully unremarkable building on MacArthur Boulevard in northwest Washington, D.C., an area of the city once solidly blue-collar but now stately and rich.

The faux federalist two-story brick town house, with turn-of-the-century wrought iron railings stretching from the sidewalk to the broad wooden porch, had fallen into disrepair. And now, converted into multiple offices, it was rarely visited. There was a behind-the-counter buzz-in coin dealer, a wine seller specializing in racks of dusty, overpriced bottles and a realtor whose hours coincided with the local elementary school calendar.

The primary tenant, Blaylock & Wolfe, a private security and surveillance analysis firm, subsidized the rent of the other three businesses, although the stuffy owners had no clue and instead congratulated themselves on their talent for spotting rental gold. Such misguided arrogance was a cultivated outcome for the firm because it helped keep up appearances on MacArthur Boulevard.

The firm contracted with the National Security Agency to sift through a haystack of low-value intelligence data with the hope of identifying needles of actionable information. Blaylock & Wolfe operated three subterranean floors of supercomputers powered by massive servers hidden behind two sets of secured-access doors, and it employed a small herd of analysts.

Despite what they told impressionable young ladies in the bars of Georgetown on their nights off, the two men were not spies. They were data analysts with mid-level security clearance who spent five nights a week sorting through and categorizing a staggering amount of digital recordings and low-resolution photos of low-priority targets casually recorded by a network of surveillance devices stretching across the country and around the globe.

"I don't know," his friend said. "Some small towns are nice enough. Let's take a look." He pulled up the satellite map on the big screen and typed in the coordinates. A pixelated image of a ramshackle town with a ribbon of highway cutting through it, surrounded by a sea of blue-gray sagebrush and ringed by snowcapped mountains, slowly took shape.

"Holy crap, you cannot even call that piece of shit a town," said the second man. "More like a wide spot in a poorly maintained road."

His friend stood and stretched, bending at the waist to either side, then sat again. "Right, and he doesn't even live in town. Zoom in on his bunker."

With a few clicks of the keyboard, the perspective shifted to a trailer in the center of a graveyard of old cars, washing machines and, inexplicably, what looked like a Chinese fighter plane with one wing.

"No place like home," the man said. "You can see how he might get a little lonely and stir-crazy out there. But even so, his ramblings are off the charts in the paranoia category."

"To be fair, if people knew even half the stuff we know," his colleague said, "they probably wouldn't believe us either."

"True enough," he said. "And we don't even know the good stuff. But seriously, UFOs and cattle mutilators? Really? Didn't you say this guy was some kind of weapons expert?"

He touched the screen and a photo appeared of a middle-aged man, unshaven, with intense green eyes peering gravely out from under a grease-blackened baseball cap. "Says here that before the accident, he was some kind of crazy-good engineer. He was involved in serious shit and got captured in Iraq, before the first war. He got worked over pretty good and then he went all Unabomber. That's why they keep an eye on him."

"I doubt national security will ever face much of a threat from him anymore. Seriously, listen to this," said the first man, as he unplugged his headphones and turned the volume higher.

A crackly voice came through. *"I will not debate the ethics of eating humans during breakfast."*

"That's him?" the second analyst asked.

"Yeah."

"What the hell is he going on about? Zombies? The pros and cons of post-nuclear-holocaust cannibalism?" He shook his head. "I'm gonna go have a smoke. Want to come?"

"No, I'm trying to quit. You go on."

"Call me if he starts talking about Bigfoot again."

After he left, his colleague slipped his headphones back on and opened up the channel.

He could hear a woman's voice: "...*said Lizzie was convening a meeting of the most powerful vampires to figure out what to do.*"

The man hit Pause purposefully, a memory brushing up against his thoughts. He fished out his phone and texted a contact.

You said you know someone willing to pay for info on vampires. Might have something.

Two minutes later, the phone rang.

<u>ONE</u>

"This is the darkest goddamned night I've ever seen," Tucker said. He had one hand on the wheel of his pickup truck, guiding it down the two-lane highway, and the other around Lizzie's shoulder.

She was snuggled in close, leaving the passenger seat to Rex, who panted happily, tongue lolled out and glad to be in motion.

"That's probably not the best way to characterize our wedding night," Lizzie said.

"I don't mean poetry dark, like dark night of the soul or nothing," Tucker said. He pushed his cowboy hat back and peered out of the cracked windshield up toward the heavens. "I just mean it's really hard to see. There's no moon, and even the stars seem a little farther away than usual. A little dimmer."

"I hope it's not an omen," Lizzie said. She watched the sagebrush and barbed wire fence sliding by on either side, illuminated by the ghostly glow of the headlights, as if looking for something long lost. But the empty range gave away no secrets.

"It's not an omen," Tucker said. "Pretty sure it's just a dark night."

"My cowboy," she said, looking at him tenderly. "Always so practical. So very, very practical." She traced her fingers across the edge of his jaw, tickling loose a smile.

He swatted at her fingers, but only halfheartedly, and then returned his hand to the wheel and his attention to the taillights ahead.

On a normal night, this stretch of highway would be deserted, but this was not a normal night. Nothing was normal in LonePine anymore, not since things had gone all sideways and undead.

They were driving in the middle of a convoy of five vehicles, including two heavily armored SUVs, toward Jake's Crossing, the truckstop where Tucker and Lizzie were to be married. It was also the truckstop where, not two months back, he proposed to Lizzie.

A convoy was required for any outing these days. To avoid questions, everyone in LonePine thought Lizzie was the subject of a documentary movie, which is why one guard followed her through the lens of what appeared to be a video camera. In reality, it was a .50 caliber machine pistol loaded with subsonic hardwood bullets.

As the convoy rolled closer to LonePine, Tucker picked up the radio. "Breaker, breaker, this here's the Midnight Cowboy. You got your ears on, Red Scare?"

There was a pained silence, and Tucker grinned at the thought of Rurik glaring at the beat-up pickup truck in front of him.

Rurik was in the back seat of the SUV behind Tucker and Lizzie. He was drinking champagne, worth more per bottle than most people in LonePine made in a year, mixed with platelets, brooding and letting his senses wash out over the sleeping human families scattered sporadically throughout the valley. Though he missed

Russia and his tribe dearly, he stayed in Wyoming to oversee the undead elements of Lizzie's security detail. A masterful tactician since the days of the Crusades, he was trying his best to turn recent events to his favor.

That Tucker, a pest of a human, was marrying the most powerful vampire in the world, a woman who, by simply expressing an allegiance or even a fondness for one tribe, could tip the balance of power among the nine tribes, chafed the Russian like a yoke of barbed wire.

"Come in, Red Scare," Tucker said again, interrupting his thoughts. "Rurik, I won't stop until you answer. I can do this all night."

"Seriously, he will do this all night," a voice cut in. It was Lenny, Tucker's longtime friend. "He was a trucker in another life," Lenny said.

Lenny was at the front of the line of cars, driving a rusted-out old pickup truck with a high-performance engine and an extreme suspension hidden under the battered frame. It also sported a remote-controlled 40 mm minigun bolted to the bed, concealed inside a rusty barbecue grill, and twin rocket launchers behind the headlights that could shoot a wooden fence post straight and true for two hundred yards. He was itching to try it out on a line of vampires, but in the two months since the conference, all had been quiet. Even the Reptiles, thus far, seemed willing to abide by the brokered peace.

"Dammit, Lenny, I expect my best friend to use the CB voice," Tucker said. "Come in, Red Scare?"

Rurik gnashed his teeth and fantasized about twisting the cowboy's head from his neck like a chicken destined for the pot, and the thought of him wobbling around headless on his bowlegs, crashing into things, eased his anger. He snatched up the radio.

Tucker heard a crackle of static and then a cold voice. "What do you want?"

"Like I said, it ain't no fun if you don't use a trucker voice," Tucker said. "Now come on, get in the spirit of things. It's my wedding night. Consider it your gift to me."

There was more silence. "I assumed letting you live all these months was gift enough," Rurik said at last.

"Aww, negatory, Red Scare, you're breaking up. Come again?"

"Fine," Rurik said. His voice was flat and sharp, and Tucker could almost hear the tension in his jaws making his teeth squeak together. "This is Siberian Nightmare. Ten-four, little buddy."

"It's good buddy, not little buddy," Tucker said. "I don't think you are really trying." He grinned and dropped the radio back into the stand.

Lizzie smiled at his backwoods bravado. She knew Tucker hated Rurik, and for good reason. He was shrewd and powerful and wanted Lizzie. Wanted her to exist only in the vampire world and assume her legacy. And, it seemed, wanted her in other ways too.

Convoys and armed guards and fake entourages and mysterious vampire suitors, and all for a wedding? Things can get so complicated, she thought, petting Rex idly. He trembled at the attention, and looked up at her with his big, serious eyes.

Grizzled white hair was starting to sprout up on his forehead and behind his ears, hinting at his age. He'd been Tucker's only companion for a decade until Lizzie entered the picture less than a year ago. Rex's life had gotten a lot better with her around, and he loved her for it.

A truckstop wedding was not the matrimonial event Lizzie envisioned as a child. In those fantasies, there were so many beautiful flowers — orchids and lilies and white roses — at a little chapel overlooking a river. She was wearing a long, elegant white dress and white doves were released at the crucial moment, and then, after champagne toasts around a four-tier cake with marzipan pearls, a horse-drawn carriage would whisk them away to some luxurious honeymoon destination.

As she got older, she hated herself for dreaming about that kind of wedding, ultimately dismissing the entire notion as a hopelessly patriarchal remnant of a deranged fairy tale. But a tiny piece of her still fantasized about what a day of total love and commitment would feel like, and the sweetness and chaos of planning a wedding.

Tonight, that little girl wedding fantasy was being completely, thoroughly deconstructed.

Her carriage was a mud-spattered three-quarter-ton pickup truck and the ceremony was being held at a truckstop in tiny LonePine, courtesy of a befuddled preacher roused from the hospital chapel.

Lenny's wife, June, and his niece Rose, and a few friends close enough to not be offended by the thought of a midnight wedding were the only people who would be attending.

And instead of a beautiful, glowing bride, she was pale, undead and pregnant, ballooned up to the bursting point, with swollen ankles, an almost crippling hunger for more blood — even though Tucker had only recently offered a vein up to her — and a narrow window of time before the dawn would claim her life and send her consciousness streaming back into the Meta.

At least she'd finally found the right person.

And at least her toenails looked perfect. Earlier, she labored over painting them a brilliant shade of pink, channeling her self-conscious insecurity into the polish.

She laughed out loud at the sheer ridiculousness of it all, and Tucker caught her eyes in the rearview. "What's so funny?"

"Oh, nothing," she said. "And everything. I think I'm just happy."

"You *think* you're happy?"

"I know I am," Lizzie said.

"That's a good way to be on our wedding night, right?" he asked.

She squeezed his hand, but not too hard. "I guess so. Yes. I don't know. It worries me a little. I'm not used to being happy. Even when I was, you know, not a vampire, I had a hard time making sense of happy. It seemed like a waste of time or something. I always thought only weak people were happy. I wanted to be complicated."

Tucker snorted. "You don't have to worry about that."

She punched him lightly on the arm. "Don't wreck our special night. I just mean that everything seems so perfect now. I miss your dad, of course, and I know you do too, but everything else feels right. The part of me that has to second-guess everything is starting to worry, but not because I think things will go bad, I just wonder if I can keep this up, if we can sustain this. Now that I've finally experienced it, I don't think I can ever not be this happy again."

Tucker shook his head. "So you're worried because you are happy that you are happy?"

"A little, I guess. I'm not really worried, but I finally know what happiness feels like and I don't ever want it to change. Not one little bit from this moment." She touched the swell of her stomach. "We've been through so much, and there's still all the vampire stuff to deal with, but it feels manageable. We're about to be a family, about to be married. I don't ever want to come down from this." Her eyes sparkled with happy, uncried tears.

"You're not making a whole lot of sense." He held his arm out. "Maybe you need a little more blood?"

"Don't treat me like a baby," she said. "Just because I get a little wound up, it doesn't mean you should just assume I need to eat something. Or that I need a nap or something."

Tucker pulled his hat lower. "I'm not sure what I need to say here."

She sighed. "Nothing. Just ignore me."

"You know that's impossible."

As the few lights of LonePine drew closer, she sat up straight and ran her fingers through her thick honey-blonde hair, checking it in the mirror and catching Tucker watching her appreciatively. "Don't you ever worry?" she asked.

"All the time. I just don't dwell on it because it doesn't do much good. Plus I like to think that happy is kind of the natural state for humans."

A shadow of disappointment dimmed her smile.

"And vampires," Tucker added quickly. "It just seems like we're the ones who get in our own way most of the time."

"But not tonight," she said as he wheeled into the parking lot of the truckstop. "We won't get in our own way tonight, will we?" It was almost a plea.

"Nope. Tonight, we finally get going in the right direction together," Tucker said. He parked by the big front window of the diner, the rest of the vehicles taking strategic spots around the parking lot. Guards spilled out and took up surreptitious positions, hands resting on stubby machine pistols hidden under tailored coats.

"We're here," he said. "Are you still sure you want to go through with this?"

"I'm sure if you are," she said.

"I've never been more sure of anything in my life," Tucker said. "We may not be happy every single day of our life together, but we can damn well plan on being mostly not unhappy forever."

"Deal," she said, slipping her arm through his.

TWO

Unlike most men of the cloth, Reverend Jeremiah Coles had witnessed an actual miracle.

A simple, God-fearing man, Jeremiah served as a chaplain in the Army, helping the boys in the first Iraq war and, later, in Afghanistan for a few years, before retiring to the family ranch in LonePine and volunteering at the nearby hospital. That's where he saw the miracle.

A man on the brink of death, a man with a bullet in his gut and his spine, a man he sat with into the night watching life slip away — that man arose from the nearly dead, the surely dead, and walked out of the hospital fit as a fiddle only to disappear under even more mysterious circumstances.

Obviously, a divine hand was at work.

His faith was strong before, but afterward it was unyielding.

The kind of religious certainty that accompanied such a genuine miracle filled him with peace, and a little bit of I-told-you-so reinvigorated his preaching fervor. It was a welcome relief after a lifetime of discipline and austerity that through the years had slowly started giving way to doubt. He owed his renewed conviction to Marion, wherever he was, so when a member of the film crew following Tucker's fiancée around woke him up at ten o'clock and asked if he'd officiate at their wedding, how could he say no? A generous contribution to the hospice didn't hurt either.

They failed to mention the wedding would take place at Jake's Crossing, or he might have reconsidered.

The reverend sat yawning at the counter on a red vinyl swivel stool and clinked his coffee cup down next to his marrying bible when Tucker and Lizzie walked in. Tucker's dog, Rex, who seemed a little too comfortable being inside, was close on their heels.

The reverend spun his stool around and waved. "There's the happy couple," he said, silently hoping this wouldn't take long. He couldn't remember the last time he'd been awake after eight thirty.

"Evening, Reverend," Tucker said, crossing over to shake his hand. "Pleased you could make it."

"It's an ungodly hour to get married," the reverend said. He chanced a quick look at Lizzie's belly and smiled. "Better late than never, I suppose."

"Reverend Coles," Lizzie said, kissing him lightly on the cheek. "It's sweet of you to come out so late. The pregnancy is messing with my sleep schedule."

He nodded and slapped his hat on. "I get that, but a truckstop? It seems so, I don't know, not a church."

"We didn't want to wait," Tucker said. "We got a wild hair to get this done before the baby comes along and Vernon was kind enough to rent us the whole place tonight, so we could tie the knot official-like. He even left the bar open and the kitchen fired up so we can eat and drink our fill. 'Course, we have to do our own cooking."

"I think a truckstop wedding is cool as shit," Rose said. She was sitting in a booth with her Aunt June, and slipped out to hug Lizzie and give Tucker a peck on the cheek. "So romantic. Hank Williams senior on the jukebox, an open bar *in* a bar, and after you two lovebirds go off on your honeymoon back to your trailer, we can eat pancakes and smoke cigarettes and drink bad coffee until we're sick."

"I really wish you'd quit the smoking," Lenny said, walking in from outside. He was more nervous than usual, worried the Reptiles would make an attempt on Lizzie's life with her out in the open.

"Oh, Uncle Lenny," Rose said. "What if cigarettes are really good for you? What if they actually prevent cancer and the government just wants us to stop smoking them to sell more pharmaceuticals to sick people?" She slumped back into the red vinyl booth.

Lenny paused to think that through, his conspiracy neurons firing in rapid sequence.

"Don't tease your uncle," June said.

June was tired but smiling, a near-permanent condition that not even twenty years of marriage to a paranoid weapons expert could change. She wore a new dress from the Emporium, with scratchy fold lines still visible from years of lying sequestered on the shelf, and clutched a bouquet of blue plastic flowers that would not have looked out of place on top of a grave. She held them out to Lizzie. "Sorry," she said. "I wanted to bring a nice bouquet, but Betty Jean's was closed and I know better than to disturb her after Bunco night. Consider these something borrowed *and* something blue."

"They're so lovely," Lizzie said, hugging June. "Thank you."

"If you plan on throwing those at any point, don't aim them in my direction," Rose said, lighting a cigarette.

"I really appreciate you all coming out," Tucker said. "Let's get this show on the road so we can all go back to bed."

"That's the best idea I've heard all night," Reverend Coles said, motioning for Lizzie and Tucker to join him by the jukebox. He bent down and unplugged it in the middle of a George Strait song.

The guards took their places around the room, acting nonchalant but keeping their hands close to their guns, one of them pretending to film the ceremony. Rurik pulled up a folding chair and sat near the couple, watching Lizzie closely through half-slitted eyes.

Tucker made a mental note to stick the wooden letter opener he now carried on a chain around his neck into the vampire's black heart if he objected.

"I think we know why we're gathered here tonight," Reverend Coles said. "So I'm gonna skip the preamble and get right to the good stuff."

Tucker took Lizzie's hand and looked deep into her eyes, a river of emotions swirling between them. His heart was pounding at the thought of finally marrying this woman, this love of his life. Actually, he realized, his heart was thudding along harder than it should, out of control. And his knees felt weak. This is what love feels like, he thought. Even his vision was a little blurry and he felt sick to his stomach. Like a goddamned schoolboy, he thought.

"Do you, Tucker, take Lizzie to be your lawfully wedded wife from this late hour until forever?" Reverend Coles asked. "Will you love, honor, comfort and cherish her from this day — or, actually, this night — forward, forsaking all others, keeping only unto her for as long as you both shall live?"

"Lizzie, I don't, I can't..." Tucker stammered.

She looked up at him, startled, and he was staring at her, a blank, puzzled look on his face.

Her heart missed a beat, hearing the opposite of what she expected, then watched, horrified as Tucker slowly sank to one knee, reaching for the pistol under his jacket, only to topple face-first to the floor. She stifled a gasp and reached down to him, hearing more thuds as bodies fell: Lenny, then the reverend, June and Rose, the human guards, and then Rex, who, with a confused *woof*, fell flat in midleap as he tried to get closer to Lizzie to protect her.

Every human in the room slumped and fell like stalks of wheat in front of a scythe. She could feel it in her body now too. Something poisonous and chemical that was having only a small effect on the vampires.

Rurik was up and reaching out for her, shouting. "Get the Queen to safety. We are under attack!"

Two of the undead guards yanked machine pistols out of shoulder holsters only to stagger under a hail of wooden arrows and dissolve into dust.

She saw Rurik dodge a rain of arrows that thudded into the wall, then an explosion split the room and he was gone from her view as the force of the fireball slammed her into the jukebox. Groggy and stunned, she struggled to her feet, clenched her fists, and looked for someone to kill. She could feel humans moving close now, appearing suddenly in the realm of her senses.

"You move, he dies," a man said, stepping in from the night through the smoking edge of the wall. He was wearing a gas mask and body armor, and had a cross-bow pistol aimed at her with one hand and a machine pistol in the other aimed at Tucker's head.

"How did you get past the guards?" she asked.

"We were in the walk-in cooler. For a long time, I might add. Lined it with reflective foil to keep our hot little blood flow off your little internal radar."

More men, eight in all, materialized out of the smoke and rubble, armed and pointing crossbows in her direction and nervously watching for the undead. Another vampire guard struggled up out of the rubble of the collapsed wall, roaring, and half a dozen crossbow bolts pierced him. With an oath, he dissolved to ash in a flash of green smoke.

"The good news is, the arrows work. The bad news is, I don't think I will ever get used that," the leader said. He kept his gun aimed at Tucker and tossed an oddly shaped pair of handcuffs in her direction. They landed near her feet.

"Strip," he said, the gas mask distorting his words, "and put those on."

"No," she said.

"I will ask precisely one more time. If you don't do exactly as I say, he dies, then you die, and I'll shoot an arrow into your belly first, then all the rest of them die." He gestured toward Lenny, Rose and June slumped over in the booth, Rose's hair fanned out over the ashtray.

Ears ringing, she let her senses wash out over the men and the fallen bodies, felt heartbeats erratic and faint in her friends and in Tucker. Felt the adrenaline in her assailants driving their hearts faster. They were humans. All of them. She couldn't sense Rurik, and feared the worst.

"What have you done to them?"

"Fentanyl. The same stuff they used in Russia at that theater a while back. It's likely most of them will make it, if you do what I ask. Waste any more time, or if any vampire so much as casts a shadow in this room, and everyone dies."

She slipped out of her dress with a shrug and stood defiantly in front of them, her swelling breasts barely contained in the lacy blue bra and her stomach taut as a drum. "Is this is how you get your jollies, staring at pregnant women?"

"You're a pregnant vampire. Not a woman. And no. I get my jollies by completing my mission. Now put the cuffs on."

She kneeled and picked them up, snapping them in place hesitantly and then testing them surreptitiously, but to no avail.

"Don't bother. These are perfect for your species. Braided titanium strands. We tested them under extreme circumstances." He motioned with the crossbow. "Let's go, outside now."

"What is this about?" she asked, stepping through the shattered door into the darkness, shivering out of habit at the cool night air on her exposed skin.

"Don't know, don't care," he said, pulling off his gas mask. "We were paid to acquire you with minimal fuss and we've done that."

He dropped her dress on the cement of the parking lot and pulled a small pouch from his gear belt and then scattered ashes in and around the dress. "I understand your type has a nasty habit of combusting in sunlight. By the time the effects of the gas wear off, it will be dawn and they'll wake up to your cremains."

Her heart sank at the devastation she knew Tucker would feel, seeing her dress and the ashes. She studied his face, burning the details into her mind.

He gestured toward a nondescript tractor trailer in the parking lot, the back open, and at the top of the ramp she could see benches, military gear and a cramped modular metal cell at the very front. In the distance, she could hear sirens and knew Bart Braver would arrive in seconds.

"If you stall, we kill the cops and firefighters too."

She hesitated.

"Look at it this way," he said, "if they wanted you dead, you'd already be dead. Get in."

She walked up the steps and squatted down in the cell and he locked the door behind her, the men taking up positions on their seats as the engine roared to life and the truck pulled out onto the highway.

The leader pulled a radio from his tactical vest. "Package secured. Rendezvous at the airfield."

THREE

Tucker opened his eyes to the gray light of dawn, the first fingers of sunshine reaching lazily over the mountain-splintered horizon. His thoughts scattered like autumn straw in the wind and nothing made sense. Cold, fresh air blew across his face and he heard the noisy chatter of magpies and crows, so he knew he was outside, but the ground was soft. A mattress. Were they camping?

He felt something at his hand and looked down to see Rex staring at him worriedly, and licking softly, deliberately at Tucker's fingers.

What he meant to say was what the hell is going on, but the words were lost as he felt a wave of nausea wash through him, and vomited painfully. Rex saw it coming and deftly moved to the side. "Sorry, boy," Tucker said. "I don't know what's wrong with me, but we'll get that cleaned up."

He tried to sit up, but there was a belt across his chest and he stared at it stupidly, only slowly realizing he was on a gurney at the back of an ambulance and looking out across a parking lot cluttered with more ambulances and emergency workers walking through the smoking wreckage of Jake's Crossing. And then it all came rushing back — Lizzie, the wedding ceremony, the room spinning, and a shadowy movement from the corner of his eyes before it went dark.

Darkness was not a problem now, with the dawn breaking. Bringing the sun. The unforgiving and terminal sun. "Jesus Christ, Lizzie," he said with a curse, fumbling the strap open with clumsy fingers and staggering off the gurney. His knees buckled and he toppled out of the ambulance, sprawling onto the pavement.

"Take it easy, Tucker," Bart Braver said, sprinting over from his squad car to help Tucker stand unsteadily. "There's been a bad accident. A gas leak. The truckstop blew up. I have to tell you this and it's going to be hard to hear. There were casualties. That Russian fellow, Lizzie's friend, he's dead, Tucker." He jerked his thumb toward a black plastic body bag. "I'm real sorry."

"Put him in the morgue," Tucker said, knowing Rurik would be fine as long as his body was kept out of the deadly rays. "We've got to get Lizzie out of the sun," he said, shrugging Bart's hand off him.

"Tucker, wait."

"No, goddammit, get Lizzie out of the sun. Get her body out of the sun."

Bart caught him hard by the upper arm and stopped him. "Tucker. We can't find Lizzie. She's not here."

"No," Tucker shouted, staggering off toward the smoking wreckage of the building. "It can't be too late."

Rex was running ahead and found her dress first, twisted up with ash spilling out of the cloth folds, the gritty particles swirled up by the early morning breeze. He sniffed at it curiously while Tucker sank to his knees in disbelief and pulled the fabric close to his heart.

<u>FOUR</u>

Tucker sat on the deck of the double-wide in Dad's old rocking chair with his head in his hands and a half-empty bottle of whiskey at his feet. Every few minutes, he seized the bottle by the neck and took a deep pull, then swiped away at the stubborn tears gathering at the corners of his eyes and cursed.

Rex sat near his boots, trembling expectantly each time Tucker reached for the bottle, mistaking the motion as intended for him. Tucker looked with bleary eyes out across the sagebrush and to the mountains in the distance, gleaming with snow like alabaster cathedral spires.

"I don't know what I'm going to do, boy," he said, voice cracking.

It was cold, but even though he was in his shirt-sleeves, he didn't feel it.

"It's my own goddamned fault," he muttered. "Thinking we could ever be happy. Happiness is all bullshit. She was fucking right to be worried."

He punched the post next to him and felt the skin split between his knuckles, but no pain. "That's gonna hurt tomorrow," he said, holding his hand up and watching in drunken fascination as the blood trickled down the back of it and onto his wrist. "Shame to waste all this," he said, thinking of Lizzie and their nightly ritual, and then he collapsed in on himself in torment, letting rage wash through him, savoring it.

He leapt to his feet, accidentally stepping on Rex in the process, and flung the bottle out beyond the sagebrush line.

Rex *yipped* in fear and pain, jumping up, and Tucker stumbled down to him. "Shhh, wait. I'm sorry, boy. I'm so sorry." He hugged Rex too hard but Rex let him, licking at his face, at the tears falling now in earnest.

"Come on," Tucker said. "Let's get that bottle back. It ain't empty."

Rex stayed behind on the deck, head cocked to the side and one ear up, as Tucker wobbled down the steps, missed the last one, and fell sideways into the gravel. He thought about getting up but then just rolled over onto his belly and let out a sigh.

He was still there thirty minutes later when a truck pulled up. Recognizing Lenny, Rex barked his friendly bark. Lenny parked and walked over to his fallen friend.

"Tucker, it's me," Lenny said. "You, uh, comfortable down there in the dirt or do you maybe want to go inside?"

"Inside might be okay," Tucker mumbled.

Lenny caught him by the crook of his arm and helped him up.

"How're June and Rose?" Tucker asked.

"They're going to be all right," Lenny said. "Actually, everyone is going to be fine. There was an awful lot of puking, so much puking, but no lasting damage."

Tucker only made it a few steps before he pushed Lenny's arms away and hunched over, throwing up. "Pretty sure that's just the whiskey," he said when he finished, wiping his mouth with his sleeve.

Lenny nodded and guided him, unsteady, toward the trailer. "I'm real sorry about Lizzie," he said.

"It don't make no sense at all," Tucker said.

Lenny helped him up the steps and inside the trailer. "Nothing about this whole goddamn thing has made sense from day one. I'm gonna make you some coffee," Lenny said.

Tucker fell into the recliner and Rex plopped down beside him.

As the coffee percolated, Lenny rummaged in the fridge and pulled out some food. "I'm going to make a little something, just in case you want to soak up some of the alcohol in your bloodstream."

He fried two eggs and then used the same pan to sizzle three slices of bologna on both sides, toasted and buttered two slices of store-bought bread, and slid the plate on the coffee table in front of Tucker, who took it in his lap and picked silently at the food.

"Ain't you gonna at least try it?" Lenny asked.

"Sure, if you want," Tucker said. "But don't really see the point. In much of anything."

"You'll get through this," Lenny said. "It won't be easy, nor quick. Just put one boot in front of the other until you get some place closer to vengeance."

"That sounds like a mighty fine and sensible idea," Tucker said.

"Then sober up and start thinking it through," Lenny said, topping off Tucker's coffee. "I need to get back and check on June and Rose. I'll look in again on you directly."

After Lenny left, Tucker put the food down on the floor for Rex, who barked excitedly at his good fortune, and then Tucker lay flat down on the floor to watch Rex eat. Soon, an uneasy sleep came, filled with vivid, insane dreams of Lizzie dissolving into atoms and whirling away in a glowing mushroom cloud. Even in his dream, a terrible grief came over him like a wet velvet curtain.

When he woke, he felt twice as sad but half as cloudy. He put on his jacket, nuzzled Rex's ears, and they drove to LonePine. The highway was deserted, and after a few miles of driving the familiar macadam, without even checking with his brain first, his hands turned the truck onto the dirt road leading to the town cemetery.

Spring was returning and bringing with it flashes of green along the rivers and creeks and in the grasslands lining the narrow road. It was that perfect time in the afternoon when the sunlight was long and golden and rich, making every tree, every blade of grass and every tumbleweed caught up in the barbed wire fences seem otherworldly and begging for attention.

He eased his truck over the rattling cattle guard and onto the narrow gravel road winding between the old plots, heading slowly toward the back right corner past rows of gravestones, most with faded plastic flowers set around them.

Nothing looks as final as a fresh grave, he thought, parking in front of a pair of headstones. One was weathered and faded, the sparse grass in front of it well established, and the other only recently chiseled, the earth still showing the shovel marks.

"Jesus, this is weird," he said to the tombstones of his parents. "I haven't seen y'all together in a long time." He slumped against the hood of his truck and watched Rex nose around the grave and then stretch out with a sigh next to the flowers.

He looked out over the dusty hills stretching up and away from LonePine. It was perfectly quiet, not even a car on the highway. Two sleek turkey vultures circled high above, so far away as to be just dark crescents, riding the thermals and watching the grassland below for any sign of movement that might indicate a free meal. He watched them circle farther and farther down the valley, losing them in the swell of thunderclouds — big, ragged and cumulous — forming above the mountains.

"Looks like rain," he said, realizing how ridiculous it sounded.

"I'm real sorry about the way things turned out," he said at last. "But mostly I'm sorry that I'm stuck here by myself while y'all are together up there in the Meta with Lizzie."

"That's all I've got to say." He clenched his jaw. "Come on, boy, let's go to town."

Rex hopped in the truck and whined softly, as if saying good-bye, and then stared stonily ahead as Tucker made his way to the sheriff's office.

Deputy Braver was sitting at his desk drinking vending-machine coffee from a paper cup with five playing cards printed at random on the side. Coffee cup poker was usually a big hit at the station, but not after an explosion.

He stood at the sight of Tucker and hurried across the room to meet him. "Tucker, still no word on Lizzie. We got everyone looking for her. I'm guessing she must have hit her head in the explosion and wandered off."

Tucker nodded, knowing better. "Thanks Bart, I appreciate the effort."

"Y'all weren't, you know, having trouble, were you?" Bart asked.

Tucker thought about the months of intrigues with vampire tribes, the attempts on her life, and them both wrestling with her need for human blood. "Nah, no troubles. Perfect bliss."

"Real sorry about your friend, the Russian."

"He's not my friend," Tucker said, checking his watch. "By the way, where is he?"

Bart jerked his thumb to indicate the back room. "In a body bag in the back. We're trying to find next of kin."

"Try Satan," Tucker muttered.

"What's that?"

"Nothing," Tucker said. "What time does the sun go down these days?"

"I don't know," Bart said. "Any minute now I hope. It's been a long day."

"Bart, do you remember that time I told you Lizzie was a vampire?"

Bart held his hands up. "I was on the tail end of a triple shift and I hadn't eaten much. I saw some weird stuff that night, stuff that couldn't happen, stuff that didn't happen."

"There really ain't no easy way to come at this," Tucker said.

There was a loud crash in the back and Bart stood. "Hold on," he said.

The door banged open and Rurik, his clothes hanging in tatters yet still somehow appearing regal, strode in. "Where is she?"

Bart, his hand dropping to his pistol and mouth hanging open, stammered. "Y-you were dead."

"You cleverly state the obvious," Rurik said, looking past him to Tucker. "Where is Lizzie?"

"She's dead," Tucker whispered. "Gone."

Rurik scowled and swiped at the door frame, which exploded in splinters under his fist. "Then we are ruined. We are all ruined."

FIVE

At the familiar first notes of "Send in the Clowns," Elita looked curiously into the fear-widened eyes of the severed head she was holding aloft by a hank of greasy hair. Just seconds before, she separated it from a body now walking jerkily, pilotless, toward the wall, while fountaining black blood up to the ceiling.

Her phone was ringing and the tone meant Tucker was calling.

She dropped the head, losing interest before it even reached the floor and combusted into smoky dust.

There were three other vampires in the room, two males and one female; just minutes before there had been four. They were Reptiles, her own kind, unwilling to come into the fold and accept the hesitantly offered peace with the Royals. She was encouraging them to take the long view, a message not well received by the current audience of Reptile leaders. But, if anything, Elita could be relentlessly persuasive, which explained why her slender arms were covered with sticky blood, chunky gore and vampire ash up to her elbows.

The recalcitrant vampires, the survivors, looked at one another worriedly as the body lurched into the wall, fell backward and burst into foul green flames that consumed it quickly, leaving faint scorch marks on the carpet. He had been the toughest among them and she popped his off head like a cork from a bottle of cheap champagne. They stared at her with a mixture of fear, hatred and respect.

She held up a bloody finger. "Let's hit pause," she said. "Can we agree on that?"

Tucker rarely called her, and the first night of his honeymoon with Lizzie seemed an odd time to change habits. She slipped her phone out of the back pocket of her straight-leg jeans that fit like a coat of blue paint.

"How's the honeymoon, cowboy? Another eight-second ride?" she purred, then stopped, eyes narrowing and face darkening into unholy rage. "What happened?" She listened, stress tightening her muscles. "When?"

One of the vampires — a thin, pale man — moved nervously, and she covered the mouthpiece and glared at him. "If you interrupt me, I will turn you into pulled pork and keep the pieces alive in a bucket for a decade," she hissed. "This conversation is very important to me, even more important than the point I was making to Reginald."

She returned her attention to Tucker. "Yes, yes, I can hear the anguish in your voice and I understand that humans are prone to hysterics about such things, but I don't think…"

The chastened vampire turned to his compatriots. "I don't care who she is," he whispered, "we can take her," he snarled. "We have the numbers."

He drew a large knife — a curved Gurkha blade designed to put fearsome chopping power into the front edge — and, emboldened, his male friend produced a stainless steel automatic from his shoulder holster. It was a big, shiny .50 caliber, and they grinned.

"I don't know about this," the girl said, shrinking back to the wall.

"Hang up and die, bitch," the knife wielder said. "We'll never make peace with the Royals."

Elita sighed. "Tucker, let me interrupt your little pity party. Lizzie isn't dead. At least I don't think she is. But I'm in the middle of something and I have to put you on speaker." She stroked the screen and then tossed the phone onto the kitchen table. "Can you hear me?"

"Yeah, what's going on?" Tucker asked, his voice sounding tired and lost.

"I'm catching up with some old friends," Elita said.

The vampire with the knife lunged toward her, swinging the boomerang-shaped blade at her in a blur of ancient steel, but Elita was faster. She leapt forward and drove the heel of her hand into his elbow and then grabbed his wrist with her other hand and pulled down hard like he was a slot machine, snapping his arm. She plucked the knife from his now unresponsive hand and heaved it at the gunman, who was drawing a bead on her head. The blade sank deep between his eyes and he fell to his knees, dropping the big gun unfired.

"Like I said, Lizzie's not dead," Elita said to Tucker. "Not yet anyway."

There was a moment of silence as Tucker tried to process the information. "Careful with your trickery, woman," he said.

She caught the knife man by the wrist and twisted savagely, smiling as bones splintered and rubbed together and he howled. "No trickery, Tex," she said to the phone. "If she is dead, I just lost the North American territory, and all my arm twisting," she paused to laugh at her own pun, "and my cajoling have been for naught."

She thrust her hand into the gaping, open mouth of her assailant, driving her rigid fingers like a spike past his teeth and out the back of his head. His eyes crossed in fear and pain and she curved her fingers up to rip off the top half of his skull like pulling the lid from a can of cat food. He stooped to one knee as if praying, then burst into flames and dissolved away.

"Dammit," Tucker shouted through the phone. "Stop whatever you are doing and tell me what you know."

"During the repose, after I died, I mean, I sensed her in the Meta," Elita said. "Sort of. I mean, I didn't *not* sense her, and I would have."

"So she's alive?" Tucker asked.

"As alive as a vampire can be," Elita said.

"Where the hell is she, then?" Tucker asked.

"I don't know."

"A little more help here, Elita?" he said.

"Poor Tucker," she said. "Worst wedding night ever. Where's Rurik?"

"Recuperating," Tucker said. "They damn near got him last night too. His people flew in some fresh blood in the form of Russian hookers or something."

"He was always more of a lover than a fighter," Elita said. "Ask him to confirm my hunch. He knows the Meta well. Or go there yourself. I have a few loose ends to tie up here," she said, glaring at the two vampires still alive, the girl cowering against the wall and the wounded male twitching on the floor and trying to pull the knife from his head. "I will return to LonePine, against my better judgment, tomorrow. I can already taste the stupidity."

"Now ain't the time for that," Tucker started to say. "We need to…"

She disconnected the phone with a swipe of her finger, leaving a smear of brain on the screen, and then turned to the vampires.

"Shall we continue down this path, or should we talk about the future?" Elita asked. "Maybe drink a few bottles of wine, let choppy there heal up a little and see how many orgasms we can inflict upon each other before the dawn."

"That sounds a lot better than dying," the female said.

"You're smart. And pretty," Elita said. "You'll come first. Call it my own special little peace treaty."

SIX

Lizzie dreamed she was floating in a warm ocean, far from shore, buoyed gently by the salt water. She gave herself over to the rhythmic push and pull, a pulsing, symphonic silence that somehow also roared. And then there he was, as he had been since the day she first saw him, and probably even before that.

They were on the beach and Tucker wrapped his arms around her tightly. She relaxed into the swaying passion and the sweetness of his body moving with hers, back and forth in soft, silent darkness. Filled with joy and near a climax, she called out his name and with the sound, woke from her dream into a nightmare.

She was dizzy and disoriented, as if drugged. She tried to move, but her arms were bound tightly against her body and she was wrapped like a mummy or a swaddled newborn. A wave of panic began to build. She forced it back and tried to think logically, to gather data, but her mind felt sluggish, and frighteningly unfamiliar.

It was dark. Maybe she was inside a too-small sleeping bag, she thought. Maybe they were camping and Tucker was off gathering wood. Yes, that was plausible, she thought. Or maybe they simply decided to make love under the stars, or in the barn, and he'd wrapped her up tight against the cold.

"Tucker?" she called out.

A light came on overhead and Lizzie shut her eyes against it, turning her head away from the glare.

"Elizabeth," a voice said. "You are safe. We are here to help you."

"Where am I?" Lizzie asked. Her memories swirled around a truckstop, cowboys and vampires, toy soldiers and a jukebox.

"I am going to approach your bed, Elizabeth. My name is Dr. Louisa Burkett. You are safe. And we are here to help you."

"Where am I?" Lizzie asked again in a whisper, trying to steady her voice. Betray no emotion, she thought. Don't let them know you are scared and uncertain, give nothing away. Figure out which tribe this is first and how to defuse this situation.

She tried again to move her arms. The bindings held tight. She struggled to move her legs, to sit up. She pulled both ankles hard, but they were chained together and to the bed. She was weak and unable to free herself. Lizzie breathed in hard and felt the painful and familiar deep pull of hunger from inside. They were starving her. How long had she been without blood?

A woman in a white coat stood at the bottom of the bed. Another white coat appeared next to her. A man. Both of them exuded the scent of moral ambivalence.

"You are safe now, Elizabeth," the woman said. "I will say it as often as you need to hear it. You are safe. Your mother brought you here a week ago. You're safe now."

The words hit like a fist of granite. "My mother is dead," Lizzie said.

"Your mother is alive," the woman said, smiling slightly, though it did not spill over into her words.

"You are a fool," Lizzie said. "I don't know what your game is, but the other members of the Council will kill you, or I will. Either way, you're going to die for this."

The bright light was shining directly in her eyes, like an interrogation in a bad cop movie, so it was hard to see beyond a few feet. Where was she? Why couldn't she break free?

A hospital, maybe. No, too quiet, she thought. And there weren't enough people nearby. Just a few distant blips of life, too faint to categorize. She smelled sea air, and fish. The room was large, at least what she could see of it, and it had an old warehouse feel with beams and heating ducts exposed.

Her bed was in the center of a room. A bag of clear fluid hung next to her on a stainless steel pole, dripping silently into her veins.

A knot of dread tied itself into a tight ball in the pit of her stomach.

"Ms. Vaughan. Elizabeth. May I call you Elizabeth?" the woman asked without waiting for an answer. "You are safe now, Elizabeth. You are in a private hospital. Your mother brought you here."

"I told you, my mother is dead," Lizzie said. A flash of memories swarmed through her thoughts. A church and the catacombs. A jolly fat man with fangs. Her father kneeling between her thighs with a bloody mouth. She shivered involuntarily.

"Your mother is not dead, far from it," said the woman claiming to be a doctor. "And she is very worried about you."

The man in the white coat walked to the right side of the bed and checked the drip chamber on the IV line. He adjusted the clamp, flicked it twice, crisply, and watched as the drip from the plastic bag intensified. Satisfied, he returned to the foot of the bed and tapped notes into a laptop.

"That's Mark," the doctor said.

"Hello," the man said without looking up.

"Mark is one of the people who will care for you while you are here," she said. "You'll meet Helmi soon, she is your nurse. You need rest and restoration. You will receive that here. The road to mental health starts with good physical health."

"Release me now and I may be inclined toward leniency," Lizzie said, relying on an old script of imperial disdain she did not feel. "I need blood; my child needs blood to survive."

The woman nodded and Mark moved to Lizzie's side. He had shaggy, collar-length hair and an inflamed pimple in the middle of his forehead like a tiny, festering third eye. He pulled out a plastic bag of blood from a compact aluminum refrigerator beside the bed, hung it on the pole, and then inserted the needle into the tube already draining into Lizzie's vein. He flicked it, twice, with that same confident motion.

Lizzie watched as the blood began to flow. When it hit her veins, the baby moved. Relief washed through her and her strength returned but only slightly, not enough to break the ties binding her body or the leg chains.

"Let me go and you both live," she repeated.

"Please try to be calm," the doctor said. "You will be here as long as it takes to get well. Your mother feared you would harm yourself, and possibly others, perhaps even her."

"You lie," Lizzie said. "I would never hurt my mother. Never." She turned her head slightly. "I must be protected from the dawn. The sunlight will kill me. It will kill my baby."

"Elizabeth," the woman said in a gentle voice. "Your baby is fine. You are not a vampire. There is no such thing. We will help you come back to reality. It may take some time, but we are here for you. You are safe."

Her heels clicked with sharp strikes as she walked to the far wall and pulled the drapes open with a theatrical flourish. A wash of golden sunlight flooded the room. Lizzie tensed, stifling a scream, waiting for the deadly rays to trigger a terminal combustion.

Nothing happened.

"It's a beautiful day," the doctor said.

"I don't understand," Lizzie said, squinting her eyes against the harsh outside light and then looking at the blood drip.

"First, that's not real blood," the doctor said, returning to the foot of the bed. "It's colored water with nutrients and a sedative. We know you truly believe you are a vampire. This is a temporary placebo treatment until you recognize you don't need blood at all."

"I am a vampire. And I love a cowboy," Lizzie said. "Are you going to tell me that cowboys aren't real either?"

"Of course they are real," the doctor said. "Elizabeth, where were you born?"

"New York."

"Very good," the doctor said. "Do you remember what you did there?"

I think I was a journalist, Lizzie thought, but she kept that to herself. "I don't know why you are asking me all these questions, but I am not buying any of it," she said. "Untie me. Tell why you have me here."

She felt the baby kick again, weak but present, and she had a fleeting notion she could understand the taps, as if her child was typing out Morse code inside her.

"Elizabeth, can you tell me your last memory before you awoke in this room?"

She struggled to make sense of her memories. Tucker, in his cowboy hat. A truckstop. Pancakes. Rex was there. And there were vampires. Her mind felt clunky, as if she had borrowed it from someone else, her thoughts and memories and convictions awkward and unfamiliar.

"You have lost nearly five years of your life," the doctor said. "Your mind has supplanted a narrative in your memory for those years to, well, block out the pain of what really happened to you."

"What really happened to me?" Lizzie asked, both unwilling to believe in, and afraid of, whatever this woman might say.

"That's enough for now," the doctor said. "Please get some rest and we'll talk again tomorrow. Mark will stay with you."

The woman leaned over the bed and smiled tightly. Lizzie could finally see her face clearly. She was an attractive woman — in the suburbs of forty with full lips, no makeup and a careless haircut that made no attempt to conceal the strands of gray.

Oddly, she looked a little bit like Lizzie herself, only older. We could be sisters, Lizzie thought. She watched the doctor pull the blinds on the sunshine and then leave the room.

Mark smiled weakly in her direction and sat in a chair by the door. "I'll be right here if you need anything," he said, and then checked his cell phone before he began paging through an inch-thick graphic novel, glancing occasionally over at Lizzie.

She felt darkness slipping through her mind. As Lizzie struggled to keep her eyes open, she was ashamed by the fleeting pinpricks of relief, bordering on hope, which pierced her heart. Was it really all a dream? Could she go back to the life before?

<u>SEVEN</u>

For the first time maybe in his entire adult life, Tucker was not sure what to do next. And cowboys are always supposed to know what to do. Always.

He was sitting on the edge of their bed, clutching the two discarded dresses Lizzie decided were too tight for the wedding. He'd been there for three hours, trying his best to sort things out. He was caught precisely between immobilizing despair and a barely contained hopefulness; it was a push. Squeezed between those two extremes, he sat paralyzed by indecisiveness.

Rex alternated between pacing a tight circle at the foot of the bed and curling up at Tucker's boots. He was up now, wagging his stumpy tail and hoping for an invitation to jump up on the bed. He *woofed* softly once, and then again, but Tucker didn't stir, so Rex sat on his haunches and whined softly, uneasily. He was not used to seeing his man like this.

Don't drink too much whiskey, Tucker thought, running through the rules as he knew them. Be kind to your horse. Use your guns, or your fists, only as a last resort. Nothing beats broke-in boots. When push comes to shove, side with the little guy. Be careful about choosing, but once you choose, be loyal.

Rex *woofed* again.

"Of course," Tucker said. "And always be good to your dog. Can't forget that one, can we?" He patted the side of the bed and Rex bounded up, licking Tucker's hand as if it were covered in kibble gravy until Tucker finally grimaced and pulled away.

"Take it easy, let me think." Rex shimmied to the bottom of the bed and lay down quietly, wide eyes wondering, happy to be back in Tucker's good graces, but anxious.

Tucker's mind turned back to what Elita said about the Meta.

Though not everyone would agree, he'd done pretty well living his life in an uncomplicated cowboy way. But none of what he'd learned in the past, from Dad or anyone else, offered much guidance for how a cowboy in love with a vampire should act.

He'd done a lot of bad things since he met Lizzie, and not all of them were justified. Protecting her in this new world, this ancient world newly revealed, meant standing by and letting long-held moral considerations fall into the bar ditch. He'd killed bad people in cold blood, spilled their even colder blood. Innocents had been hurt or killed. Virote. Rose. Even Dad. Involuntarily, Tucker breathed in sharply and grimaced.

"And Lizzie," he said aloud. "She started out an innocent in all this too."

Rex looked up at him, surprised to hear her name, and then surprised by something else, something outside. He barked a harsh warning.

Blue heelers were bred to herd cattle, instinctively able to nip around their hooves, tripping and tricking and cajoling a group of cows to remain in a herd, bringing order to chaos across long distances. Lately, this canine instinct had been rewired and rechanneled into a finely tuned vampire sensor. When the undead were afoot, Rex was usually the first to know and sound an alarm.

"The damn Russian," Tucker said. "Come on, boy. And stay close, I'm gonna need you."

Rex jumped down from the bed and trotted right next to Tucker's boot heels, on high alert.

Tucker opened the bedroom door into the living room area of the double-wide trailer.

Jenkins was in the kitchen. "Mr. Tucker, sir," he said. "May I offer you something, some tea perhaps?"

Tucker looked at the old butler, a man who had served the best of the worst of the vampire world. "No thanks, but a shot of whiskey would be all right."

Jenkins, as if reading his mind, was already reaching for a bottle, and poured two fingers of the amber liquid into a tumbler.

"No reason to be stingy," Tucker said.

Jenkins doubled the pour. "Care for ice?"

"No sense watering it down."

He sat in the recliner, Rex sitting next to his boots with a protective, watchful demeanor. Jenkins stood, as he always did, stoically and calmly.

Tucker took a sip of the whiskey and then changed course, downing it in one long gulp. He clinked the empty glass down quietly and not, as Jenkins expected, with a theatrical slam.

"He's out there, ain't he?" Tucker said.

Jenkins nodded.

"I guess I have to go through him to get to her, don't I?" Tucker asked.

"That is an option," Jenkins said. "If you want to find out for sure."

"I do," Tucker said. "It'll kill me if it's not what I want to hear."

"Elita is not one to create false hope, I wouldn't think," Jenkins said.

"That's for sure," Tucker said. "She left California already. Said she'd be here tomorrow night."

"I trust her mission to corral the Reptilian Diaspora into submission for the establishment of their permanent homeland went well," Jenkins said.

Tucker shrugged and motioned for him to top off the whiskey. "I guess so. Don't really care anymore."

Jenkins noted the deep fatigue in Tucker's voice and wondered how long he would be able to keep up this pace.

"If Miss Elita said her experience of Lizzie is distorted, perhaps someone is going to great lengths to make you think she is dead," Jenkins said.

"That's what I'm thinking," Tucker said. "And apparently our favorite vampires can't make sense of the Meta, not like Lizzie."

"If I may be frank..." Jenkins said, preparing to ask a question. When Tucker nodded, he continued. "What makes you think you can make sense of it? What makes you think you can ascertain if she lives?"

Tucker, who was always wary of hopefulness, shrugged. "Because it's all I've got, Jenkins. I'm hoping what we share is strong enough to let me navigate whatever kind of crazy afterworld it is she lives in. I know it sounds stupid, and I don't even know if the goddamn place is real, but I'm out of options."

Jenkins noticed his own hands were shaking and poured himself a shot without thinking. "If there's anyone she will respond to in the Meta, it's you. I think, at the very least, you will find an answer."

"A lot of bad things have happened this past year, ever since I fell in with Lizzie," Tucker said.

Jenkins nodded.

"I guess I can assume there's gonna just be more of the same now pretty much until the end of my days."

"That is likely an accurate prediction," Jenkins said.

Tucker slumped back in the chair and closed his eyes, trying to work up the nerve. Jenkins watched him quietly.

When Tucker opened his eyes again, they glittered with fierce determination. "Go on and bring him in," he said quietly.

"No second thoughts?" Jenkins asked.

"Jesus, I don't have nothing but second thoughts, but I ain't gonna let her down, no matter what," Tucker said. "I can't. I just can't. There's nothing else anymore. It's just Lizzie all the way down."

Jenkins knew there was little he could offer Tucker now, except perhaps a bit of calm and order in the face of the now-permanent storm of his life.

"I will escort Mr. Rurik into the trailer," he said.

Tucker looked down at Rex, and then scratched him behind the ears.

"Jenkins, I've got one favor to ask you, just in case things don't turn out the way we hope," Tucker said.

Jenkins nodded. "Of course."

"Don't spoil him, though," Tucker said, patting Rex brusquely. "He's a cow dog, not a lap dog, no matter how he might try to con you."

EIGHT

He hadn't realized, until now, just how tall the damn Russian vampire was. There was only about eight inches between the crown of his head and the drywall ceiling of the double-wide. Christ, Tucker thought, do they get taller at night or something? It was a bit of a forced perspective, however, from his vantage slouched down in the recliner.

Rurik's face was backlit by the fake chandelier that came with the trailer, and individual strands of thick blond hair around the edge of his head shone like a fragile halo. He stood in front of Tucker, hands on hips, feet spread, looking like the angel Gabriel himself.

Tucker wondered if being a vampire kept a man from going bald. Rurik had quite a head of hair on him, and Tucker thought of how hair kept growing after death. Another reason to hate him, he thought. He pulled the brim of his hat down over his eyes, and sank deeper into the recliner. The whiskey was getting to him.

Jenkins stood silently in the trailer kitchenette.

"Does my presence offend you?" Rurik asked.

Rex growled deep in his throat and then barked.

"It offends Rexie, that's for damn sure," Tucker said. "Why don't you sit down or something? Get out of my line of sight?" He dropped his hand to the side of the recliner, searching for and then finding Rex's head and ruffling up his fur to placate him. Rex quieted down and looked up at Tucker with sad eyes, as if he knew the danger ahead.

"My preference is to stand."

Why did the vampire refuse to ever use his name, Tucker thought. The chair smelled like Dad.

Tucker suspected the suddenly wobbly state of his own brain was not just due to the whiskey, but rather more likely some kind of buildup of traumatic shock. He wondered if those horse-tranq pills the vet gave him a while back were somewhere around the trailer.

"Please don't waste my time," Rurik said.

Tucker laughed, sharp and humorless. "Ain't that about all you got? Endless time, I mean."

"Things are changing rapidly," Rurik said. "Rather than spend my hours with a pitiful human, I should be with my own, preparing for war."

"War ain't a certainty," Tucker said. "Did you see her there?" he asked, unsure he wanted to hear the answer.

"It's not that simple," Rurik said. "I sensed her presence, but it was very distant, weak and confused. Not the Lizzie I know."

The words hit Tucker hard, but at the same time the subtle jab carried hope. He was glad he was sitting down because he wasn't sure if he'd try to kill the Russian, or hug him. He realized he'd been holding his breath. Elita was telling the truth.

"You don't know her at all," Tucker said at last. "We're going to do this thing, but I can't stand the sight of you. Why don't you wait outside until it's time?"

The muscles around Rurik's eyes twitched, almost imperceptibly, and Tucker knew he'd landed a blow. The Russian wasn't used to taking orders.

Rurik wondered if he should just kill the human and drain him, and be done with his insolence once and for all. But the road to Lizzie was through this weak man, this petulant cowboy, so he stayed his hand and, with a sneer, stepped outside. Good things come to those who wait, he thought, looking out across the darkness and feeling the heartbeats of every little living thing around him for miles. And he had waited a very long time.

Tucker pulled himself out of the soft chair and stood. He might not be as tall or good-looking as Rurik, or as rich or mysterious — Christ, why *had* Lizzie picked him? Didn't matter, she picked him, she loved him, he was the one she wanted, and he was the one she needed now, he reminded himself. He was going to find her and bring her back.

"Where's there's hope, there's life," he murmured. It was something his Mom always said back in the days they'd been looking for Travis. In this case, this might not be life as Mom would have known it, but undead life was still something, as he had come to learn. He tipped his hat back and looked over at Jenkins. "Well, what do you think?"

"The timing must be exact," Jenkins said. "He must send you to the Meta at exactly the same time as he dies, so you can follow the path opened by him. Wherever Lizzie is, if she is alive and within a similar diurnal pattern, the correct time zone, she will be dying too and entering the Meta, or already there."

"Who else will be there? Elita?"

"All of the consciousnesses of every vampire facing dawn or still waiting for sunset wherever they are in the world will be there."

"Have you ever, you know, crossed over?" Tucker asked.

Jenkins shook his head. "My understanding is only theoretical."

"That's not very comforting."

"No, I imagine not," Jenkins said. "You will have a scant few minutes to seek out Miss Elizabeth before you either die and stay there, or return to your body. And I will be doing my very best to make sure you don't die."

"I appreciate that," Tucker said. "There's a lot of things I ain't done yet. Finding Lizzie being number one on the list."

When this was over, he thought, they could go on a permanent vacation. Maybe see the ocean for the first time in his life.

Tucker stood and stepped outside into the crisp Wyoming night air, standing next to Rurik. The darkness was slowly giving way to dawn. The two horses tied up behind the trailer whinnied. The moon was nearly full, but low on the horizon, sprinkling a dusting of light across the jagged mountaintops.

Rurik was looking out across the landscape to the twinkling of house lights in the distance where he had helped Lizzie consume the aging molester. Her first kill.

"She ain't even here," Tucker said, following Rurik's gaze to the old farmhouse. "You don't have to try to one-up me now."

"If she lives through whatever is happening, she will eventually be mine," Rurik said. "Whether I kill you, she comes to her senses or simply by your impending mortal death, there can be only one outcome."

"So why are you helping me now?" Tucker asked.

"Trust me when I say it is not for you I do this."

Tucker looked up at the moon and wondered if the footprints from the Apollo landing were still there. What about the flag? Was it eternal?

"Has she fed from you?" Rurik asked.

Tucker nodded.

"Good. Perhaps that will make your connection strong enough to solve this riddle."

He would never tell this monster, Tucker thought, but Lizzie feeding from him brought them closer in ways he had not imagined possible. Each time she took his blood in her mouth, he felt as if he was granting her life, and when she fed, she gazed at him with such gratitude, it filled his heart near to bursting.

"It's time," Rurik said. "The human experience of the Meta is gained only through what your kind call a near death experience. I can induce that in you by feeding on you. I am adept at keeping humans alive for as long as I wish. You should be able to enter the Meta for a few minutes before your natural regenerative processes repair the blood loss sufficiently to return."

"I don't like the sounds of 'should,'" Tucker said.

"You know it is not without risk," Rurik said.

"Jenkins will be watching my back," Tucker said. "What should I do when I am there?"

"Cowboys are good at improvising, or so I have heard," Rurik said.

"Will she be like a ghost or something?"

Rurik looked at him with a mixture of disdain and amusement. "The Meta is an energy field, not a place, and certainly not a haunted castle from some campfire story. The embodied brain is a vehicle through which that energy is filtered and translated back into a unique consciousness. When you go to the Meta, what you experience depends on how you blend into that field. It is unique for each person."

"That helps me not at all," Tucker said. "And it's almost morning."

"I can give you no more instructions. We now must put aside our differences and trust one another," Rurik said. "At least for a single day."

"I will never trust you, but you have my word I won't take advantage of the situation." Tucker noticed that Rurik's Russian accent was getting stronger. Maybe as the sun came closer to the horizon, his neurons began shutting down.

"My men will stand guard throughout the day," Rurik said. "Armed and with orders to protect my corpse. I will never trust you."

"The Winnebago Lenny renovated for Lizzie is still pretty banged up," Tucker said. "Not sure some sunlight won't get through those bullet holes. Only other place that's blacked out where you'll be safe is in the back."

"Shall we proceed to your bedroom then?" Rurik said.

NINE

"That is weird as fuck," Mark said, pointing to the corpse in the bed displayed on the monitor. He could feel the disapproving stare of Dr. Burkett from behind and caught himself. "Pardon my French."

"Coarse language is the sign of an inexpressive mind," she said.

It was morning and they were both tired from an all-nighter and from the energy required to maintain the elaborate ruse. Faking kindness is much more draining than simply being kind.

"She's really a vampire?" he asked. "For real? Like, if we let her go she'd be all *arggghhh* on our necks, all Dracula and stuff?" He emphasized his question with snapping teeth and hands like claws.

"I guess so," Louisa said. "I don't know anything about how the creatures normally function. I only know what we've observed with this specimen so far."

"What a trip," Mark said. "Shouldn't we, you know, tell the government or something? Seems like people would want to know about this. I can see some major cash in our future from *People* magazine for an exclusive."

Louisa poured herself a cup of coffee, took a sip, and then winced and threw it into the sink. "Tastes like it was brewed with bilge water," she said. "Listen to me carefully, Mark. You are to tell no one. You are here because you have a reputation in scientific circles for discretion."

"Don't worry," he said. "You're paying me enough, I wouldn't care if we had Santa Claus tied to that bed in there. But why are we fucking with her head?"

Louisa sighed. "Mark, please. Language. I need her as disoriented and docile as possible until we are able to get what we need, and until I understand the degree of her physical strength. The longer she thinks she's a traumatized rich girl with a vampire fetish, the smoother our experiments will be."

And the safer we'll be, she thought, but decided not to say that out loud.

"Got it. It's like a spy movie," Mark said. "Only in an old fish cannery."

She logged on to the computer and turned off the video loop showing a sunny outdoor scene on the high-definition television nestled against the false window in Lizzie's room.

"She really believed that was the outside world?" Mark asked.

"Apparently. I imagine it's been a while since she's seen the outside world in the daytime. Plus she's starving and weakened, and I scarred her eyes slightly with a laser. They already started healing, it's really quite remarkable, but her vision is likely not fully restored."

"Wow, that's sick," he said. "Can I do it next time?"

"Yes. Now please go get some sleep," she said. "The thing won't wake up until the sun goes down. And keep in mind, Helmi doesn't know any of this. She gets the same story as the creature. She is outside the need-to-know circle."

"What about the guards?" Mark asked, jerking his head toward the front of the building where several heavily armed men in bulletproof vests watched the door. "How much do they need to know?"

"They know enough to apply a terminal solution if necessary, but that's it."

They watched the video monitor as the exterior door swung open and a young woman with blonde hair and sparkling blue eyes walked in. She wore a baseball cap and a denim jacket over colorful scrubs with little hearts and flowers on them, as if she had most recently worked in a pediatric ward. She waved at the guard, who nodded in return, and then walked to the lab at the back of the building, waving at Dr. Burkett and Mark as she passed on the way to her locker.

"She's cute, and annoyingly chirpy," Mark said. "I'm going to enjoy lying to her."

TEN

Tucker was stretched out on his normal side of the bed next to the window, the mattress canoed by the weight and contours of his angular body. But instead of Lizzie next to him, it was the Russian, his mouth fixed to Tucker's wrist, noisily sucking the blood from a deep slice across the veins.

If I get through this, Tucker thought, I'm going to burn this fucking bed.

Jenkins watched worriedly from near the closet, a tray with gauze, tape and antiseptic at the ready.

Rurik was feeding deeply, enjoying the fact that Tucker's life was under his dominion. He could feel the cowboy's life force slipping away, and let the sour taste of Tucker's worn-out blood fill his mouth. He considered taking it all, opening the gates and draining him like a can of beer, but he needed to know too.

Tucker felt the same sleepy kind of sensuality hardening in him as when Lizzie fed on his blood, and was momentarily horrified, but then the room grew blurry and dark and he couldn't worry about it anymore because there was a gentle tug and a *pop*, and then he was freed from his own body. Floating up slowly, he was looking down at the Russian working on his wrist like a dog at a bone; the top of Jenkins's bald, worried head; the top of dusty, long-neglected cabinets; and Rex, who seemed to be watching Tucker's disembodied form, staring up at him in wide-eyed wonder as he floated on out through the trailer ceiling.

In the gray light of early dawn, Tucker stretched momentarily out across all of creation, the cold earth below and the warming sky and the mountains and the thoughts, and then he was swirling up into a circle of light brighter than the sun.

Speeding forward and yet also perfectly still, a turquoise-blue ocean came into view and Tucker found himself standing on the edge of the water, watching the waves gently break, lost in the repetition and rhythm of the movement.

So that's what an ocean looks like, he thought.

In a landslide of joy, Lizzie was next to him, her face upturned and basking in the sun, smoothing lotion on her arms and shoulders.

"Better let me put some lotion on your back, honey," she said. "You'll get burnt to a crisp out here if you aren't careful." He looked down to see he was wearing only a pair of Bermuda shorts and a pair of dilapidated boots. And his cowboy hat.

He turned to smile at her, but he was alone. He knew it was only wishful thinking he had passed through. The blue waters swirled and faded and he was again peering down at his own near-lifeless body sprawled out in the darkened trailer bedroom, as if through the wrong end of a telescope. Rurik pulled his lips from Tucker's wrist, wiping at his crimson smile, and nodded at Jenkins, who used a towel to put pressure on the cut and stem the bleeding.

From his vantage, Tucker could see dawn knifing across the mountain, and through the dark focal point he watched Rurik lie next to his body and grow still, eyes open but sightless, his body rigid.

Jesus, if the boys from the Watering Hole could see him now, he thought, sprawled out next to the handsome Russian. Handsome? What the hell was he thinking?

There was a savage pull upward and he saw lines of energy winding around him as he rose even higher, felt the earth turn, and watched the sun wobble up over LonePine. He was calm, with a growing sense of joy, and shouted down to Jenkins, who was looking at his watch worriedly as blood soaked through the towel.

"I'm okay," Tucker yelled, grinning. "Nothing to worry about, Jenks, I feel great!"

But Jenkins could not hear him, and in fact was getting farther and farther away as Tucker was drawn upward through a dark tunnel, sliding toward a brilliant golden light. Heavenly music was playing, country music. Was that Kitty Wells, he wondered? On the walls of the tunnel, images from his years in LonePine swirled past him and through him, and there in the distance, waiting in the golden light, was Dad.

"Dad! Good God, is it really you?"

"In a manner of speaking. Boy, it's good to see you, but it ain't your time. You shouldn't be here. Not yet."

"I need to find Lizzie," Tucker said, the weight of the words reverberating through the moment.

He was bathed in love and happiness as the golden light washed over him and carried away doubts.

"That's a pretty good reason," Dad said. He smiled broadly and held out his hand and then a woman's hand was suddenly grasping it too and Tucker's mother came into view. Together, his parents beamed at him.

Tucker knew, just knew, in that instant that everything was unfolding in his life as it was meant to. The clarity was consuming in its simplicity and power, and seemed to permeate each cell of his being. All these thoughts occurred simultaneously, as if he could now think more than one thought at a time.

"Mom, I've missed you so much. I promise I'll find Travis, I will. And Dad, I'm sorry about everything," Tucker said. Holy shit, was that Snort galloping up toward him in the distance? There was something else. A different, joyful, simple presence. It practically called out to him and he felt like a little boy again.

And then he felt her.

It was weak. She was scared, uncertain, but reaching out for him. The image of Lizzie at the beach on the edge of the ocean came back into focus, as his parents faded away. At the same time, he was looking down on his own lifeless body again and feeling a heavy pull back into his life.

Not yet, he thought, not ever. Lizzie and I could live in peace here in this place, with Dad and Mom, he thought. Another wave of joy and certainty passed through him.

"It's me," he shouted, not sure if he was shouting with his voice, his mind, his heart, or with a single cell. "Lizzie, honey, it's Tucker. I'm coming for you. Don't you give up."

There was a savage swat and then a spiraling, screaming loss of control, and when he opened his eyes, Jenkins was looking down at him worriedly. Rurik was next to him, stone cold.

His body felt heavy, useless and tragically decrepit. "I didn't want to come back," he whispered.

ELEVEN

Rain was beating heavily against the window, the storm blowing in off the lake, but the howls were not from the wind. The patient was up out of his chair slapping the glass and moaning, his eyes wide and heart hammering.

It was nine in the morning and his agitation caught them all off guard. He was usually so quiet and pleasant, and today they had pancakes for breakfast, his favorite. The cook always made chocolate chip pancakes special for John, JD as they all called him. And scrambled eggs and two pieces of bacon and a cup of decaf coffee. JD loved his ranch breakfast and talked about it, looked forward to it, all week.

But now the food was tipped over to the floor and he was wailing and banging on the window.

"JD," the doctor said. "What is it, what's going on? Are you in pain?"

JD looked at him, anguish in his normally placid eyes, and for a brief second, the attendant feared things were about to become violent. "Get a sedative ready," he whispered to the nurse.

"I've never seen him like this," she said, her hands shaking as she prepared a syringe.

"JD, you must calm down," he said. "Tell us how to help you."

"He needs help! Bad things have happened!" JD screamed, his broad face twisted in pain and fear.

"Who? Who needs help?" the doctor asked. "You? Do you need help? Did you have a nightmare?"

"He needs help!" the big man screamed, banging harder against the window frame. "I have to help him. I can see him there, he's in the overworld."

"Please, John, please sit down. Who is there? Who needs help?"

The patient caught his reflection in the window, face illuminated by rage, and in an instant, he stopped. He saw his breakfast, ruined on the floor, and began crying.

"Don't worry, JD, we can get you more," the nurse said, moving closer and patting his arm. "We'll do that right now."

The doctor moved into the hall, the nurse following, and clicked opened the case file. "Has he ever talked about this overworld before?"

The nurse nodded. "Yes. He says sometimes he goes to a different place. Like heaven, kind of, I think."

TWELVE

Auscor Kingman looked pensively out across the dreary Manhattan skyline, methodically shredding a copy of *BusinessWeek* and dropping the strips into and around the wastebasket.

He paused in his labors to punch the intercom button on his desk. "Where's my latte?" he snapped into the speaker.

"Coming right up, Mr. Kingman," a disembodied voice answered.

"Extra hot this time. And I mean it. Extra fucking hot, like if it doesn't burn my mouth when I take the first sip, you are completely fired."

"Yes sir."

He returned his attention to the offending magazine. *BusinessWeek* had a distribution of some 120,000 movers and shakers, captains of industry, his now snickering peers, all reading yet another damning story about him, a cover story no less. *The Continued Fall of a Once Bright Star*, the headline luridly proclaimed.

The story chronicled, again, his four-year rise to prominence with his start-up Kingtech — a technology firm specializing in missile guidance systems that, with interest cultivated from inside the Pentagon, he took public, making just south of a billion dollars, before taxes.

Fucking taxes.

A glitch in the code led to a few unfortunate US deaths, a congressional inquiry and a media firestorm about the problems identified, and ignored, during testing, all of which resulted in a terminal slide in stock price.

Auscor, of course, got out at just the right time with an inadequately large fortune and a blackened reputation.

That was all about to change. He had a new plan. War was passé. Weapons too. The revelation hit him like a thunderbolt as he mucked around in his own self pity for a few months after what he now called "the debacle."

The real money wasn't in death, he realized, but in life. A new and better fortune stood ready to be mined in death prevention. And he had just the angle.

When Kingtech began unraveling, he spent some time in a secluded property deep in the Carpathian Mountains of Romania, where a passing interest in local legends turned into an obsession. It took two years, much of his fortune, and a strain on every connection imaginable, but that legend proved to be a reality.

A hesitant knock on the door stirred him from his reveries.

"Yes."

Tommee, his assistant, came in carrying two cups of coffee and wearing oven mitts to make a point.

The garish mitts clashed dramatically with the carefully pressed pants and shirt, immaculate vest, and perfectly groomed hair sleeked into place.

The two had a long and well-established working relationship. The money, and Tommee's own masochistic streak, more than compensated for Kingman's manic passive-but-mostly-aggressive streak.

"I got you two. One extra hot and one extra extra hot. But be careful. The barista literally got third-degree burns on her hands. Literally."

"Just set them down."

Tommee set them on the edge of the desk and tucked the mitts under his arm. "The extra extra hot one is on the right. Um, my right, your left."

"Good," Auscor said, never turning his head from the task at hand.

"Another bad story?"

"Go please."

"It's just so unfair. If they knew you like I do..."

"They'd think I was a giant douche bag, just like you do," Auscor said. "Please, seriously, leave."

In the ensuing silence, Auscor returned his attention to task at hand. When the magazine was sufficiently destroyed, he took a sip of the nearest latte, stifling an oath when it burned his lips.

With a smile, he reached for a cell phone in his desk.

After punching in the number, he waited impatiently until the connection was made. "What's the latest on our little project?" he asked without preamble.

The answer took too long and he interrupted. "Yes, I know it has just been a day. I have a calendar. And I also know that Rome wasn't built in a day, but — and stop me if you heard this one — when the builders of Rome didn't make progress, Caesar put them in ham panties and fed them to the lions."

Partially distracted by a story on Bloomberg News channel, muted — thankfully — about the *BusinessWeek* article, he half listened to a stream of excuses. "Yes, fine, keep up the charade if that makes it easier, but find me something usable."

He broke the connection. "Tommee, my lattes are cold," he said into the intercom, enjoying the sigh on the other end.

THIRTEEN

Lizzie lay motionless in the hospital bed. Her uncovered belly swelled up above her hip bones. Red liquid seeped into a vein through the IV taped carelessly across the thin skin, now taut and dry like parchment, on the back of her hand. An imposing array of equipment surrounded her, beeping and blinking and whirring — a busy island of technology in the large, otherwise empty floor of the warehouse, an abandoned salmon cannery.

"Is she dead?" Helmi asked.

"No. Not dead. And even more fucked up, she doesn't age, not like you and I do," Mark said. "Dr. Burkett says she is practically immortal, or at least her cells are. It probably has something do with how deeply she sleeps, like she's doing now, almost like a coma."

"But not dead?" Helmi asked.

"Not dead," Mark repeated. "She only sleeps like this in the daytime, by the way."

Looking around, Helmi asked, "How would she even know it's daytime?" The room was blacked out with heavy curtains. "But more to the point, what do her vitals say?"

"From what we can measure, she mimics death, but trust me when I say she'll wake up like clockwork, when the sun sets. I've seen it."

"Maybe circadian rhythms play a role," Helmi said. "Or something else. Like animals, you know? How birds know how to migrate, butterflies and such."

"Yeah, fascinating, but that's not what we're here for." Despite his rising irritation, he wanted to sleep with Helmi. Hard.

She was too nice, too cute, and way too far out of his league, so he decided to act like an ass until he seeded enough doubt in her ego that she might conclude he was special. It had worked before. Women needed so much praise. Withholding it, he'd found, opened unexpected doors. And sometimes legs.

Helmi pulled back one of the curtains, hoping for a glimpse of the sea. Instead, she found the windows boarded up tightly with plyboard painted black. She noticed the nails holding it in place were new and shiny, with a starburst of fresh splinters around each hole.

"Salmon too," Helmi said, still thinking about the intelligence of animals.

"What about salmon?" Mark asked from his perch behind the EMR cart.

"Each year, they have these huge runs back to the waters where they were born. No one is really sure how they keep that knowledge."

"Neat," he said, meaning the opposite.

"You're not from around here, are you?" she asked.

"No. Are you?"

"Born and raised in Astoria. Home of the salmon. And Finnish saunas." She smiled.

"And boredom," he said.

"Tell me more about the study," Helmi said as she inspected the IV line.

"The first thing you should know is that Dr. Burkett is brilliant. Working with her is like making history. She's going to solve the human disease of aging."

"That's a funny thing to call it."

"It makes you die, so in my book, that's a disease. The secrets are in this woman's cells, or in her psychosis. But she's mentally unstable. She has delusions about being a vampire," he said.

Helmi rested her hand on Lizzie's cheek, which was icy cold. "Not an unreasonable way to think about a condition like this. Are you sure she's not dead?"

"How many times do you have to hear the same thing?" Mark asked. "She's not dead, okay? Be logical. Why would we go through such an elaborate ruse to bring a corpse here?" he said, then grimaced, realized he had revealed too much.

Helmi looked up. "Wait, is she here against her will?" She pushed a strand of nearly white blonde hair out of her eyes, tucking it neatly behind her ear.

"She is not here against her will," Mark said. "She's not fit to make decisions for her own care. Her mother asked us to help her."

Helmi walked to the foot of the bed and gently unwrapped the sheet from around Lizzie's feet. Lizzie's ankles were tied to the bed frame. The pink polish on her toes looked fresh. No chips. Helmi reached out and touched her foot. Cold. Like a corpse.

"Why is she restrained?"

"You're asking a lot of questions," Mark said. "Does it really matter?"

"It matters to me," Helmi said, focusing her pale-blue eyes directly at Mark. "Can I see the admission papers please?"

"How'd you get this job?" Mark asked.

"I answered an ad," she said. "It wasn't very clear, but it was here in Astoria."

"Yeah, Dr. Burkett said *dozens* of highly qualified people responded to the ad," he said.

Helmi understood. She needed this job badly.

"She's restrained because she tried to harm herself," Mark said. "You know Dr. Burkett, someone of her stature, would never do anything illegal. This is for the patient's own safety. Now if you are through playing Nancy Drew, girl detective, could you help me run the tests?"

Helmi turned away from Lizzie, pumped a handful of antibacterial gel into her palms and rubbed them together. A sickly orange scent filled the room. She left Lizzie's feet uncovered.

It was impossible, at least in this day and age, to conduct science without all the proper paperwork, she thought. She was being paranoid. Everything was fine. "What's first?" Helmi asked.

"Blood draw. And after that, let's push her through the MRI. Dr. Burkett wants every possible bit of ancillary data while she is in this deep sleep state," Mark said.

Mark lifted Lizzie's arm, tying the rubber tourniquet above her elbow and tapping a vein, trying to find a good spot. The arm was bruised, purplish welts covering the crook of her elbow.

"Why not just pull the blood from the IV line?" Helmi asked.

"Still with the questions? It takes too long. There's something weird about her blood. It gets thicker and slower during the day. We just have to open a vein, got it?"

"But look at her, she's bruising, that will be painful."

"What difference does it make?" Mark said. "She can't feel any of it and it will heal." He tapped the syringe again and pulled out the needle when the vial filled with blood. "You'd be surprised how fast she heals."

<u>FOURTEEN</u>

Tucker tugged at the bandages around his wrist and looked down at Rex. The dog, sensing his man was different, that some part of him had changed, sat snuggled up too close to Tucker's boots, trembling nervously and occasionally licking at the worn leather and duct tape.

Tucker was in the living room of the double-wide trailer with Rurik, though he could barely meet his eyes after sharing such an intimate near-death, and Lenny, who was growing used to the late-night phone calls.

"I felt her," Tucker said. "No question about it."

His body felt leaden and a little decayed, like part of it was newly wasted. His trip to the Meta had affected him, and he wasn't sure yet if it was for the better or worse. He was clearer that the love he felt for Lizzie was the only thing pure remaining in the world and that everything else was meaningless. He was surprised by the thought that death now seemed a reasonable option, and maybe the only way he'd ever get a little rest.

As if reading his thoughts, Rurik looked at him curiously. "You know you cannot stay there."

"Who said I want to?"

"You are mortal and your life is very narrow," Rurik said. "Accessing such an expansive reality is unsettling. Everyone is overwhelmed at first, even vampires when they are first turned. I still find the experience humbling, and I walk through this world as a god."

"A goddamned asshole," Tucker said. "You and I ain't nothing alike. It was a mite different there, that's for sure, but I'm glad to be back here in the real world," he said, even though he didn't mean it.

"How did you get there again?" Lenny asked.

"Never mind," Tucker said, massaging his wrist and looking at the blood seeping through the gauze. "Let's just say I went there, figured out what I needed to know, and then came back. No big deal."

He was posturing, buying time until he could settle into this new version of himself.

"I know the Meta," Rurik said. "What happened to you last night was a revelation, and I can only assume how your feeble faculties are now struggling to cope. It is where we all come from, and where we return. Like, I suppose, this squalid little town feels to you. But only because you still have individual senses. Stay in the Meta long enough, without returning to your body, and you lose cohesion. You lose that which is you and become a self-less, undifferentiated part of the whole."

"Maybe that wouldn't be so bad," Tucker said.

"We agree finally on a point. It would be glorious," Rurik said. "But you would no longer feel the connection to Elizabeth, or to your friends or this place. You would simply become the connection, and also everything that is not the connection."

"Dad sure seemed real enough," Tucker said.

"He was real," Rurik said. "But by this time, he has long ceased to be a single strand of life. You, however, disrupted the Meta as you arrived and assembled some traces of him there."

"So you're saying it wasn't real, what I experienced?" Tucker asked.

"It was as real, or even more real, than this reality we are in," the Russian said, slamming his palm against the coffee table for emphasis. "You brought an aspect of him into being from your own memories."

"I hate this shit," Tucker said. "It makes my head hurt." He reached down to pet Rex, who, expecting a rough-natured swat, ducked to the side. Instead, Tucker began to pet him softly and Rex lunged up into his lap, surprised, but determined by instinct to take advantage of the moment.

"You ought to be sitting in my chair," Lenny said. The effects of the gas at the truckstop left a constant ringing in his ear, and he was having trouble keeping up with the conversation. "Catch me up. Did you talk to her?"

"No," Tucker said, struggling to put his experience into words. "It was like I could feel her, and I think she could feel me. But something was wrong. Like how it feels when you've had maybe a few drinks too many and someone starts talking to you at the bar and you know you ought to know them, but you can't quite get it all worked out? That's what it felt like. Like she didn't know me, but knew she ought to."

"What do we do now?" Lenny asked.

Tucker turned to Rurik. "If I go back and feel her again, make her stay with me longer, can we find her? Can we trace her back somehow to her body?"

Rurik shook his head.

Tucker's phone buzzed, causing them all to startle a little. Rurik looked sheepish that he had reacted at all.

"It's my cousin," Tucker said. "I'm going take it. She's doing something for me." He held the phone to his ear. "Hey, Wil, thanks for what you are doing, but I got a thing going on here, it's hard to talk."

"All right," Wil said, a ragged irritation just beneath the surface of her words. "I understand, but I've got something I know you'll be interested in, even with whatever thing you have going on."

"Okay, I can spare a minute, shoot," he said.

"I've been digging around like you asked, and I'm not a hundred percent sure, but it sounds like a young man matching his description, a John Doe, was admitted into a private facility in upstate New York with serious head injuries about three years after Travis went missing. Been a ward of the state ever since. There's a slim, but very real, chance it could be him. You should go there. Like right now."

"Like I said, I got a thing going on," Tucker said.

"Hold on, I think my phone is messed up," Wil said. "It sounded like you said you can't be bothered finding out if your brother is still alive."

"Wil, I'm having a little crisis here. Please."

"You're serious?" she asked, realizing there was an unusual gravity to his voice. "What's going on? You sound, I don't know, rattled."

"I am," Tucker said. "You know how I told you my fiancée was a little different?"

"You said she came from money or something."

"Yeah, lots of money. She's a, uhm..." He struggled

to say the 'v' word and failed. "We have a lot of catching up to do, but she comes from a royal family and she's been kidnapped. Two nights ago."

"Holy shit," Wil said. "Have you called the police? You need to get the cops involved right now. It's the only way these things ever turn out well."

Tucker sighed. "There are complicating factors."

"I don't know what's going on, but I'm going to load Sake in my car. We can be there tomorrow."

"Do not do that," Tucker said. "I mean, I'd love to see you and I know Rex would love to see Sake again, but this ain't safe."

There was a long pause, and he imagined her clenching her jaw and possibly checking the automatic she always carried in a shoulder holster or the double-edged dagger tucked into her boot.

"Are you suggesting I can't take care of myself?" she asked. "Because I recall a young cowboy from twenty years ago who would disagree with you. A cowboy with a busted nose and a newfound sense of respect for his girl cousin."

"That's not what I meant," Tucker said. "I know you can handle yourself just fine. Better than me, but just trust me, until we talk, you can't get involved. You can do me a lot more good by looking into the whole Travis situation. I've got money now. I'll send you some. Lots of it," he said.

"I don't need the money," she said. "I need to help my cousin."

"I appreciate that," Tucker said. "This would help me more than you know. I made a promise to Dad."

"I'm real sorry I missed his funeral," she said. "It was so sudden."

"Thanks," Tucker said. "I know you were there in spirit. But let me ask you this before you go, if you were looking to find someone who'd been kidnapped, what's the first thing you'd do?"

She was silent for a minute, thinking. "You said you had security?"

"Yeah," Tucker said. "On account of her, uhm, royal status. We got ambushed at the worst possible time."

"During sex?"

"The second worst, then," Tucker said. "It was during our wedding."

"Yikes," Wil said. "And, also, thanks for the invite."

"Wil, seriously, not now," Tucker said.

"Look, when it comes to a caper like that, there's no such thing as a coincidence. Whoever did it knew you'd be vulnerable so you need to figure out how the info got leaked. Look in the least obvious spot first. Someone got inside your security and they would do it where you least expect it."

Tucker sighed, thoughts spinning. "Thanks. Stay in touch," he said.

"I'm heading east," Wil said. "You call me if you need anything. I can turn around anytime."

"What did Wil say?" Lenny asked as Tucker broke the connection. Lenny had a soft spot for Wil, a tough, confident woman who knew almost as much about weapons as he did.

Tucker studied him curiously. "She said we need to check your house for bugs," he said at last.

FIFTEEN

"I have never been so disappointed in myself," Lenny whispered. He was crestfallen to the point of nausea that his long-cultivated paranoia failed to insulate him from unwanted surveillance.

He and Tucker stood in the bowels of Lenny's bunker and looked across the room at a small electronic device, no bigger than a pencil eraser, on the kitchen table. It was now under an overturned soup bowl, which was under an overturned mixing bowl. A small radio tuned to an evangelical station, the most annoying white noise either of them could think of, was blaring beside it to drown their conversation.

"I can't believe I missed it," Lenny said. "I can't believe the federal government has been listening to me all these years."

"How do you suppose they even got it inside?" Tucker asked. He was holding a pad of paper upon which he had written '*Remember the script*,' and was jabbing the pencil at it resolutely.

Lenny nodded, anguish in his eyes. Even though he was playing a part, he was telling the truth. "Tucker, that's what kills me. I carried it in myself. I always thought those damned old videodisc players would be good for something. I bought six of them at the dollar store maybe ten years ago. I had one hooked up to the CB to record and analyze the chatter. The bug was inside."

"I'm just impressed you were able to find it now." He turned the page where he had written '*We think this is the only one.*'

"Really wasn't that big of a deal," Lenny said. "I mean, it's pretty sophisticated, but your suspicious cousin made me start from scratch. I was so sure of myself, I hadn't swept the whole place in years. You can bet that won't happen again," he said grimly. "The price of pride." He looked at Tucker. "I am responsible for what's happened to Lizzie."

"Don't think of it like that," Tucker said, sensing Lenny was about to lose his cool. He pointed at the pad and then motioned for Lenny to calm down. "If someone was this desperate, they would have figured out some way to get her."

"At least we found all the bugs," Lenny said, almost choking on the lie. He found six more in addition to the one under the enamelware and knew those six were currently transmitting every word spoken between the two men. "Who do you suppose is behind all this?"

"I don't know. Rurik swears it ain't the Royals. He's been in touch with all the tribes. Elita says the Reptiles would have just tortured and killed you. Snooping is not their strong suit."

"Now what?"

"They tip their hand," Tucker said, turning the page of the notebook quietly. He had written '*old granary*' and underlined it savagely. "If we get them to bite, we're going to track the bugs back to the source and rain hellfire on whoever was listening to you, whoever kidnapped my fiancée. Come on, let's make contact."

He motioned for Lenny to join him and they sat down at the table, turned the radio off and lifted the two bowls so the bug was exposed.

Tucker picked it up and held it like a microphone. "Hey, bug-listening people. We are on to you. We know who you are, and we know where you are, and believe me when I say you have messed with the wrong people. We're coming for you, and we're coming for the people you work for. You've got twenty-four hours to get her back to me, unharmed, or a pissed-off vampire will be the least of your worries. You've been warned."

He put the bowls back over the bug, turned on the radio, and they retreated to the doorway again.

"Think they heard?" Lenny asked.

"I think so," Tucker said.

"Now what?" Lenny asked.

"It's likely they'll send some heavy hitters our way. We need to move into the bunker under the old granary. It would take a small army to pry us out of there. Then we just wait for them to contact us. Let's go."

They returned to the surface, where June was waiting and worriedly wringing her hands. "I sure hope they were listening," Tucker said.

They were.

Within minutes, a pale, nervous and underpaid analyst in the offices of Blaylock & Wolfe in D.C. was having an awkward and heated conversation with his co-worker as he dialed a rarely used number on his cell.

SIXTEEN

Whatever this species was, it did not appear to be threatened by the repeated insults to her biology. She appeared unable to die, at least not in the way humans died. Still, the photos showed bruising from the battery of tests, and her pain last night had been significant.

So the creature experienced pain, and although her intent was not to be cruel, cruelty, nevertheless, was an outcome. Louisa knew this was an unfortunate but often necessary step for the greater good.

In many ways, this female was the perfect subject — sentient, able to communicate, exceptionally resilient, and genetically similar to humans — and one that offered the potential of accelerated results.

If results came faster, fewer other animals would be needed for research. Research with this new creature therefore, she rationalized, ultimately helped lessen the cumulative cruelty.

She nodded, pleased that the rationalization made good logical sense.

She could make a small fortune cloning the female and selling her genetic progeny, or at least her cell lines, to the constellation of research facilities around the world. But a small fortune did not interest her.

Instead, yesterday, she sent the full suite of backup samples to Portland, pulling in the last of her owed favors from a discreet lab tech to get them sequenced. That included the promise of silence, though it was likely unneeded. No one wanted to be associated with her anymore since the mishap two years ago. The judgment had been swift and final, her scientific ostracism complete. She shrugged, thinking about it. She would prove them all wrong.

As Louisa scrolled through the blood work data one more time, her cell phone vibrated. Kingman, of course. It was always only Kingman.

Not now, Louisa thought. She turned the cell phone over, hiding his name as it buzzed and vibrated angrily, and then beeped once in message-fueled indignation.

Okay, she thought, reeling in her wandering mind, time to recap. What did she know at this point? The bulk of the samples had been collected and the next phase, the analysis, could now begin in earnest.

Specifically, her aim was to understand the genetic basis of this creature, and why it apparently neither aged nor experienced disease. There were several plausible hypotheses. Maybe the subject carried an aging antigen. Or perhaps her immortality was linked to supercharged T cells. It could be a disproportionately high number of leukocytes. Once she figured out which was right, she would work backward to identify the code. But she would need a few lucky breaks along the way if she was going to get this done on Kingman's timetable.

One step at a time was all she could do. Hypothesize. Collect. Analyze. Review. Repeat. And breathe. Don't forget to breathe. Repeat again and again until she had enough information to try and synthesize a compound. It was one giant biological mystery story, and she was the detective.

She opened the manila envelope with the subject's personal belongings. There was nothing of note other than an antique necklace, a pendant crucifix with a thorny rose wrapped around it and a delicate crescent moon dotted with what looked like crushed emeralds. It fell into her hand and she pocketed the necklace, thinking it could prove useful in tonight's interview.

She stood and stretched her long, thin arms, clasping them above her head, bending side to side. She was tired, and wondered if she could adjust to sleeping by day when the creature was in her deep sleep. Her cell phone vibrated again. She could not continue ignoring him. He would just keep calling.

"Yes?" she answered.

"Dr. Burkett. Don't avoid my calls in the future. Your progress?"

"Steady."

"That would be great if I was a tortoise, but I'm a hare. And I'm a hare that doesn't rest. Please be more precise."

"I'm waiting for the first analysis," she said.

"Pretend you're playing in your little science sand-box for actual money. What's your hunch?"

"The pace depends on how closely matched to humans her overall genome is. We need it to be close."

"I bet even you, a scientist, I bet you're praying now," Auscor said.

She could hear the cold disdain in his voice. It wasn't the first time.

"When do you start tests on the secondary subject?" he asked.

"When we've finished with the mother," Louisa said.

"Keep pressing," Auscor said. "I want everything, her biology and also her story, her history. How did she get to be like this and where can we find others? We may need more than one specimen, dozens, hundreds even. See what you can find out."

"I intend to interview her again tonight."

"You have what you need for that?" he asked.

"The biographical details in her dossier are sparse," she said.

"Can't be helped," Auscor said. "You've got everything I could find, and I had some expensive people looking. I trust you don't need to get inside the heads of the monkeys you test on, or the rats?"

"They aren't in a position to break free and kill me," she said. "Or talk to me. Or lie to me. Or give me insight into their own biology that could speed us along by light-years in this research."

"It's what makes science so darn exciting," he said. "Anything else you need to complain about?"

"The accommodations are wretched, and it smells like fish," she said.

"At least you're at the beach." He disconnected.

Louisa pulled off her glasses and rubbed her eyes. She would welcome a little divine intervention now. In the meantime, back to the data in hand. She opened her laptop and stretched out on the military cot where she had slept for the past few days. There was a new e-mail from the lab in Portland:

Tissue sample compromised. Unable to sequence. Decomposing? Blood sample also contaminated with unknown substance. Low viscosity. Leukocytes proactively separating out, red blood cells degraded. Unable to perform standard tests. Bad sampling?

Louisa looked over her sampling notes and saw nothing anomalous. She quickly keyed in a reply:

Sampling was perfect. Will get more. In the meantime, please identify blood contaminant. Let me know the second you have more information. I can come to Portland if necessary.

She sent the e-mail and stared at the screen.

That last part was motivational. If he thought Louisa might actually come, he'd get it done faster. Still, she would collect new samples tonight, repeating the process exactly. This was a setback, but she knew she was in for a long slog. The prepared mind, she repeated to herself. Focus on being adept at interpreting whatever comes out of this.

Just fifteen years ago — how time flies like a dying bird, she thought — Louisa was the one, a scientific ingénue destined for a great career, the postdoc with multiple offers and a young investigator award. She had a fully funded lab at thirty-three.

Despite brilliance and money, and a natural ease at navigating the cutthroat envy of her academic peers, she was not the blessed one in the musical chairs of scientific discovery. There were no molecules, no buildings, no drugs named for her. Her line of inquiry proved unfruitful, a dead end, a thread relegated to history as a failure at worst, and at best an arcane piece of information about a path no one else ever need walk again. Important to the accumulation of knowledge, yes, but a guarantee of anonymity in scientific history.

No one remembered the mapmaker who figured out which way *not* to go, only those who found the right route that opened up new worlds. Only the trailblazers received accolades.

After decades of painstaking bench work, she looked back in bemused disbelief at the wasted years piled up behind her and at this unexpected finish outside the winner's circle. Occasionally, she wondered if science had been a foolhardy life choice. At this moment, looking out across a fishy warehouse at a confused vampire chained to the bed, the answer seemed clear.

Louisa had expected all of it to be black-and-white, rigorous and linear, logical. But it turned out science contained as much folly and serendipity as any other human endeavor.

Eventually, she lost her funding, her lab shut down and the rumors started swirling about the compromises she made as her desperation grew. Next came the damning report. Just when she gave up and resigned herself to embracing mediocrity, even failure, she met Kingman. He had done his research well, identifying her, a brilliant scientist on her last legs, desperate for relevance and with nothing to lose.

And why not, she thought. With no children and no partner, at least not at the moment, it was now or, quite literally, never.

In the last month, Louisa learned that with enough money anything was possible, including capturing a mythical creature, transforming an abandoned fish cannery into a secure biomedical lab and the distinct possibility of resurrecting her own scientific career. It was a final chance to make a lasting contribution to human health, to make the world better and to perhaps receive a little recognition in the process. That's all she ever wanted.

She turned to her laptop and opened the file marked 'neuroscans.' Mark had compiled the hourly scans from last night into a single chrono-clip. She hit Play. Eleven neurological images flowed across the laptop screen like gravel on the bed of a meandering river. She hit Replay and watched the details.

During the middle scans, the exterior of the brain was briefly hot, the circumference lit by a thin blue line. And there, right at the base of the skull, posterior to the thalamus region, a small dot — invisible in the first scan — flared up and then grew progressively wider until it was the size of a nickel by the fifth scan. At the end of the sequence, just like that, it was gone, shut down, and the brain returned to a lifeless state.

Louisa watched a third time. Was she seeing this right? When the creature was dead by all other measures, its brain was alive in a way she'd never seen, or heard of, before.

As the possibility of what this signified hit her, Louisa's heart skipped three beats.

SEVENTEEN

The mood in the room was skeptical and tense, the default setting, and Auscor was not pleased. He kept a library of business books in the memory palace of his mind and was rapidly sifting through strategies, everything from nonverbal mirroring to subliminal guidepost planting, but nothing seemed able to redirect the flow, nor supplant his irritation.

He was meeting with three big-money men from Dearborn Investments. The men controlled access to literally billions in investment capital. They were dressed in nearly identical dark-blue suits; two had dark-red ties and the most senior, a man who likely fancied himself an iconoclast, wore a light-blue tie.

Auscor had pulled the last of his few remaining strings to get them in this room and so far had been unable to impress them in the slightest.

The iconoclast was looking at the prospectus, his fingers steepled in front of his face. "Auscor, we want to back you on something, but this seems too far afield from what we know and expect from you. And, frankly, a bit dubious."

"I'm not even sure exactly what we're talking about here," the second man said. He flashed a wide, pleasant, empty smile.

"What we're talking about is near immortality," Auscor said. "I am *this* close to unlocking the secrets of a life free from the fear of disease. An ability to withstand trauma. Aging without the effects of aging. There are military applications, of course, but mostly I'm talking about a reasonably priced, failsafe method of living longer and better. Who doesn't want that? Even the poorest bastards in the world would want in on it."

"Are you talking vitamins here?" the man asked. "Some sort of supplement?"

"Genetic modification with the need for regular treatment," Auscor said. "Our target market is the entire human population. And boomerang customer potential is off the charts."

The third man looked up from the confidential and hastily prepared prospectus impatiently. "Wouldn't that lead to resource competition? You know, more hunger or poverty or whatever?"

"I don't see any of the science here," said the second man. The thought of a product that appealed to every single living human was piquing his interest and making his brain salivate greedily.

Auscor fought back the urge to scream at the three douche-keteers and throw them out the window. "We are finalizing the research and it is proprietary at this point, you can understand. You are going to have to trust me on this."

The maverick sat back in his chair. "We do trust you, Auscor," he said, meaning exactly the opposite. "But our clients need more than just your word and our recommendation. You understand."

"Of course," he said, knowing their word alone could free up $100 million or more in five minutes.

A knock at the door surprised all of them, and they looked up as Tommee bustled in, worried. The men were not used to thinking anything else took precedence over their time.

"Tommee," Auscor said coldly. "Was I unclear about the importance of this meeting?"

"No," Tommee said. "But you have an urgent message. On the red phone. Several messages, actually."

Auscor stood up quickly. "Gentleman, excuse me. It should come as no surprise that you are not the only investors I've been talking to. Give me five minutes."

The three men exchanged curious looks at each other from over their starched collars, suddenly slightly more interested.

Auscor slammed the door to his office and snatched the special cell phone off the desk and listened to the messages. "Dammit," he muttered, and dialed a number.

"They're on to us," he said. "Double security around the project. And turn the extraction team around and send it back to LonePine to clean this up."

He listened impatiently to the voice on the other end.

"Let me be as clear as possible then, Blaine, is it?" Auscor said. "We do not have time for meddling cowboys. So send as many of them as you can."

EIGHTEEN

"I say we just hit them out here in the open," one of the mercenaries said. "Be done with it."

The four men, all in dark tactical gear, were watching the truck in front of them intently, the headlights of their rented SUV barely illuminating the battered old three-quarter-ton and the two men, and one dog, inside.

"Stick to the plan," Clive, the leader of the group, said. He was in the passenger seat holding an assault rifle, a lethal Israeli bullpup design with a grenade launcher under the barrel, against his leg while simultaneously considering the outcome of just blowing the truck off the road. "No," he said, mostly to himself. "No loose ends. The one on the right, apparently, is some kind of an improvised weapons guy. We need to follow them into their bunker and torch it from the inside out. Make sure the data are contained."

The driver grimaced, irritated at someone who used "data" correctly.

After the truckstop job, most of the mercenaries from the Controlled Marketing Corporation, ex-soldiers unable or unwilling to return to civilian life, disbanded and headed back to their hometowns, or home countries, for the mandatory cooling-off period after a mission. Only four of them were in a position to return quickly.

Ordinarily, Clive wouldn't lead a team this small on this type of job, but the money was impossibly good and CMC was committed to high-quality customer service.

"Think they'll have vampires with them?" one of the men asked. "They creep me out."

"Probably," Clive said. "But we have crossbows and thermite grenades. Remember, they are tough and fast, but they die even easier than humans if you have the right tools. And we have the right tools."

They followed the truck out past the tiny little town, smiling — pleased with themselves — at the sight of the charred and boarded-up façade of the truckstop.

"Anyone die from the gas?" one of the men in the backseat asked.

"Not sure," Clive said. "Probably not." He looked at the map on his phone. "According the satellite photos, the granary is about five miles off. Let's pass them and get there first."

The driver tromped the gas and the SUV surged forward around the truck.

Tucker looked to his left and watched the car passing them, the four men inside looking stolidly forward. He waved; they ignored him and raced out of sight.

"Think that's them?" Lenny asked.

"No doubt," Tucker said. "And they look like real badasses."

Lenny checked his harness for the fifth time. "I hope this works."

"It will. We just got to get inside without getting shot."

Five miles later, the headlights revealed the sign to Wheat Lane and Tucker turned off the highway and aimed his truck toward the old grain silo at the end of the rutted gravel road.

Built in the 1950s, the silo was eighty feet tall and fifteen feet in diameter, with walls of thick, cold concrete. A rusty conveyor belt angled up to the top from a still-functional but rickety wooden storehouse nestled up close to the massive structure, like it had been hatched from the silo itself.

Tucker parked near the door at the base of the silo, killed the engine, and sighed. "If I was them, I'd wait until we got inside. If I'm wrong, we'll likely take a bullet in the brain the second we step out of the truck."

"Why don't you go first, then," Lenny said. "Ain't no sense in us both dying."

"Fair enough," Tucker said. "I'll leave the keys in the ignition. Come on, Rex."

Rex, not understanding what was at stake, perked up and followed Tucker out in an excited leap from the front seat of the truck.

The night was cool and Tucker stood for a moment looking up at the stars, imagining the bad guys peering at him through night scopes, itching to perforate his skull. His thoughts flashed to Lizzie, the way she felt in his arms and, after his trip to the Meta, the way she felt in his thoughts.

He took a deep breath and walked toward the door feigning nonchalance, but his muscles tensed, expecting a bullet. Nothing happened. "Lenny, come on," he said. "The text message said they'd call in ten minutes." He disappeared into the silo and Lenny got out and hurried after him.

The leader of the mercenaries, hidden with his men in the old house, watched them through the scope of his gun. After Tucker and Lenny entered the silo, Clive stood silently and motioned his team forward at a quick trot, pausing them at the door with an upraised fist. They all checked their weapons once more and then, with a nod of his head, burst in, two high and two low, rifles up, fingers on the triggers and the lights on their gun barrels crisscrossing the darkened interior.

Tucker, holding Rex tight to his chest, was standing against the far wall with Lenny beside him. The rifles steadied onto the two men.

"Not much of a bunker," the leader said.

"Nope, really more of a trap," Tucker said and then, with a savage tug and a surprised yelp from Rex, he shot up into the darkness, followed by Lenny. The four men were momentarily stunned to see their targets fly up into the shadows, but recovered quickly and began firing into the rafters above. Tucker, Lenny and Rex had already zipped out of sight as two bone-jarring thuds shook the earth in front of the door.

"Shit," the leader snarled, and lunged for the exit, but the door slammed shut and locked into place. "Grenade, quick," he said, but then stopped, realizing they would all die in the constrained explosion. "Belay that. We can shoot our way out. The door is corrugated metal."

They stepped back in unison and began shooting, but a dull mechanical rumble shook the sides of the silo as the conveyor belt roared to life and an avalanche of wheat began raining down from above.

"Shoot faster," Clive yelled as the grain fell heavily and was soon up to their knees, the musty air filled with chaff and dust that burned and choked their lungs.

Outside, boots echoed against metal as Tucker, still holding a ruffled and disgruntled Rex, and Lenny raced down the lonely spiral staircase snaking around the silo and joined Rurik and Elita on the ground. The ropes the two vampires used to lift Tucker and Lenny, holding the ends and throwing themselves off the top of the tower as ballast, undead weight, were now piled on the ground. Elita was smoking a clove cigarette.

They waited together silently, an unlikely band of humans and vampires — plus one dog — united, if uneasily, in their common desire to bring Lizzie home. Standing out of range of the bullets shredding the door, grain spilling out of the holes, they watched and waited until the shots trailed off and the men started to yell, panicked, as they contemplated suffocation under a mountain of wheat.

"That worked out pretty well," Tucker said. He dropped Rex to the ground and watched as he stretched and wagged the stump of his tail excitedly, ready for another ride.

"We still have to get them to talk," Lenny said.

"Leave that part to me," Elita said. She was wearing a vintage Blondie T-shirt, the arms cut out to reveal an impossible-to-overlook neon-purple bra, and silvery tights with leggings over black-and-white Chuck Taylor high-top sneakers. "Think it's up to their necks?"

"Yep," Tucker said, hitting the Stop button. He felt a pang of conscience, wondering for an instant if he was letting things go too far, so much violence, but when he considered what these men had done to Lizzie, his rage built quickly. "They don't deserve no mercy," he coldly whispered to himself.

"This should be fun. And I'm starving," Elita said, smiling broadly.

She grabbed a length of metal pipe leaning against the concrete and sprinted up the stairs, Rurik following. At the top, Elita looked through the skylight and peered down into the darkened silo. Far below them, a layer of wheat mostly covered the lights of the mercenaries. She cracked a chemical flare to life and dropped it, slithered through the skylight opening, and threw herself down with a snarl to land catlike on the surface of the grain. Rurik joined her seconds later.

The four men were immobilized, the wheat up to their necks, their heads poking up like mushrooms. They had abandoned their guns, trying desperately to swim and struggle to stay above the suffocating flow of wheat. They were panting and wild-eyed.

One of them, an older mercenary with a savage scar down his cheek, was terrified, and begged and cried out when he saw the two vampires land like bloodthirsty comets between them.

"Hey fellows, looks like you are up to your necks in trouble," Elita said, and laughed. "Now listen, I need information. When I get it, whoever is still alive stays that way."

"Go to hell, bitch," the leader said.

"Do not taunt us, human," Rurik said. "You have stumbled into something much larger than your pathetic little lives."

The scared mercenary was not so tough. "Jesus, tell her what you know, Clive."

"Shut the hell up," Clive said. "Remember your training. We cannot lose control of the situation."

Elita smiled. "Oh, sweetie, you have no control of the situation. You never did." She walked to the scared man, sinking up to her ankles in the wheat with each step. "I guess we know who doesn't have anything useful to add." She turned, held the pipe out like a golf club, and with an exaggerated swing, cracked it into the scared man's head with a wet *thunk*. He didn't have time to cry out as the force ripped his head from his pinned body and sent it bouncing off the cement wall. "Fore," she said. "Or should I say three."

Blood bubbled up out of the stump and she dropped to her knees to drink from it hungrily like a child at a water fountain until the flow subsided.

"Your turn," she said to Rurik.

He smiled at her appreciatively and then turned to the horrified men.

"You killed my people, you stole my queen, and we will know who is behind this and why."

"I won't tell you," Clive said, but it lacked conviction. He was a hard man who had done terrible things for money, but the sight of Elita, blood dripping from her chin to her shirt, shook him to the core.

"Please, Jesus, Clive," one of the others said.

Rurik spun, bent down and seized him by his hair and yanked him, kicking and struggling, free from the imprisoning grain like a carrot from the ground. The man shrieked and fumbled for the crossbow pistol at his belt but Rurik swatted his hands, breaking his forearms.

He spun the man back into Elita, who snaked her arms around his shoulders and held him fast, nuzzling her bloody chin into his neck. Rurik shook a dagger loose from his sleeve and flicked it across the man's neck. The blade was so small, so sharp, that at first it seemed nothing happened other than a thin red line was suddenly drawn across his throat.

Rurik slapped the back of his open hand across the man's cheek and the brutal, twisting torque revealed the depth of the cut as blood sprayed out in an arc. The man tried to cry out, but he could only manage a wet gurgle as Rurik fastened his mouth to the now-gaping wound and drank.

"Always prone to the dramatic gesture," Rurik said to Elita, smiling a crimson smile. The blood was flowing through him and he felt desire stirring. She felt it too and dropped the drained husk of a man to kiss Rurik hard. He pushed the blood from his mouth into hers and she swooned and bit his lip and pulled his hips into hers.

"Oh Jesus, no," the two men said as the vampires fell heavily into the grain, the bloodlust driving their actions. Rurik swiped her shirt away from her and pulled the bra loose as she tugged at his belt and fumbled for his iron erection. She screamed in pleasure as he entered her, raking her nails down his back and shredding the skin as he roared in approval.

Outside, Lenny looked at Tucker. "What, uhm... what do you think's going on in there?"

"Sounds like they are, you know, getting a little information and, uhm, maybe having a little sex."

"I'm so glad we are not in there," Lenny said.

"Me too," Tucker said.

"I guess it's good to have some downtime," he said.

Tucker was silent, his brow furrowed, and Lenny was reminded of that same look on his friends' face in fifth grade playing dodge ball.

"Course, it gives me a little *too* much time to think about things," Lenny said.

"Things like what?" Tucker asked.

"How they, you know, kind of act like wild animals. Even though they're smart and can talk about things better than you and me, what's going on in there is like lions on a gazelle."

"Lizzie ain't like that," Tucker said.

"I didn't say she was," Lenny said. "It's just curious is all."

"There's a difference between them and us all right," Tucker said. "And between us and animals. But we're all kind of the same too. And Lizzie is still Lizzie."

Rich, sensuous laughter rolled out of the silo, drowning out the screams.

"Elita has a scary laugh," Lenny said. "Kind of like a female version of Johnny Carson, only mean and sexy."

Tucker gave Lenny a pained look. "Johnny Carson?"

Lenny shrugged.

Tucker took off his hat and dusted grains of wheat from the brim. "I may never eat a piece of toast again."

NINETEEN

"I am so goddamned tired," Tucker said, sinking into a booth.

They were in the Watering Hole, deserted at the late hour except for three chronic alcoholics, permanent fixtures, slumped at the bar arguing without passion about doping in professional sports, politics and the efficacy of polio vaccines.

"Humans are weak by design," Elita said. She was wearing a combat vest taken from the corpse of one of the mercenaries after ditching her blood-soaked T-shirt. She made Tucker stop at the Gas N' Get for cigarettes and bought a dozen toy keychains, Japanese-inspired anime cats with oversized eyes, and clipped them through the various loops of the vest normally reserved for weapons of war.

"Says the vampire who gets a goddamned twelve-hour death vacation every day," Tucker said. He caught the attention of Clarissa behind the bar and she came over reluctantly, keeping her eyes averted from Rurik.

Clarissa had been tending bar at the Watering Hole for sixteen years, starting right after her sophomore year in college when it became clear the academic path was not for her. In a town where beauty was a commodity, even though a bit faded and worn, she was practically immune to the hopeful eyes of her patrons, but there was something about the Russian that made Clarissa feel nervous and small.

A few months back, he tipped her more than two thousand dollars. Normally, that would put any man in her good graces and just one genuine smile away from her luxurious pillow-top bed, but the sight of him raised the small hairs on the back of her neck and simultaneously made her desperate to please him. Even now, her hands were shaking on the verge of fear, but all she could think about was a rendezvous in the walk-in cooler for a quick, rough fuck, though something told her it would be anything but quick.

"Beer and whiskey for me," Tucker said when she paused at the table.

"Ginger ale," Lenny said. He was still so upset about the surveillance he wouldn't allow himself even the temporary absolution or solace of a drink.

"I think you know my preferences," Rurik said, enjoying the sway he had over her.

"Vodka, ice-cold," she mumbled, flushing.

Elita, feeling languorous after feeding and an orgasm, enjoyed the rush of pheromones and the interplay of serotonins and oxytocin in the addled woman's brain.

"I'll take a Pimm's Cup," she said.

"Sorry, we don't have Pimm's," Clarissa said. "Can I get you something else?"

"What would you recommend?" Elita asked coyly. "Other than a sweaty tussle on a hotel bed with a handsome Russian?"

Clarissa blushed and stammered, and then darted toward the bar. "I'll take a port," Elita shouted after her. "A double."

"That was mean," Lenny said. "Are you jealous or something?"

Elita rolled her eyes. "Of her? Oh, yes, terribly jealous. Rurik and I had a perfectly lovely, mutually pleasing blood fuck and suddenly you think we're going steady? Your puerile notions about sex never fail to amuse."

"Maybe, but not too many people I know stop their murdering to fool around in a silo," Tucker said. "I just wish you could have gotten a name."

"I tried," Elita said. "I was very insistent. Apparently, there is a fail-safe in place to prevent the extraction of too much useful information. Firewalls around who knows what." She pulled a crumpled sheet of paper from her pocket with a telephone number finger-painted on it in now-dried blood. "At least I got a number. Not to mention chaff in unusual places."

Tucker snatched the paper away from her as Clarissa brought the drinks, slopping the vodka a little as she hurriedly slid it in front of Rurik, then retreated to the bar.

"My cousin Wil already traced it for me," Tucker said. "It belongs to a PR firm in D.C. called Controlled Marketing Corporation. She said they're not the 'help a celebrity recover from a sex tape' kind of PR firm, more the 'help a genocidal dictator rebuild his name' kind."

"I've heard of CMC," Lenny said. "Ex-CIA types run it. Tight with the Pentagon and some big-name defense contractors. Pretty sure one of the big shots was involved on a project I was working on back in the day. Rumor had it one their opponents ended up disappeared. And we're talking about a congressman."

Elita took a sip of the port, grimaced and spit it slowly back into the cup in a thin stream. "That is truly awful. But on the bright side, CMC sounds like my kind of place. Who knew corporate America could have such a sordid pedigree?"

"Uhm, pretty much everyone," Tucker said. "We have a meeting with them tomorrow. Flying out in the morning, you in your coffins and me and Lenny in first class where we can get a little sleep."

"How did you set something up so quick with a company run by a bunch of spooks?" Lenny asked.

"Wil flashed a wire transfer account. It's amazing what hundreds of millions in undead money can do. They think I'm some kind of oilman from Texas looking to invest in grazing land underneath a soon-to-be-harvested Amazon rain forest."

He downed the whiskey. "I'm gonna go home and break the news to Rex that he has to fly again, which he hates." He stood and looked at Rurik and Elita. "I want you two to promise me you'll check for Lizzie when you go to the Meta. If you can, tell her I'm coming for her."

"I'll put a sticky note on my soul before I die," Elita said. "Come on, Rurik, I'm bored. I challenge you to a game of shuffleboard before dawn. Loser has to watch the winner seduce the waitress."

"Y'all leave Clarissa alone," Tucker said. "She's a nice woman."

"Don't worry, I won't bite," Elita said. "Unless she's into that."

TWENTY

The phone on the rolling table vibrated and Louisa opened her eyes reluctantly. They felt gritty and gummy, a function of too little and always fitful sleep on the scratchy cot, she surmised.

She sat up slowly and looked at her watch. The female would be waking soon and Louisa was eager to get back to work. The feeling of being on the brink of a significant discovery, and excited about the research, was intoxicating. She wanted that feeling more than sleep.

Louisa rubbed her eyes hard until little floaters of light flared behind her closed eyelids, then stood and walked to the window. Against a dusky sunset, a tanker slid up the Columbia River escorted by two Coast Guard boats. A helicopter buzzed above, heading out to sea, no doubt delivering a bar pilot to the tanker from Russia or South Korea, or wherever its provenance. The ship was heavily loaded and rode low in the water, moving slowly, methodically, grimly. Louisa thought of a pregnant woman with a bellyful of shiny new Toyotas, Black Sea oil or moldy Russian grain with gleaming Kalashnikovs tucked away inside.

She looked down at her phone. An urgent e-mail from the lab. And then another popped in.

Never seen anything like it before. Blood changing by the minute. Leukocytes nearly triple normal amount. Unknown contaminant now multiplying. Tissue samples still decomposed state. Problem: unable to sequence.

That is unexpected, she thought. Why would the blood be changing? She looked out the window as the crimson-orange sliver of sun slipped past the horizon. She thought about the data embedded in the chrono-clip.

Louisa stared at the sky where it met the ocean, thinking, integrating the lab results into the full context of the information she had so far, and parsing this new data into various hypotheses.

Of course. The disproportionate volume of leukocytes might suggest the white blood cells controlled the anti-aging element of the female's physiology. Could it be that simple? Stimulating human bone marrow to generate additional white blood cells was a reasonable therapeutic target. Kingman's dream of a compound to combat aging just took about ten steps forward, she thought.

She opened the second e-mail from the lab.

Contaminant in blood appears to have neural signature. Is that possible? What in the hell are you working on?

Louisa reconstructed the neuroscans in her head as she realized that a lightning bolt of serendipity was in the process of striking a prepared mind, and this time, finally, it was her mind.

TWENTY-ONE

The untangling began, as it always did, with a heavy, all-pervading sense of sadness that meant her body was pulling her back into the flesh. There was the gradual dimming of exuberance, a shrinking of unbounded freedom and the tired realization that fetters of undead flesh were once again encircling her soul.

When she returned from the Meta, it was always with a splinter of regret lodged just beneath the surface of her thoughts and a sick feeling in her stomach. That feeling was soon replaced by the hunger, and with a flood of confidence and strength.

Elita opened her eyes to see a pale, worried face looming over hers and she flinched and drew back, ashamed at a moment of...not fear, exactly; it was more akin to informed worry. But it was only Tucker, and she relaxed and sat up in the coffin to stretch and take stock of her newly reclaimed life.

"Was she there?" Tucker asked, his voice sharpened by concern.

Elita nodded, feeling Rurik coming to life nearby. "Yes. But even more distant. Still not of her own mind."

They were in a luxurious room looking over...in the distance she could see the Washington monument and on to the Capitol dome. Washington, D.C., then.

"Jesus," Tucker said. "What the hell is going on? Could you, you know, feel where she was?"

Elita shook her head.

Rex was stretched out on the soft leather couch, his head on his crossed paws, watching the two vampires with resigned canine disdain.

"I felt her as well," Rurik said. "There is only a very brief moment when we are fully in control of our faculties as we enter and exit the Meta, but I could certainly sense her both times. But not all of her."

"This is killing me," Tucker said. "I don't know what to do, and that ain't a place I'm used to being."

Elita stood and stretched. "I've got news for you, cowboy, if you ever felt like you were in control of any situation...," she said. Her voice trailed off when she saw the hurt and sorrow flaring in his eyes, and she laid her hand on his arm. He flinched and she could feel the blood pulsing underneath his skin. "We'll find her. I'm sure of it."

"Do you have a plan for tonight?" Rurik asked, stepping from his coffin and surveying the room.

Tucker thought for a moment that perhaps he had become a little too comfortable spending undead money, using it to rent an entire floor of a hotel in Crystal City and tipping the staff outrageously to haul the two coffins upstairs. They thought it was for a wake for his dear old Mawmaw and Pawpaw, who so loved each other they died within minutes.

"We've got a meeting set up at CMC in an hour," Tucker said. "I told them my partner was flying in from Russia and this was the earliest we could meet. Elita, you're my secretary."

"They're called administrative assistants these days," she said. "More like an executive assistant for a woman of my pedigree."

"Call it whatever you want, but grab a steno pad and a pen, and let's get going," Tucker said.

"Steno pad?" Elita said. "LonePine really is in the dark ages. Even I know steno pads fell out of favor twenty years ago, and I have never been in an office for anything other than sport or sex."

"Bring whatever you want and let's go," Tucker said. "Act professional, at least until we can feel this guy out. We need information, not murder and mayhem."

"In a perfect world, we'll have both," Elita said.

Tucker turned to Rurik. "Rurik, you've got ties to the Russian mob and deep pockets from the oil grab. I'm a Texas rancher sitting on family oil and refineries. I want to use lots of your money and none of your name and you want to use a little of my money and all of my name to start a feedlot in Brazil. There are some native folks in the way and we need their help winning the PR war. At any cost. They were salivating so much at the prospect, I thought it would drip through the phone."

"I'm still not sure why we don't just find one of them in their home, invite ourselves in, and then get serious about finding Lizzie," Elita said. "By torturing them and killing them," she added, as if her intentions weren't obvious.

"Because all we've got is a phone number," Tucker said. "We don't even know if they are involved yet, so if you and Smiling Jack here start feasting on the wrong folks, the people we're looking for will go to ground and we might never find Lizzie."

"It is possible this is a trap," Rurik said. "Do you have any weapons?"

"Yeah," Tucker said, nodding. "Two vampires."

He pulled his hat on and motioned for Rex to follow. "They don't exactly let you walk into a secured building run by mercenaries and spies carrying a bunch of guns." He patted a leather sheath on his belt. "But I've got my folding knife."

"That should serve us well against mercenaries and spies," Elita said.

TWENTY-TWO

Lizzie was gradually aware she was awake, slowly drifting into the realization that she was someone who was somewhere.

A heavily starched pillowcase pushed up against her cheek; her heart beat faster than it should and each breath was noticeable, hard to take in and harder still to keep in. The act of breathing itself seemed to injure her anew, each pulse sending out shocks of dull pain.

Someone else was in the room with her, someone with hot, satisfying blood coursing through their veins.

Lizzie moved her head to take in the room and an intense pain shot through her neck and then into the base of her skull. There was a bank of machines whirring and clicking and blowing heat. Most of them seemed connected to her somehow; she traced the snake of cables and cords and wires to her own pale arm, her chest and, it seemed, to a band around her skull.

The woman in the white coat had her back to Lizzie. The same woman who was there when she last died. Slowly, Lizzie remembered again.

"I'm thirsty," Lizzie whispered, not meaning to, but her voice was weak. She felt fragile and the hunger was carving out her insides.

The woman started at the sound of Lizzie's voice and turned.

A flash of surprise flitted across the doctor's face like the shadow of a bird across rough pavement, and she stopped fiddling with the machine she was attending, pouring a cup of water from a nearby plastic pitcher and handing it to Lizzie. When she saw Lizzie could not lift her arm, the doctor sighed and dribbled the water through Lizzie's chapped lips.

The cool water snaked down her throat, indescribably comforting. She turned back toward the heavily curtained window. Was he dead? He, Tucker, her cowboy. She pulled hard again on vague memories about a wedding night at the truckstop, half-remembered explosions, and then nothing. She had no idea how much time had passed since that night, or even if that night was real.

Lizzie inhaled deeply, once, twice, ignoring the pain as she caught her breath and held on to it, willing her heart to stop pounding against her ribs. A moment passed and the loudest beeps began to slow and the whooshing sounds in her ears subsided.

She moved her legs and found herself still bound, then tried the same with her arms. Bound, but not as tightly, it seemed. Any normal vampire could break free, she thought. If vampires were normal.

"Why are you doing this to me?" Lizzie asked, her voice still weak but growing stronger.

The doctor stared at her curiously without responding.

"I want my child to live," Lizzie said. She was less concerned about her own future; under any circumstances, it seemed a choice between awful and more awful, but she needed two, maybe three more months of life for their child.

"Tell me about yourself," Louisa asked.

"Is her life at risk?" Lizzie asked.

"The fetus? Possibly."

She blinked back tears. "Why?"

"You are sick, not just in your mind," Louisa said. "It is unlikely your child will survive without some sort of intervention. For the sake of you both, we have to test you thoroughly to determine what form that intervention might take."

The plan to keep the creature unsure of itself, meek and uncertain, seemed to be working, Louisa thought.

"I will kill you all," Lizzie said.

Well, maybe not.

Louisa weighed her next words carefully. "Lizzie, the first step of your recovery is to move away from violence," she said. "I can understand the impulse, given what happened to you — violence and reckless behavior have consumed you for more than a year, which, in turn was the culmination of four years of deep depression. That's why your mother brought you here."

"What do you want from me?" Lizzie asked.

"Full cooperation," Louisa said.

"Submission," Lizzie said, shutting her eyes. Even my eyes hurt, she thought.

She pondered all the ways she wanted to kill the doctor, and she suddenly understood the world as seen through Elita's eyes.

Elita. Why hadn't she come for her yet? Or Rurik. Did they even exist?

"I need blood," Lizzie said.

The woman nodded to the male nurse. His name was Mark, Lizzie dimly remembered.

Mark hooked a pint bag of pale blood to the IV pole. Within a few seconds, Lizzie felt the diluted red blood cells enter her body. Her mind cleared and the unfamiliar sluggishness lifted, opening a window, slightly, to lucidity.

"You are not a vampire," the doctor said.

"You know nothing about me," Lizzie said.

"I know you are not a vampire," the doctor said. "There is no such thing. This is fake blood, sugar water, a placebo to your delusion. You have a powerful, but disturbed mind. To help you recover from your psychotic break, we must first understand the stories you tell yourself and why. Then we can peel away the layers, like an onion, to reveal your core psychic wound."

Louisa was intent in her performance. Whatever those things were in the creature's blood, the cells with the neural signature, that was the key, she was now sure. There would be no turning back. She felt a pang of remorse that the research was taking her in a direction Kingman had not yet authorized. But no unreasonable resources had been expended at this point. Not yet. But tonight, this female must be persuaded to tell her more. She would need a clear-eyed proposal for Kingman.

The study design Louisa originally devised included caging and anesthetizing the creature for all the tests and sample extractions, but the unknown aspects of her physiology brought unacceptably high risks with this approach. There was no way to know how long the creature would stay under or if it could be trusted to do no harm to itself. She reluctantly discarded this first study design, given she had access only to one subject.

Instead, she came up with this plan — psychological confusion combined with very limited feeding to keep the subject in a constantly weakened state. It was more complicated, and now in hindsight seemed questionable, but still had less probability of subject extermination, which would necessarily result in study termination.

Even so, this alternative design was by no means risk-free. This creature was not human and Louisa had to remember that, no matter how sympathetically it might present itself. The next few nights would have to be delicately scripted.

"Is my mother really alive?" Lizzie whispered, immediately cursing herself for the weakness of the question.

"Yes," Louisa said. "But you won't be permitted to see her, or anyone, for several days, weeks even. You have hard work ahead of you to bring your mind and body back into balance."

"I don't believe you."

Louisa pulled the necklace from her lab coat pocket and dangled it in front of Lizzie.

"Do you recognize this necklace?" she asked. It was a hunch; it was equally possible a lover had given it to her or she had bought it at some antique store. Light reflected off the gemstones.

"Where did you get that?"

Louisa pocketed the necklace again. "Your mother gave it to me to show you, as proof she was thinking of you. You can have it when you get better."

"Why am I chained?"

"Restrained. It seemed more compassionate than a cage or a medically induced coma."

"All these tests, these things you are doing to me…why?" Lizzie asked.

"You are unique in terms of your genetic profile as it potentially correlates to your mental pathology. If we can isolate the gene, we may be able to understand your condition. I believe it's related to why you sleep so much, and so deeply."

Lies, but close enough to the truth that Louisa felt she'd remain believable.

"I thought you were just drugging me," Lizzie said. "If I am not a vampire, if all these memories are false, invented, then whose baby is this?"

"I don't know," Louisa said. "We don't know the details. Just that the child is connected to the event that caused your breakdown."

Lizzie closed her eyes, trying to remember. "Was it violent?"

"You were raped," Louisa said.

Lizzie's eyes flared open in surprise. "By whom?" An image flashed through her mind of being chained, naked, and her father crouching before her, bloody and triumphant.

"The police never caught your assailant," Louisa said. "You were not helpful , you had been drinking. The attack was violent. You created a fantasy world in which the horror was replaced by a more palatable story about vampires. We are working to untangle your delusions from reality, and from your medical condition."

As Louisa pulled details from thin air to support the narrative she needed for her research priorities, Lizzie struggled to fill in details from her own life that would match the story.

"It's not make-believe," Lizzie said, as she let the events of the past six months replay through her thoughts. So much had happened and so fast, piling on top of one another, a mountain of insanity, there had been no time to consider what it all meant. Louisa had to be lying.

"I am not delusional," she said. Her voice sounded unconvincing, even to herself.

Louisa smiled slightly. "Are you the only vampire in the world?" she asked.

"No," Lizzie said. "Of course not."

"How many are there?"

"Five hundred twenty-five thousand six hundred eighty-six," she said. "Maybe eighty seven."

Louisa arched her eyebrow. "Of course, because of the child. How do you know this so specifically?"

"The census."

"So organized, this fantasy world of yours."

"It has to be," Lizzie said. "There is conflict between the two species. War has lasted thousands of years."

"Really? Tell me more."

Lizzie told her about first reading the census in the ancient book when she learned the difference between the types of vampires, the Royals and the Reptiles, and how only humans of the correct lineage could be turned.

"You mean there is a specific genetic signature?" Louisa asked.

"I suppose lineage and genes are more or less synonymous," Lizzie said.

"Latent?"

"That's your area of expertise, not mine," Lizzie said.

Oddly, it almost felt reassuring to talk so openly about it all, especially to someone who might help her see it objectively. Doctors always helped, she thought. They always knew the answers and they could always be trusted, even when they chained you to a bed.

Despite this unexpected desire for confession, her cautious nature held sway. Lizzie gave Louisa only the bare bones, not mentioning that in her blood, and in the blood of the child, flowed the unique power to turn any human regardless of lineage. A power that existed outside the constraints of science and rationalism. She also left out how Tucker figured into the whole scenario.

That the doctor failed to ask about Tucker told Lizzie this woman likely had never been to LonePine, or the truckstop, and therefore had not been directly involved in her abduction. Maybe Tucker was safe. Or maybe he did not exist. Maybe this woman was telling her the truth. She shook her head, trying to sort it all out.

"Good girl," Louisa said, pleased that uncertainty and lies and triple doses of narcotics seemed to be loosening her tongue. "Your candor will help you recover your faculties more quickly so we can move forward with the treatment."

She knew she would have to be careful about the dosing; she did not want the creature to become truly delusional. Or die. Not until she had what she needed.

TWENTY-THREE

The passenger window was partially down so Rex, sitting in the front seat next to the uniformed driver, could sniff the mish-mash of new urban scents: bus exhaust, late-night restaurant kitchens, freshly pressed macadam and the intriguing stench from the garbage truck trundling along in front of the limo.

In the backseat, Tucker, Rurik and Elita embraced their roles. Elita wore a gray skirt and white blouse, provocatively unbuttoned, with her hair up in a tight, sleek bun. Oversized retro glasses completed the sexiest librarian look since the very earliest days of librarians in ancient Alexandria.

Rurik chose to play toward his youthful looks, ironic given his age, wearing a trendy Burberry trench coat, a gauzy scarf and lightly tinted blue spectacles that gave him a faraway hipster, clubber look.

Tucker was dressed exactly the same as always — plaid shirt with snap-button pockets, worn jeans, boots with a few duct tape patches over the leather and his trusty cowboy hat — and still he felt uncomfortable.

Rurik insisted on arriving in style to play the part of money, even though practical Tucker wanted to walk the few blocks. Rurik, a military tactician, won the argument. The limo snaked into the parking lot of a gleaming office building just a hop, skip and appropriation away from the Pentagon.

"This here's the place," Tucker said. "Remember what we're here for."

"Of course, Mr. Tucker," Elita purred.

They assumed their respective roles the second they entered the rented limo for the sake of security, rightly expecting their conversation would be broadcast to a security team in the bowels of the CMC building.

"Wait here," Tucker said to the driver as they exited the limo, Rex in tow.

At the glass doors at the front of the building, a smiling man and woman stood to welcome them.

"Mr. Tucker," the man said. "I'm Blaine Daniels, we spoke on the phone. Pleasure to meet you. And this is my executive assistant, Greta."

Tucker saw a told-you-so smile haunt the corners of Elita's mouth.

"Nice to meet y'all," Tucker said, shaking his hand and trying his hardest to be even more country. "And thanks for meeting us at night. We had a jam-packed day."

"You'd be surprised how many of our clients prefer night meetings," Blaine said. "Please follow me. We have a conference room reserved upstairs."

"With a view of the Potomac, I hope," Tucker said.

"Of course."

They followed Blaine and Greta to the elevator bank, Rex slinking along almost guiltily at being inside such an upscale building.

Tucker noticed Blaine held his hands tight against his sides, and his fingers were closed in on each other, making his hands look slightly deformed, like the claws of an angry crab.

Elita let her senses wash out over the two, feeling a satisfying sense of evil emanating from both. Or perhaps it was simply lack of morality. Easy to confuse the two, she thought, though it mattered little. Since casting her lot with Lizzie, Elita embraced the Royal coda of feeding only on humans who had, or would, perpetrate evil. The PR firm was a veritable buffet. She lightly licked her lips. There will be blood, she thought.

The elevator opened on the third floor and the group walked through long rows of cubicles, many of them occupied, even at the late hour, by people working diligently on reports and presentations and factually ambiguous stories to shape media coverage. At the far wall, a glass-walled conference room overlooked the Potomac and tributaries of highways, the urban streams of light feeding into and across the dark ribbon of water.

Inside the conference room, a large, coffin-shaped desk of exotic wood burnished to a high gleam reflected the overhead lights; three folders with the company seal embossed in copper foil lay on the table.

"Right in here," Blaine said. "Let's talk about your project, but first, what would you like to drink?"

"I wouldn't say no to a whiskey," Tucker said, "but the little lady better pass. One of us needs to stay sharp. How about you, Boris?"

Rurik smiled tiredly. "I keep telling you, Tex, my name is Piotr." He looked at Greta, dressed in almost an exact copy of Elita's outfit, only with her blouse slightly less revealing, and opened himself to the pulse of blood in her soft neck. "Champagne," he said, "mixed with a splash of Campari."

"Fantastic. Greta, would you grab those drinks and a dog bed and some treats for our four-legged friend?"

Rex perked up at the 't' word.

"Right away, Mr. Daniels," Greta said with a smile before hurrying off.

Blaine pulled the door closed and motioned for everyone to sit, which they did, their backs to the river view and all in a neat row like schoolchildren. Blaine sat down ceremoniously in the empty seat behind the mahogany desk facing them. "Let's get down to business. If you will open up your prospectus," he said, placing his phone on the desk near his hand.

Tucker opened the folder to find one single sheet of paper with a crisply typed sentence: '*How stupid do you think we are?*'

"Shit," Tucker said, looking up.

In a heartbeat, Elita pushed her chair over and stood, ready to throw herself across the desk at Blaine, but he smiled and wagged his finger above his phone.

"Let's not get hasty. There are explosives under the desk with enough kindling to *poof* any vampires into dust and to fill human insides with an unpleasant amount of splinters." He looked down at the table. "I'm shielded, of course. Another twitch from any of you, and you go boom from the waist down."

Four beefy men in casual street clothes filed in and took positions at the door. Three of them held brutal crossbows with laser sights, two aimed on Rurik and one on Elita.

She looked down at the crimson dot on her chest. "Just one on me?" she said. "I'm insulted."

The other guard held gleaming .50 caliber handguns in each hand, both aimed at Tucker, who slowly, carefully, placed his hands palm down on the desk. "Does this mean I won't be getting that whiskey?" he asked.

"We're not uncivilized," Blaine said. He nodded to Greta, standing patiently in the hall.

"I took the liberty of bringing champagne for the lady," she said. "Since she's clearly not your assistant."

"Thank you," Elita said, vindicated.

Greta placed the tray at the head of the desk and stepped back.

"You can understand why I won't let her get too close to you, though?" Blaine said. "We don't want another unfortunate human shield situation to lead to a vacant position. I've invested significant time training her just the way I want her."

Tucker pulled the tray closer, took the tumbler of whiskey and sipped. He whistled beneath his breath and Rex perked up. "Damn, that's good whiskey."

He put the empty glass on the tray as Elita picked up a champagne flute and drained it.

"This doesn't have to get all hard," Tucker said. He looked at the guards. "Correction. Harder. We just want information."

"We don't disclose information about our clients," Blaine said. "It's kind of our thing. That, and, of course, always being prepared. Even for vampires, which I never, ever thought I would have to say."

He leaned forward, finger still close to the phone, and spoke directly to Tucker. "We found records on you. Boring records, but all the expected stuff. These other two though, not a peep. Fascinating. I really thought I had the lost the ability to be surprised. That I had grown too…I don't know…"

"Cynical?" Greta asked.

"Exactly right. Cynical. But you made my night. Can you do any, I don't know, vampire things?"

"Drain your blood from the stump of your neck," Rurik said flatly.

"Ooh, very horror show," Blaine said. "But words don't convince me of much these days. A professional side effect, I suppose."

"Here's the thing," Tucker said. "I'm pretty sure one of your clients is the bastard who kidnapped my lady."

"We are involved in many business ventures."

"Lizzie is not a goddamn venture," Tucker said angrily, making ready to stand and eliciting a growl from Rex, who suddenly realized things were tense and treats were not forthcoming. "She's a pregnant woman who wasn't hurting a goddamn soul."

"Easy," Blaine said, his finger near the screen of his phone. "Remember the whole thing about blowing your legs off? From what I understand, she's not a woman, she's a thing, just like these two. But I don't even really care about that. We provide a service and our business plan requires us to be unencumbered by issues of morality or even facts. Results are what matter. And discretion."

"Can we buy the information?"

"It's not for sale," Blaine said. "Someone always comes along with more money, but we only have one reputation. And I don't think you have the resources to become our only client."

"You'd be surprised at how much money I could shake loose for Lizzie," Tucker said.

"You'll have to do better than comically exaggerated checking accounts," Blaine said. "No one has that kind of money."

"I actually do have that kind of money," Tucker said. "Vampires are pretty good at saving for a rainy day, or a sunny day, I guess."

"You'll pardon me for not believing you," Blaine said.

"Then I think we're at what they call an impasse," Tucker said.

"No, not really," Blaine said. "Either you leave of your own volition, or we will escort you out, or escort pieces of you out, if that's your choice." He looked at his watch. "But could you make a decision soon? Greta and I are attending a show tonight."

"We'll go," Tucker said, resigned.

Elita drained the last drops of her champagne and then picked up Rurik's glass and finished it as well. "No sense letting it go to waste," she said, setting the flute back on the tray and winking at Rurik.

"Before we walk you out, could you please hand over the knife in your belt," Blaine said.

"I've had this a long time," Tucker said. "I'd prefer to keep it."

"It's really nonnegotiable," Blaine said.

Tucker shrugged and carefully removed the folding knife from the battered leather sheath and tossed it on the table.

Blaine opened it, tested the edge and whistled. "Sharp. But is this really how you prepare to meet your foe? Bringing a knife to a gunfight? Pathetic."

Tucker glared as Blaine dropped the knife on the middle of the desk and motioned for them to leave.

TWENTY-FOUR

The girl nurse stood at the foot of the bed, her blonde hair pulled back into a tight ponytail and her bright, kind eyes focused intently on Lizzie. "My name is Helmi," she said. "Do you need anything?"

Lizzie tried to smile back, but it felt like a grimace. The pain was taking its toll.

Louisa had excused herself a few minutes earlier for what she called a "bio-break," and so they had the room momentarily to themselves.

When she was human, Lizzie thought, she reported on crime stories in which the victim was so brutally traumatized they made up a false reality just to cope. There was always someone like this in those stories — a kind nurse or a whore with a heart of gold.

"Helmi, let me go," she whispered. "My name is Lizzie and I don't belong here."

"Your mind is injured," Helmi said gently. "We want to help you. Is there anything I can do for you now, in this room?"

Lizzie shook her head. Helmi tapped on the watery blood bag hanging from the IV pole, and Lizzie felt a little stronger as the liquid dripped into her vein faster, but not by much.

The door to the room opened. "I need an additional sample of cerebrospinal fluid," Louisa said. "Prepare her for a lumbar puncture."

"This will be her third spinal tap," Helmi said.

"I'm aware of that," Louisa said. "Be ready to proceed after I've conducted the next phase of my interview with the subject."

"Yes, Doctor," Helmi said, hustling from the room.

"And prepare for the possibility of direct brain tissue sampling as well," Louisa called after her. "I have a neurosurgeon on call to walk us through it."

Kingman wanted the treasure that would come from saving humanity from old age. Louisa would do what she could to make that dream a reality for him, and for the world. From this alone she would become part of scientific lore and she would help improve the lot of all humans. But the neural signatures on the creature's blood opened up another door, a door to the holy grail of human consciousness, and a chance to test a theory she'd long held.

"I need blood," Lizzie said. "Surely you have some test monkeys in the back. I could drain some of them."

"Animals for animals," Louisa said, snapping open the electronic medical record, but then quickly checked herself. Wrong script. She took a deep breath to refocus.

"I am not an animal," Lizzie said.

Louisa pushed her glasses onto her head. Partial truth was always easiest, she thought. But it was necessary to adjust the study design slightly to accommodate the new research direction that focused on the creature's neurological aspects.

Louisa's fingers tingled and she felt suddenly giddy, as if she'd had a second glass of champagne. This new line of inquiry perfectly matched her long-dormant dissertation thesis. Maybe she was right all along, and it had been a mistake to switch directions so long ago. Maybe giving up on it was the reason her scientific career sputtered out.

But to test the hypothesis, she would need much more cooperation from the creature, and quickly. Time was limited.

"Eventually, I will kill you," Lizzie said. Her voice was still weak and scratchy, as if she'd chain-smoked a dozen cigarettes.

"I know you are damaged because of the unspeakable evil that has befallen you, and by the evil you committed in turn," Louisa forced herself to say.

"What evil?" Lizzie asked.

"You killed the man who raped you. Stabbed him to death," Louisa said. "It is understandable you would invent a bloody, death-centric story to explain your actions, even to yourself."

Lizzie's mind flashed back to New Mexico and the death of her father at her own hands — his thick, evil blood flooding her mouth. There was something else. A man on a rough bed, his hands bound, naked, begging for his life. She remembered his blood too, a wife and daughter numb with fear. And a Russian.

"Because of the trauma, you lost your identity, and any sense of morality," Louisa said. "I can try to cure you, but in the process, I want to learn from you."

"Cure me how?"

"I think you understand."

Lizzie felt glimmers of the woman she once was, the reporter with the omnivorous curiosity and a penchant for good wine. A life that once seemed so stressful and complicated now seemed so simple and desirable. She wanted it back. Maybe there was still a chance.

"What happens to you when you sleep?"

"It is not sleep," Lizzie said. "It's death."

"It can't be death," Louisa said. "You wouldn't be here talking to me."

Lizzie looked up at the ceiling, at the thick wooden beams exposed there. She wondered about the age of the building. It seemed solid, as if built long ago.

"I want to understand what happens to you when you go into the deep sleep," Louisa said. "Do you recall anything from those hours?"

"Can you make me normal again?" Lizzie asked.

Louisa pulled on latex gloves, snapping them at her wrist. "What do you consider normal?"

"Human," Lizzie said. "I want to be human again."

TWENTY-FIVE

"Come on, chop-chop," Blaine said. "Let's go. Time to head back to your little ghost town in Wyoming and you all to get back in your coffins or wherever vampires live, or die."

No one moved. Elita looked down at the crimson dot on her chest, cast there by the laser sight on a crossbow aimed in her direction, the wooden shaft just the twitch of a restless finger away from impaling her and ending her undead existence. Eyes sparkling with barely contained rage, she shifted her gaze to Tucker's knife discarded casually on the table.

If Blaine saw the object of her interest, he chose to ignore it and instead motioned brusquely at the door. "Seriously, time to go. Don't make this more embarrassing than it already is. Leave now with whatever's left of your dignity and spend some time on the flight back reflecting on the perils of facing a superior enemy with inferior preparation."

"We might," Tucker said, smiling evenly. "But y'all might want to ruminate on the shortcomings of over-confidence. Now, Lenny," he said.

Blaine looked at him curiously, but before he could speak, there was a distant, muffled boom that shook the walls and caused the lights in the entire building to flicker and die.

In the ensuing darkness, there was a chaotic rush of movement, wordless cursing and then gunshots. The huge pistols boomed four times, blossoming with muzzle flashes that lit the room in dizzying bursts, revealing careening shadows and acrid smoke that captured the crisscross of the ruby laser sights.

The crossbows twanged, sending deadly bolts whistling through the bedlam. Two *thunked* solidly into the backs of now-empty chairs, the third skidded off the tabletop and crashed through the window and out into the night.

Next came wet, slapping, splintering sounds, and then screams that mostly trailed off into pained gurgles. And rich, joyous female laughter.

Within seconds, the backup power kicked on emergency lights to reveal in their feeble glow a gruesome tableau of death in the disordered conference room. The three guards who had most recently held crossbows now held their own slit throats; two were sitting slumped against the blood-spattered glass wall with their legs splayed out. One was kneeling and staring in horror at the waterfall of blood gushing between his fingers, splashing down his chest and soaking into the gray carpet.

Elita was standing by the door, Tucker's knife in her hand. The blade was coated in blood and gore dripping onto the white sleeve of her blouse. She was licking the back of her hand slyly, like a cat and smiling triumphantly.

Rurik was crouched over the shooter who was writhing on the floor, both his arms broken and bent downward at ridiculous angles, bone shards poking through the skin, and two shattered champagne flutes buried deep in his stomach. The Russian tossed one of the big pistols to Tucker, who made sure a round was seated in the chamber and placed it on the conference table aimed in the direction of Blaine's stomach.

The PR man sat stock-still, face pale. Greta was crouched on the floor beside him, her hands over her ears and her mouth open in a silent scream.

"See, we were prepared," Tucker said. There were two splintered holes on the desk in front of him where slugs bored deep into the wood, and a crease along the top of his chair where the exposed cotton fibers showed just how close another slug had come to coring his head.

Blaine, stunned, looked down at the tabletop for his phone hoping still to trigger the explosive charges, but Tucker held it.

"I think you may miss your show tonight," Tucker said. "Unless of course you just want to save us all some time and tell us who hired you, and where Lizzie is. And then you can be on your merry way."

"More men are on the way," Blaine said, voice cracking.

"Good, I'm hungry," Elita said. "And I love East Coast men." She knelt down beside one of the guards and pulled his pale, trembling hand away from his throat, clamping her mouth on the wound and sucking with wet, loud gulps. Greta sobbed uncontrollably at the sight.

"I know," Tucker said. "It's gross. I never get used to it. But you don't have to end up like them. Just tell us what we need to know and you two walk."

"W-w-we can't disclose, you know, client names," Blaine stammered.

Tucker stood and put his boot against the desk. "A little help?" he said to Rurik.

Together, they turned the desk and pushed it up against the window. Tucker pulled his phone from his jacket. It was connected to Lenny, who had been listening the whole time.

"You ready?" Tucker asked, then nodded. "Good, because we're coming out, and unlike vampires, people don't bounce. You want to tell me your plan?"

He paused. "'Trust me' is not a plan." He listened intently. "All right, if you say so. Watch out below."

He turned to Elita. "Can I have my knife back?"

Elita wiped it on her skirt and handed it to him. "It was sharp. A little less so now."

He closed it and tucked it back into the sheath. "I'm gonna blow the window," he said. "You grab him," he said to Elita, pointing at Blaine. "And you grab Greta," he said to Rurik. "I'll get Rex and out we go, all at once. Lenny has something lined up below to catch us."

"Something like what?" Elita asked, using a handful of tissues to dab the blood from her chin and cheeks like she was seated in front of a makeup mirror.

"Does it matter? You're practically indestructible."

"True, but I didn't get to be this old by not looking *before* I leap."

"Let's argue on the ground," Rurik said. "More are on their way, and the police, likely."

"Last chance," Tucker said to Blaine. "If we take you with us, things are going to get really weird for you, and for Greta."

"Tell him, Blaine," Greta begged.

"Can't c-c-compromise our promise to c-clients," Blaine stuttered.

"A good trooper to the end," Elita said. "Let's take this party somewhere more private."

Tucker pulled Rex close, cradling his head against his chest and pressing his free hand over the dog's exposed ear, he then used his thumb to press a big, red button on the screen of Blaine's phone with the word "boom" in it. There was a flash and *whoomph* of air as the directional explosives shredded the window and blew kindling out into the night.

"Geronimo," Tucker said, holding Rex tight. With a running start, he leapt out of the window. To his right, Elita was dragging Blaine by his hair and to his left, Rurik had a swooning Greta in his arms.

They plummeted down three stories toward a brightly colored structure in the carefully manicured lawn below.

Tucker hit first and felt a whoosh of air and, gratefully, cushioned support.

He struggled up out of the deflating fabric with Rex wriggling loose.

"A bounce castle?" he said to Lenny. "That was your great plan? A goddamn bounce castle?"

Rurik, with a now-unconscious Greta over his shoulder, pushed his way past them toward the rental minivan idling nearby.

"This was a stroke of sheer genius," Lenny said. "It's basically a giant airbag. I had to work my ass off to find one, and get enough compressed air cylinders to blow it up in time. I spent half the day rummaging around a U-tow salvage yard in Frederick for airbag modules to blow it up quick-like."

Blaine squeaked in fear as Elita pulled him from the rapidly deflating castle by the scruff of his neck. "We are going to have so much fun together," she said, pushing him toward the car.

"We just gonna leave it here?" Tucker asked.

"Yeah, and let's get going before either the cops or the clowns get here," Lenny said.

"A bounce castle," Tucker muttered.

Shouts and shots from overhead and a distant siren caused him to hurry his reveries and chase Rex into the back door of the van.

TWENTY-SIX

The ocean felt closer, the air saltier, and the odor of dead fish stronger. Lizzie's senses were heightened, even if the rest of her body was weakened.

"Tell me what happens when you go into the deep sleep," Louisa asked again.

"Have you ever been in love?" Lizzie asked.

Louisa considered the question, and then looked at her watch. 4:52 a.m. She needed to make this work. There would not be another chance. The creature's near-death would come on soon, and she was reaching the point of exhaustion herself.

"Once. Yes, I was in love," Louisa said.

"I wasn't talking to you," Lizzie said. "I meant the other one." She nodded toward Helmi, who was watching Lizzie's heart monitor, but now looked up cautiously.

"Answer her," Louisa said tiredly, only half paying attention now as she pictured the third neuroscan in her mind, examining it from every angle, making sure it really fit her hypothesis.

"No, I haven't been in love," Helmi said. "Not yet."

"Thank you for telling me that," Lizzie said. "For sharing." Her eyes burned and everything seemed fuzzy. "You're very pretty, I think, and nice. It will happen soon enough." She closed her eyes and Louisa thought she had lost her again.

"What about you?" Lizzie said after a few minutes, looking at Louisa.

"I already said yes. Why else do you want to know?"

"It's not a trick question," Lizzie said. "I'm just making conversation while you have me strapped to this bed drilling holes in my spine. Seems like a fair trade. What's the harm? Tell me about when you were in love."

"It was during my university days," Louisa said.

"That was a long time ago, I bet," Lizzie said. "Were you a virgin?"

"Really? That's what you want to know?"

"Humor the crazy lady who thinks she's a vampire," Lizzie said.

"Fine. Yes, I was." Louisa felt her neck flushing.

Sensing the rush of blood in the doctor, a painful pang of hunger stabbed through Lizzie.

Louisa noticed Lizzie's pupils dilating, and that Lizzie was staring at the fragile skin around her throat hungrily. Louisa felt a tingle of fear and Lizzie saw it, and in that moment Lizzie felt stronger than she had in days.

But this is not the time, Lizzie thought, and she worked to still her heart and her hunger. Deep breaths, she told herself, deep breaths. Not a vampire. Not real. Even if it is real, I don't want it to be real, she thought, any of it. She remembered her human days when she did yoga — not very well, of course, but the breath control exercises seemed to have stuck. She let the oxygen flood deep into her lungs and then willed it even lower, into her stomach, her thighs, and pushed her breath down into her toes.

Louisa knew she was being tested, and it was a test she intended to win. She would finish the conversation and get the information she wanted. The moment called for measured words.

"I thought he was brilliant and I believed he was my future," Louisa said, a little too loudly. "When he touched me, I melted."

"Interesting word choice. What happened?"

"All happy loves are similar, all breakups are uniquely tragic in their own way, yes?"

"Tolstoy," Lizzie said, thinking again of the Russian, who probably wasn't real. With difficulty, she reined in her thoughts. Reality did not exist beyond this moment between her and her captor.

"Poorly paraphrased," Louisa said. "Turns out I meant nothing to him. He wouldn't leave his wife. I was heartbroken."

"Did you love again?" Lizzie asked.

Helmi was watching them closely, near frozen by the intensity between the two women.

"Not really. Not like that. I have a dog, a German shepherd. Her name is Deena. It's a love of a sort. I don't have time for any other kind these days. I don't miss it."

"Fair enough," Lizzie said. "Your question from before, I travel to the Meta."

"What is the Meta?" Louisa asked, opening her notebook.

"My cells, my brain, myself — whatever that is, whatever I am — I transcend my body, at least it feels that way. I suppose it could all be a lucid dream too. It feels like something that starts in my blood."

"Good. I need more blood samples and fluid from your spine," Louisa said. "While you sleep this cycle, I'll also conduct additional neurological scans and electrophysiological studies. Helmi, please bring what's needed from the supply room."

Helmi nodded and left.

"I asked you something before. I need to know," Lizzie said. She looked up at Louisa, her eyes betraying a desperate hope as she struggled to stop her lower lip from trembling.

Louisa felt a surge of pity for this female. She was so pretty, even in this weakened, sickly state.

What was happening? She could not, would not, allow herself to become attached to the subject. Louisa was too close to knowledge, and empathy was an obstacle. One chance left for success. Discipline now was crucial. The flush overtook Louisa's cheeks, and she paused before responding.

"I think I can help you, but I can't promise. I don't know how you came to be what you are, but it is irrelevant to my research as currently designed. This is what you are now, a genetic aberration. A reversal of fortune, a tiny downturn on the evolutionary scale."

"How do you know I am below you?" Lizzie asked. "Maybe I'm above you. I think I'm above."

The thought had not occurred to Louisa.

"If I am a new version of humanity, an improvement, an advancement, so to speak, that makes you a lesser adaptation," Lizzie said. "Then you are the animal, not me. I can see how my kind would be inclined to treat you as simple prey, something lesser on the food chain."

Lizzie's mind felt newly clear.

Louisa made a mental note to increase the dose; she needed her malleable, although this idea was an interesting development. She began to process the possibility that the creature represented a different evolutionary vector than she originally assumed.

"Answer me now," Lizzie said. "Can you turn me back into a human?" If this curse of hers, this delusional world of violence and intrigue could be stripped away and sealed off, she and Tucker could live out their lives. If Tucker was even real. Her thoughts scattered like startled pigeons whenever she tried to focus.

Louisa looked back at Lizzie silently. Her original assumption had to be right. Humans were at the pinnacle of evolution, thus far. Intentional genetic manipulation might one day change that, but this thing, this blood-sucking creature, was far from intentional; she was an aberration.

"I will commit to studying that later," she said. "If you agree to help me understand this place you call the Meta and how you access it."

She hoped this would satisfy the creature. Lizzie seemed to nod slightly, but Louisa could not be certain.

Helmi came back into the room and placed several wrapped items on the nearby shelves.

"Let's proceed," Louisa said. "Prepare the subject for a round of blood draws, and prep her for an EP study and more MRI scans. But first, the spinal fluid."

"Yes, ma'am," Helmi said. She picked up a long needle and placed it on the table.

"Turn over on your side," Louisa said. "And pull your legs up to your chest, a fetal position."

"My legs are chained."

"I won't unchain you," Louisa said. "Do your best. Position yourself so I can reach your back."

"It's impossible," Lizzie said, her voice breaking into a sob. "Why not wait until I am in the Meta?"

"We have detected a difference in your neural cells based on time of day," Louisa responded sternly, but then softened her tone. "Please, you must cooperate, so I can help you later."

Lizzie wanted to believe her. She inched onto her side, bending her knees, nestling them as best she could beneath her pregnant belly. She felt the baby softly kick against her thigh.

"This is a spinal tap; it will hurt, but afterwards, we'll give you an additional bag of blood."

"I have the anesthetic prepared," Helmi said.

"A contamination risk," Louisa said brusquely.

She took a deep breath to steady her hand and then plunged the three-inch needle deep into the small of Lizzie's back.

The pain sent a bolt of lightning careening from Lizzie's spine to her brain and then out into every nerve ending. Louisa pulled out the bloody fluid agonizingly slowly. As the seconds and then minutes passed, Lizzie panted and cursed, but refused to scream, saliva trailing out of the side of her mouth.

Helmi steadied Lizzie's shoulder with one hand and with the other handed the doctor a sterile wipe. As Louisa used it to slide the needle out, Helmi turned back to the supply cabinet to hide her tearing eyes.

"You are an evil woman," Lizzie whispered through gritted teeth.

"I will help humanity," she said. "Sometimes, this requires sacrifice."

"Of your ethics?" Lizzie asked.

"I don't expect you to understand," Louisa said, wanting to say something kinder, but held back, keeping herself firmly focused on her goal.

Louisa gave Helmi the used needle to discard.

Lizzie exhaled as the worst of the pain subsided. She pressed her face into the pillow and let all the anger and hate inside her uncoil out in a long, painful scream. She strained against the shackles and felt them squeak and weaken, and felt a pulse of adrenaline as the two humans recoiled in fear. Only one of them, Helmi, tempered that fear with empathy.

The sun wobbled up over the edge of the horizon.

TWENTY-SEVEN

The heart monitor went flat with a soft chirp, a sound that in hospital rooms around the world was the first note in a subsequent symphony of mourning and grief as an individual human story collapsed in on itself. Helmi went into action as Lizzie died, relying on her training by instinct.

"Code blue, get the crash cart," she shouted, but Louisa casually cut her off.

"She's not dead," Louisa said. "How many times must you be told? She has gone into her deep sleep state. Prep the EP study. I want results within an hour."

Helmi was momentarily adrift, stoically holding the defibrillator paddles, still certain that saving life must always be the priority. "But her vitals, Dr. Burkett, we must respond."

"Come up to speed on the protocols," Louisa said, waving her hand toward Helmi dismissively. Distracted, she turned her attention to the still form on the bed and unconsciously chewed on her lower lip. Abruptly, she left the research room, almost colliding with Mark, who stood to the side as she passed silently by.

Helmi placed the equipment back onto the crash cart, quietly organizing it, making sure it was ready for the next possible use. She looked at Mark, her gaze questioning, but he just shrugged, unmoved.

"Let's get her ready for the next test," Mark said.

Helmi gathered her wits and turned resolutely to the lifeless body, pulled back Lizzie's long blonde hair — now clumped and dirty — and began to cut it short. The locks fell onto the pillow as Mark prepared to shave her head. He slipped a laser onto the tray, unnoticed by Helmi, because he soon would scar Lizzie's pupils again.

In her workroom, Louisa pulled up the data record for the blood. The technician had added a clever lime-green dye that attached to the unknown contaminant cells, making them easier to see in the scans. Another chapter in the endless detective story, thought Louisa. In the images taken earlier in the sample night, the lime-green substance now circulated throughout the liquid. She compared it to images taken just after the sun had risen. The contaminants shrank in on themselves, now nearly imperceptible.

Louisa pulled out a vial of blood and put it in the centrifuge, watching intently as the circular motion soon separated out the heaviest layer of plasma. It expectedly sank to the bottom of the vial, but there was another layer now too, impossibly thin, at the base below the plasma. Whatever it was, it had to be the differentiating factor that resulted in the female's deep, deathlike sleep.

She removed the vial, stepping over to the large windows of the old cannery. The smell of decades of salmon flesh deboned, pulverized and squirted into cans permeated the hundred-year-old wooden structure.

Louisa thought about an image from a film she'd seen long ago in which a woman, maybe Susan Sarandon, tried to wash the stink of fish from her hands with lemons. Over the sink, each night, after she got home from the fish market where she worked, the woman rubbed her hands with cut lemons until the juice covered her fingers like invisible gloves. Louisa tried to remember if she liked the movie but couldn't recall any other scenes.

She opened the window and cool ocean air blew into the room carrying the cry of seagulls.

Such pedestrian thoughts of old movies and raucous seabirds could not distract her long from the decision she was weighing.

It wouldn't be the first time. There was a long history of scientists using themselves as experimental subjects, Louisa thought. The downside was that if anything happened to her, the research would come immediately to a crashing halt. But the upside, well…she shuddered with excitement. The upside was knowledge, and the only risk was death. And what was death, really, to her anymore other than the end of another line of inquiry?

She walked back the workroom and tapped out a message to Kingman with the file name 'Read only if I am dead,' and then encrypted it and scheduled the delivery for hours later so she could easily turn it off, if she lived through it.

Louisa used a syringe to siphon off the plasma, leaving just the unknown substance, a scant few drops, in the bottom of the test tube. She squirted in enough sterile water to half fill the tube, shook it quickly, and popped the cap off. She sucked in a ragged breath, then downed the blood like a shot of rough-cut whiskey and stretched out on the cot.

Within seconds, her breathing became labored and she panicked, but just as quickly, the distress subsided. A sense of peaceful resolution filled her from the nucleus of every cell outward, while above her, a constellation of stars wheeled slowly around and pulsed with a cosmic heartbeat, and she was alone inside a gravely silent, living planetarium.

Floating through the universe, she heard her mother's voice behind her, long dead, soothing, and then her mother's laughter, always infectious. Louisa felt a radiant euphoria, and that this moment was the only one moment in time that had ever existed, that she belonged here, that she was deeply loved.

Without warning, she began to plummet, away from the ether, like a stone falling through air, landing inside an inky, musty darkness. The temperature dropped, goose bumps rose across her skin. She pushed at the top of the darkness, at the sides, and kicked at the bottom. Nothing. She could not move, and she heard the sounds of something — was it dirt? — falling on the top of the box. Louisa screamed, but her voice was silent. And then she woke, her hands gripping the sides of the cot and tears streaming down her face.

She sat up quickly, calming her breath and her mind. What the hell was that?

TWENTY-EIGHT

The Weary Traveler Motel had seen better days, but not much better.

During the mayoral reign of the infamous Marion Barry several decades prior, the New York Avenue corridor into the District from neighboring northeast cities, near Bladensburg Road, was a sinkhole of poverty and crime, with rent-a-room-by-the-hour deals for trysting government workers on their lunch break.

More recently, like much of the close-in District, the area had become partially gentrified and was now interspersed with a few tourist hotels mostly on the north side, catering to the wide-eyed visitors endlessly streaming into the city to observe the towering marble edifices of the federal government.

Today, the low-rent love nest motels of the past were mostly demolished to make way for the influx of new wealth, but a few remained, steadfast symbols of a different city. These two-story walk-ups — with pot-holed parking areas surrounded by abandoned car lots, abandoned industrial buildings and the omnipresent fast food restaurants serving tourists from across the street — clung to life like mold that no amount of bleach could scrub clean.

The Weary Traveler, one of the last of these stubborn, decaying motels, was bordered on two sides by a parking lot filled with mostly defunct cars and surrounded by a razor-wire-topped fence and, on the other side, a check cashing service with inch-thick glass service windows. In front, the motel and its denizens were buffeted by the continuous roar of New York Avenue traffic and the clatter of arriving and departing trains.

It was the kind of place where bad things happened on a daily, sometimes hourly basis, but the goings-on were unnoticed or, more likely, ignored by the nearby Metro police station.

There were currently five residents in the Weary Traveler. One of them was Blaine Daniels, recently of Controlled Marketing Corporation.

When he opened his eyes, he was staring at a cracked ceiling and a dusty fan wobbling slowly and ineffectively. He tried to rub his eyes, but his hands refused to cooperate. Upon further investigation, he saw orange twine, braided four layers strong, binding his wrists and ankles to a bed frame. He tested it curiously, then with growing urgency, and finally with panicked strength that caused the orange fibers to cut deep into his wrists. The rope was unyielding.

Worse, he realized he was completely naked and tied to a bed that smelled sour and recently soiled. He wondered if the smell was from him. A man used to giving orders, he now felt doubly vulnerable and his teeth chattered softly from the cold and growing fear.

He craned his neck, eyes wild and wide, to take stock. It was a hotel room, and not the type he was used to patronizing. A cheap place where money bought anonymity but not service, and certainly not hygiene.

"Good, you're awake," a male voice drawled. The cowboy. "Elita plays rough. I wasn't sure you were ever going to wake up."

Tucker was sitting in a threadbare easy chair, jacket collar turned up and hat pulled low. He stood suddenly and draped a towel over Blaine's privates. "Not really interested in looking at your shriveled little pecker while we talk," he said.

"You need to let me go," Blaine said. "This is illegal."

Tucker laughed, a harsh snort. "Mr. Daniels, you, of all people, should not be clinging to the law," he said. "You are in a real pickle here. You have information I need, information that will save the life of my fiancée. I reckon I would do just about anything to get my Lizzie back. As for them two in the next room, they want her back pretty bad too. And they'll do just about anything they please because they're goddamned vampires." He paused. "Are you hearing me?"

"I have rights," Blaine said, voice cracking.

"What you have is a long night ahead of you, and very little chance of seeing the sunrise," Tucker said. "They got Greta in the next room." He jerked his thumb toward the door. "They've been working her over ever since the sun went down. Seems she don't have much in the way of useful information. She sure wishes she did, because it might have gone a lot easier for her. But she didn't, so now they are just sort of playing with her. Like, you know, how a cat keeps messing with a mouse, poking at it and throwing it around. On account of vampires have a cruel streak."

"Why are you helping them?" Blaine asked.

"Really? You come to *my* town, to LonePine, and blow up *my* wedding and steal *my* fiancée, and you have the nerve to question *my* motivation? You help murderers and dictators, all for a buck, and you ask me how I live with *my* decisions?"

"I'm sorry," Blaine said. "It's all just a terrible misunderstanding. Let me go and I will get it all sorted out. Make some calls."

Tucker held his hand up. "Nah, see, I don't think you can do a goddamn thing to convince the people you work for to play nice. You just need to tell me who took Lizzie. It's the only way you end up only a little hurt. And then you better pray she is okay when I find her or else I'm coming back and I'll be pissed."

"I...I can't reveal client information," Blaine stuttered bravely, despite his genuine terror.

"You're loyal and I can respect that," Tucker said. He jerked his head toward the adjoining room. "They won't. They'll just see it as a challenge."

A high-pitched, keening wail knifed through the wall, and Blaine grew even paler.

"Yep, that was Greta," Tucker said. "Guess she ain't dead yet."

The door between the rooms swung open suddenly and Elita stood there, framed by sobs and panting and wet, thudding sounds spilling around her from the darkened room.

"No more," a weak voice murmured behind her. "Please, God, no more."

Elita slammed the door shut and grinned wickedly. A sheen of blood shimmered on her lips and stained the front of her blouse. "I see the second course is awake," she said. "I adore this motel. That poor wretch has been begging us to stop for hours, and not so much as a peep from the managers."

She was holding a straight-edged razor, the blade coated in blood, in one hand. She *tutted* her disapproval at the sight of the towel across Blaine's middle. She snatched it free and tossed it across the room.

"Tucker, you have no idea how much blood we can get from down here," she said, tracing the tip of the razor across his scrotum.

"I've castrated a lot of calves," Tucker said. "I don't think I'd be that surprised."

"Mmm, maybe a little," she said, bending close. "I should tell you, peach, it's going to feel good at first," she murmured, pressing the blade more insistently against the puckered skin. "When I open things up a little and start sucking. But that will pass quickly, because I tend to get excited and use my teeth more than I should."

"Auscor Kingman," Blaine said, writhing against the ropes. "It's Auscor Kingman. The tech guy. He did it. That's all I know. I swear. Auscor Kingman. Please."

Elita frowned. "That was too easy. Please say I can finish him off."

"Nope," Tucker said. "I want him alive and mostly in one piece. We're not killers."

She laughed. "Speak for yourself, Bronco Billy."

"Seriously," Tucker said. "He's a bad guy, but just a

businessman. No better or worse than anyone who hides behind profits and cell phones and shareholders. Have some fun, drink some blood and make him regret his decisions, but leave him alive and with his parts intact."

"I accept your conditions reluctantly," she said, "but only because I can sense his evil is superficial and probably redeemable. As much as it pains me, I know Lizzie would want it that way. So we'll just have a little fun, instead."

Rurik opened the door, nude and smeared in blood, a rock-hard erection pointing out like a dowsing rod directly at Elita. "She has passed out again," he said. "And after only a mere handful of orgasms. I am in need of satisfaction and she sleeps as if dead."

"We have what we need," Tucker said, looking pointedly away from the Russian. "You and Elita can have your fun with this one."

"I don't understand," Blaine said. "Greta?"

"Is alive," Elita said. "She'll wake up a little anemic and sexually satisfied like she's never been before. There's something about the feeding process that turns on the sex machine for humans. Once we found out she was not the slightest bit evil, only easily manipulated, and didn't know anything, we just wanted to make it sound like she was dying."

"But it will not be from pleasure you beg me to stop," Rurik said with a scowl, crossing the room with his erection bobbing.

"Okay, well, that's about it for me," Tucker said. "I'm gonna step outside and let you all get acquainted. Remember this night, and what happens to people like you when you sell your soul."

Blaine begged him to stay, but Elita was on him in a flash and, with her hand clamped over his mouth, dragged the razor lightly across his chest and lapped at the blood that welled up. As Tucker pulled the door shut, Rurik was pushing Elita's skirt up around her hips exposing her ass, a turquoise thong separating her cheeks. Tucker paused just long enough to admire what was revealed there and, sensing his gaze, Elita turned her head and grinned happily at him as she pulled her shirt off. She turned to face him, her breasts exposed, but Tucker shut the door quickly, trapping her laughter behind him.

Outside, Lenny sat on the smoking bench looking out over the parking lot. He had one hand under his coat resting on the handle of a pistol, watching for CMC mercenaries. Rex sat beside him, watching for Tucker. The motel sign was blinking, lighting them in a sickly red glow. Under it, the No Vacancy sign was lit because they had rented all fourteen units, ostensibly for a porn film shoot.

Rex, excited, jumped down and trotted over to meet Tucker, who bent down and patted his head.

"What's going on in there?" Lenny asked.

Tucker sat down on the bench. "A little sport, but they'll both live."

A discarded French fry container blew by on the ground. Silently, they watched the wind carry it into the gutter.

"We live in a very fucked-up world," Tucker said.

Lenny didn't answer, knowing there wasn't much he could say to improve Tucker's situation. It had been fucked-up since the moment Tucker met Lizzie. City girls and cowboys were like oil and water to begin with, Lenny thought, and that was without the undead wrinkle. Not that it mattered anymore. Love, and pending fatherhood, trumped it all.

"When you were in the war, did you see bad stuff like all this killing and maiming?" Tucker asked. He saw pain flare in Lenny's eyes and wished he could take the question back. Even after all this time, Lenny didn't talk about those years. "Sorry, you don't need to answer."

Piercing sirens broke the nighttime silence and the two men watched a convoy of motorcycle cops and squad cars speed down New York Avenue toward the Capitol, escorting three black SUVs.

"That the president?" Lenny asked.

"Could be, I guess," Tucker said. "Seems kind of late for that."

"I heard they call his limo 'the beast,'" Lenny said.

"Why is that?"

"It's fortified with so much armor and such, it weighs a couple of tons," Lenny said.

"Makes sense. He's got a lot of people gunning for him." Tucker patted the space in between them and Rex jumped onto the bench. He sat straight up, his head high, looking ahead, proud to be one of the guys. "I'd still rather have your custom Winnebago."

They listened to the traffic and roaring by and the wail of car alarms and honking taxis.

"I've seen worse, actually," Lenny said at last.

Tucker looked at him curiously.

"You asked me about my time in the service," Lenny said. "I've seen much worse."

"How can it possibly be worse than what we've seen?"

"We've seen some bad stuff, but mostly it comes down to intent," Lenny said. "When things go according to plan, these vampires are mostly removing the kinds of evil bastards I saw in the war from the human gene pool."

"That's a fine line," Tucker said.

"Not really," Lenny said. "After seeing the torture humans can inflict on other humans, on children, babies even, just for the sake of it, seems like vampires at least have their reasons."

They sat quietly. Tucker worried that he'd caused his friend to dredge up painful memories. Rex jumped off the bench and sniffed at what he hoped was an old French fry but turned out to be a twig, and then lifted his leg by the curb. Steam rose up from the piss flowing into the gutter.

Another few minutes passed and Tucker felt like a sense of equilibrium between them had been restored. "We got a name," he said. "Auscor Kingman."

"The tech guy?"

"Guess so. You know of him?"

"Don't you ever watch the news?" Lenny asked. "He made like a gazillion dollars and then his company tanked. What the hell would he want Lizzie for?"

"I aim to ask him. Come on, let's collect our vampires and get going," Tucker said.

TWENTY-NINE

"This is the place," Wilhelmina said. "You ready?"

She didn't expect an answer, not verbally anyway, because she was talking to her dog, Sake. They were sitting in a rental car in a scenic pullout next to Lake Pleasant.

The picturesque private lake, about an hour east of Utica, New York, the City of Possibilities, was nestled against the edge of the Adirondacks. Overlooking a particularly lovely stretch of shore was a sprawling and decidedly old-fashioned building on several lush acres of well-manicured lawn. A three-story former spa, for the last fifty years the building housed the Mount Shaker Institute and Rehabilitation Center. It was the last stop in Wil's cross-country quest.

She wheeled the car across the road and into the parking lot. "You stay here," she said to Sake, who looked at her curiously. Wil cracked the window two inches. "Anybody reaches in, hold them until I get back."

Sake, a well-trained Akita who managed to make her hundred-pound frame seem at once threatening and delicate, watched seriously, intently as Wil followed the smooth, wheelchair-friendly path to the front door.

Judging by the architecture, the place had been built in the early 1900s, though elements — the fence, a separate but connected dining area — looked decidedly modern.

At the main door, a printed sign indicated the buzzer, and she pressed it and peered inside.

In the reception area, a young nurse sat expectantly, her smile affixed to her face like a devotional poster. She seemed out of place in the secured interior. Some people are just truly happy, Wil thought.

"Hello. Welcome to Mount Shaker," the nurse said into the intercom. "How may I help you?" She had a lilting, cheerful voice that grated on the part of Wil's brain that had just flown all night across the country.

"My name is Wilhelmina Clarion. Wil. I called earlier."

"Oh, yes," the woman said. "Please come in."

The door buzzed and opened and Wil met her at the desk. The woman, Gretchen according to her name tag, stood and smiled even wider. "You wanted to visit one of our patients. A John Doe, ward of the state."

"Yes, that John Doe is likely my cousin," Wil said.

The woman's mouth dropped open as her good heart surged up and crashed like a tsunami over her professional demeanor. "Oh my God, that would be so awesome," she said. "The poor guy has been here for years, since before I even started, and he's never had a single visitor. He's a sweetie, but he sure doesn't talk much." She picked up her phone and buzzed the intercom.

"Dr. Miller, Wil Clarion is here to meet John Doe."

There was a garbled, crackly response Wil couldn't understand and Gretchen smiled. "He'll be right out."

By the time the words left her mouth, a pleasant-looking man in a white coat was hurrying down the hall toward them. He was burly, like a misplaced lumberjack, with a closely trimmed reddish beard — shot through with gray — and a precise flattop haircut. Probably ex-military, Wil thought. His hands looked soft but competent as he hurried to slide a key card at his waist against the reader on the interior glass door, allowing him entry into the reception area.

"Miss Clarion, I'm Dr. Miller." He shook her hand excitedly, as Wil winced at the 'Miss.' "So very good of you to come all this way. You can imagine how excited we are to think John has family. He's been dreadfully alone since he arrived all those years back. We are all very fond of him."

He escorted her down a narrow hallway lined with dormitory-style rooms. "Your records indicate he was admitted eighteen years ago?" Wil asked.

"He arrived with a severe brain injury. He'd been shot several times in the torso, and once in the hand, but the worst was a bullet that pierced his brain through the right parietal lobe. He's otherwise healthy, but has a hard time talking or sustaining focus."

"Travis disappeared from a high school class trip to Chicago about twenty years ago," Wil said. "From a little town in Wyoming."

"He does seem to have a ranch background," the doctor said.

"I'm having a hard time not getting my hopes up a little," Wil said.

The door to his room was open and the doctor entered first. "JD, you have a visitor."

A man sat next to the window overlooking the lake. He was big, soft and pale, his hands folded in his lap, and he turned to look at her with vacant eyes that slowly gathered clarity. Wil felt tears welling up and slipping down her cheeks.

"Travis, it's me," she said. "Your cousin Wil. It's been a very long time."

He smiled gently and nodded. "I am sorry about the mustard," he said. "The yellow mustard, very sorry. That won't come out."

Wil lunged forward and threw her arms around his shoulders and buried her face in his soft neck, crying and laughing at once.

"Do you know what he means?" Dr. Miller asked, confused.

Wil looked back at the doctor, tears streaming down her face. "The last time I saw Travis, we were at a picnic in LonePine. Tucker dared him to squirt mustard on me and it got all over my dress. We got into a terrible fight."

"Sorry, yellow mustard," Travis said softly, patting her arm.

Wil sank down to her knees, her voice cracking with emotion. "Tucker sent me here, Travis," she said. "Do you understand me? Tucker sent me."

Travis looked at her, his eyes wide. "I knew he wouldn't leave me here forever. Not after I felt him in the overworld."

"Okay, I don't know what that means," Wil said.

THIRTY

Exhausted at the end of another long shift, Helmi slipped out of the old cannery building and into the gray Astoria morning. Clouds and fog blanketed the river and the hills, clinging to the trees and the long span of the Megler Bridge like a shroud.

Helmi was distressed and unsettled by how Dr. Burkett treated that poor pregnant woman who thought she was a vampire.

Of course, with her sleeping disorder, pale skin and intense animosity, she sure *seemed* like a vampire. Helmi wondered if anything could be done for her.

Standing on the edge of the soggy, splintered dock looking out over the Columbia River, Helmi turned her collar up against the light, misty rain and took a deep breath, hoping the fresh air flowing through her body could help suppress her doubts.

A tanker slid by in the deepest part of the channel, serenely anticipating the chaos at the bar ahead where the river currents fought with the surging Pacific Ocean. Seagulls, ever present in Astoria, wheeled above, shrieking and dive-bombing and chastising all those who dared pass beneath. She shoved her hands into her pockets and made her way to the footpath leading downtown.

The trolley, popular with the tourists staying in the nearby luxury hotels, clattered by on its first run of the morning and the conductor, a man she knew from around town though his name currently escaped her (Clevis? Cletis? Carol?) dinged the bell and waved.

Closer to town, the farmers market was slowly taking shape as artists and artisans, bakers, honey peddlers and a few actual farmers set up their booths. She wandered through the tables admiring sand paintings, flattened beer-bottle clocks and fresh baguettes. At the sight of the bread, her stomach growled and she decided to stop by the Finnish Sauna for breakfast.

Owned by her parents, the Finnish Sauna was actually a restaurant and, at night, a bar. For decades, it had been an actual sauna, frequented by actual Finns, but closed in the 1950s, locked in a decaying orbit with the fishing industry and mostly immune to the recent resurgence in tourist attractions.

Astoria was an old city, one of the oldest on the West Coast. Built to serve trappers, the town grew into a fishery hub, attracting Europeans who knew what to do with the bountiful waters — Swedes and Norwegians and, famously, Finns.

The city had a rich Finnish legacy that was clearly visible in Helmi both physically, with her blonde hair, blue eyes and sprinkle of freckles, and in her solid, centered disposition.

Her father, Oley, married her mother, Kiia, both direct descendants of first generation Finns. Both grandfathers worked the fishing boats and then later in the canneries. Both grandmothers kept tidy, modest homes and cooked an abundance of meals to feed the bustling families.

Helmi's father worked the canneries as well, until an accident took three of his fingers. She was twelve when it happened and remembered visiting him at the hospital, where his normal jovial nature was momentarily shipwrecked as he wrestled with the prospects of providing for his family, and in a drug-swaddled cocoon tried to scratch itchy fingers no longer attached to his hand.

Oregon Kist gave him a decent settlement, and with the money they bought the old, long-defunct Finnish Sauna, once the high point of Finn social life (at least for the men) and converted it to a restaurant.

It never made much, not like working in the cannery — now just as gone as his fingers — but the work was not as backbreaking and considerably less dangerous. Her mother did the baking, her father did the cooking, and they had a modest little two-bedroom apartment attached to the back of the building. A small, good life in a small, good town.

Helmi pushed the door to the restaurant open, smiling at her dad, who was behind the counter flipping eggs.

"Good morning, Helmi," he said cheerfully, waving the familiar two-fingered salute.

"Morning, Pops," she said. "Where's Mom?"

"Still in bed, I imagine." He jerked his head toward the stairs. "We had a long night last night, with some late drinkers."

"Were you one of them?"

He smiled sheepishly. "Maybe a little. Come, sit, have some breakfast. I will make 'eggs Helmi,' just the way you like them. Scrambled, with lots of cheese."

"Sounds delicious," she said, taking a seat at the counter and running her fingers absently over the antique tiles preserved from the original sauna.

He poured steaming hot coffee into a thick mug, and she wrapped both hands around it to drive off the chill.

"How was work?" he asked, walking into the kitchen but maintaining eye contact through the order window.

"Weird."

"I wish you could tell me more about it," he said, diverting his attention to an omelet pan where he began slow-scrambling three farm-fresh eggs.

"Me too."

When hired, Helmi signed a nondisclosure agreement that spelled out, in no uncertain terms, the severe legal consequences of sharing any details about the project with anyone, including family.

In the interview, Dr. Burkett made it clear that discretion was as important, possibly more important, than nursing and research skills.

She never should have taken the job; she knew right off that something was weird. She should have trusted her instincts. But the money was irresistible and her student debt was daunting.

Her dad returned with a plate heaped with eggs and cheddar cheese, a side of roasted potatoes and a toasted bagel. He slid it in front of her and wiped his hands on his apron.

"Are you sure this job is for you?" he asked.

She took a bite before answering. "Dr. Burkett is a genius," Helmi said. "I should be honored to be working with her. And this project will likely change the world."

"And yet you don't seem very happy."

"I'm tired," she said. "Up three nights in a row. I guess I'd better get used to it. I'm going to go crash for a few hours after I'm done eating, then I have to go back and work another shift."

"Your mother will be sorry to have missed you."

"I'll stop by on my way in this afternoon."

He returned to the grill to make an order of French toast for the couple at the two-top, leaving her alone with her eggs and her thoughts for a moment.

She couldn't get the sad, frightened eyes of that poor crazy woman, Elizabeth, out of her mind. Being cursed with a feeble brain and a potentially beneficial genetic disorder didn't seem like reason enough to treat her like a lab animal.

She had been told the security and isolation were due to the potential reach of competing labs, but Helmi was beginning to wonder if it had more to do with hiding probably illegal, or at the very least unethical, activities.

Was a greater good worth that price?

Her thoughts were interrupted by a muted curse from her father who had been chatting with customers at a table near the window.

"Damn kids," he muttered, spying two shabbily dressed hitchhikers along the highway, backpacks loaded down, gleefully throwing rocks at a stray dog, all ribs and sharp angles, its tail down as it limped out of range.

He threw the door open and bellowed across the street. "You two knock that off this instant. Leave that poor thing alone."

"Fuck off," the boy said, and they both flipped him middle fingers.

"Yeah, I will fuck off right into the middle of you both," he shouted, stalking out across the highway, regardless of the traffic.

Helmi was already up and at the door, her phone in hand. "I've called the cops," she called across the street.

"Fuck off too, skank," the girl yelled back.

"I will throttle you both," her dad was shouting as traffic came screeching to a stop, the drivers surprised to see a tall, angry apron-clad Finn missing three fingers and waving wildly in the middle of the coastal highway.

"Dad, forget about them," Helmi said, watching the two hitchhikers trot away from a potential confrontation with the police.

"And do not come back," he shouted, making an incomplete fist and shaking it at their retreating backs. The dog, surprised to find a savior, scurried across the street in his direction.

"Looks like you made a friend," Helmi said.

"You wait here," he said, "I will get him a bite to eat."

The dog eyed her warily until Oley returned with a tin pie plate full of scraps and then watched, smiling, as the starving dog devoured the food.

"Not even a stray dog deserves to be treated like a stray dog," he said.

THIRTY-ONE

"This makes me plenty nervous," Lenny said as he and Tucker strolled through Times Square.

"Which part?" Tucker asked. "Meeting a crazy billionaire who may try to kill us in broad daylight, completely unarmed and without Rurik and Elita to watch over us, or just being in New York in general?"

"Mostly the second part. It's been a long time since I been around this many people," Lenny said. "Kind of forgot how big the world can be."

After a quick flight from D.C. to New York, Rex and the two vampires were holed up in the penthouse suite of Sofitel on 44th, ensconced behind a Do Not Disturb sign and some well-placed bribes.

Money, Tucker was learning, really could buy almost anything, including discretion. The vampires were in a darkened interior room, the TV blaring on the porn channel to discourage curious housecleaners. Rex, who was growing a little hard of hearing anyway, was snoring happily on the overstuffed couch among the remains of cheese crackers ferreted from the criminally overpriced minibar.

Even in the chilly weather, Times Square was bustling with gawking, sloppily dressed tourists shoulder to shoulder with well-dressed locals, uniformed garbage men and policemen doing their best to control the refuse and beady-eyed peddlers squatting over blankets laden with souvenirs, knockoff purses and scarves, made-to-order Tee-shirts and slowly degrading watches. Tucker, a veteran of Gotham on this, his second trip, and growing increasingly agitated as Lizzie's kidnapping stretched on, blocked it all out as he chewed on warm candied nuts from a cone of wax paper purchased from a street-corner vendor.

"You get used to it," Tucker said. "I mean, I wouldn't *want* to get used to it, but it's not so bad in short bursts. Nuts?"

"A little bit," Lenny said, then realized they were talking about two different things. "No thanks."

They made their way past the soaring walls of urban canyons, flashing and gyrating with huge pulsating neon screens airing dizzying ads for everything from candy to lingerie, or else trumpeting the latest, greatest Broadway shows.

"Yes, just a little overwhelming," Lenny said, then stopped stock-still. "Jesus jumping Christ, look at that guy." He pointed to a cowboy in nothing but white underpants, boots and a hat, strumming his guitar and posing for pictures with wide-eyed, giggling high school girls and taking donations for every picture snapped.

Tucker and Lenny walked closer and looked at him curiously. The man nodded and grinned, somehow able to look relaxed while tensing every well-defined muscle on his body. "Howdy, boys."

Tucker fished out his wallet and handed the man a crisp one-hundred-dollar bill. "Add this to your clothing fund," he said. "If you ever get back west, you're gonna need britches."

They continued along, borne forward by the surging currents of pedestrians until they circled back close to their hotel, and Lenny pointed at the street sign. "This here's the place where Kingman said to meet," he said, and they walked up the cross street to a nondescript diner, The Red Flame. "We're a little early."

"We'll have the element of surprise," Tucker said. "And we can have a bite to eat. All this flying around has me hungry. I need to be thinking clearly."

Inside, the place was mostly empty, because, as the owner explained in a thick Greek accent, "It was a very busy, very busy morning, but the tables just turned over."

Tucker and Lenny scanned the dining room but saw no obvious hired muscle. Instead, in a sea of empty and unbussed tables, a few were filled with what appeared to be a mix of exhausted and over-stimulated tourists with bags of mementoes purchased from nearby flagship stores and a few blue-collar types with callused hands and tired feet recovering from manual labor jobs. Some were talking or texting, others were reading magazines and newspapers.

A dark-eyed, curvy hostess showed them to an empty booth and handed them menus, smiling uncomfortably as Lenny tried, and failed, to not look down her blouse.

When the waitress stopped by with coffee, Tucker ordered a fried egg sandwich with cheese. Lenny ordered a grilled cheese and a chocolate egg cream. "Always wanted to try one," he said.

Another bright-eyed waitress delivered the food in three trips, and Lenny slurped his egg cream happily.

"There's something odd about this place," Tucker said, squirting mustard and then raining drops of hot sauce onto his egg sandwich.

"There's certainly something odd about this," Lenny said, pointing to the half-empty glass and foamy chocolate bubbles. "And delicious. There's no egg and no cream, but it's real good."

Tucker scanned the room and then stood suddenly. "I got to use the can," he said.

When he returned and sat down, Lenny was looking mournfully at the empty glass. Tucker picked up his sandwich just as a man in a sweater vest and aviator glasses walked through the door.

"That's our guy," Tucker said, recognizing Auscor from the Internet.

"Shorter than I expected," Lenny said.

"Aren't they all," Tucker said.

Auscor crossed the room without waiting for the hostess, pulled off his sunglasses, and slid into the booth next to Lenny. "Let's cut to the chase," he said. "You should know right off, you are outgunned." He snapped his fingers and said, "Now, people."

The owner flipped the sign to Closed and locked the door, then turned to stand next to the cash register, his hands clasped in front of his apron.

Every person in the diner, with the exception of the buxom hostess, stopped what they were doing and drew guns from under their jackets or out of the shopping bags. Most of the guns were quite large, and every single one of them was aimed at Tucker or Lenny.

"Holy shit," Lenny said. "I didn't see that coming."

"Yeah, I like to think several moves ahead of my opponents," Auscor said. "And my new besties from CMC are pretty irritated you keep wriggling out of their clutches. That's why they sent over the extras. So many highly trained, expensive people. Did I mention you are outgunned? Oh, and in case it slipped your mind, here in the daylight, your little undead friends won't be swooping in to save you. If you want to live through the next few minutes, you'll be very cautious about sudden moves."

"No sudden moves," Tucker said. "Got it." He carefully put his sandwich back on the plate.

"Would it be possible to get another egg cream soda while we wait?" Lenny asked.

"No," Auscor said. "You are upsetting my plans, and for that, you have to be detained. Or killed. Your choice really."

"We'll take detained, for sure," Lenny said.

"Wait a minute," Tucker said. "Not so fast."

"Are you saying we should pick 'killed'?" Lenny asked. "Because I would probably argue that."

"I'm saying those ain't our only options," Tucker said. "The thing is, you have my fiancée and I want her back."

"What I have is an animal," Auscor said. "A predator. Can I get a cup of coffee?" he said loudly, and the hostess startled, looked at the owner.

"He's not talking to you, sweetheart. I am. Bring me some coffee. Very, very hot coffee."

He watched her bustle toward the kitchen and then returned his attention to Tucker. "That thing you think you love feeds on humans. She is not for you, Tex."

"You know I'm from Wyoming, right?" Tucker asked.

"I don't care where you are from," Auscor said. "Make your peace with this. Find yourself a nice little cowgirl and raise up a brood of redneck kids. Vampires and humans, especially cowboy humans, don't mix."

"That's not really your call to make," Tucker said.

"Actually, it is my call," Auscor said. "I have her. I am going to use her to develop a cure for aging and become fabulously wealthy. Fabulously wealthier, I should say. You don't know where she is, and in a few minutes, you won't be free to find her until it's way too late. I'm pretty sure she won't make it. And she shouldn't make it. She is an abomination. A useful abomination, but a crime against nature nonetheless. I'm doing you a favor, cowboy."

The hostess returned to deliver his coffee and he took a sip and then caught her hand. "Wait. I said hot. It's like the opposite of what this is. Let's pretend all that money I just gave your boss entitles me to a hot cup of fucking coffee."

She snatched her hand free, glared at him and then disappeared back into the kitchen.

"You are a mean man," Lenny said. "And you really ought not to talk about Tucker's lady that way. She's real nice. And she hasn't hardly killed no one at all, not to speak of, anyway."

"Less than you killed with your broken missile thing," Tucker said.

"I would love to spend a pleasant afternoon chatting about the ethical considerations of extracting useful data from a different species that will improve the lot of human existence," Auscor said, "but I have an important meeting to attend on the other side of the country and it's a long drive to the airport. Go along quietly with my people, and I give my word I'll pass along your tender feelings to your little vampiress. If, you know, it comes up."

Neither Tucker nor Lenny responded. They both sat quietly, unmoving, like statues.

"Nothing else then?" Auscor asked, standing abruptly. "Good. Since I won't be getting any fucking coffee, take them to the holding facility, figure out where they were staying, go there and kill the vampires," he said. "Wait, belay that kill order. Let me find out from the good doctor if two more subjects would be helpful to her research."

"I can't let you leave until I know where she is," Tucker said. "And you better pray she's all right when I find her."

Auscor looked around the restaurant at all the guns pointed in their direction. "You're not going to let me leave?" He was truly taken aback. "How do you see yourself stopping me, much less getting out of this one?"

"I don't," Tucker said. "But I knew something was off about this place. Then it hit me. No kids. Not a single child in here. I figured you stacked the place with hired muscle. So I slipped into the pisser and called the cops. I used my best Western twang and told them I thought I heard two of them 'Al Cajuns' talking about blowing up a bomb in Times Square. I imagine they got this whole block cordoned off by now. The way I understand it, New York has some of the toughest gun laws in the country. Good luck explaining all of this hardware to a bunch of homeland security types."

Auscor responded without losing a beat. "You will be detained as well."

"I doubt it. We ain't packing. We're just two wide-eyed good old boys from the sticks in town to sightsee. We got nothing to explain. As for all the rest of y'all, well, I imagine they are gonna want to know why you are ready for World War Three."

An ominous, shadowy figure in a helmet tapped at the door and the guns inside wavered.

"Hello, anyone in there?" a voice called.

Auscor scowled, then nodded. The guns disappeared.

Tucker caught Lenny's eye and they both stood as the owner turned the lock and swung the door open to reveal a bewildered mailman in a standard issue pith helmet, his hand inside a low-slung bag of mail.

"What's going on?" he asked. "Never seen you locked up during the middle of the day."

Tucker and Lenny were already up and running for the door.

"Go boys, I'll slow them down," the owner said.

The hired guns from CMC leapt up, only to slam to a halt as the owner locked the door in their faces and stood blocking it, his arms crossed.

Auscor's face contorted with rage. "What the fuck are you doing?" he asked, watching through the blinds as Tucker and Lenny disappeared down the street.

The owner pulled a stack of hundreds from his pocket and threw it Auscor. "You can keep your money, *sweetheart*," he said. "No one disrespects my daughter, not for any price."

THIRTY-TWO

That they came did not really surprise Louisa. An offer of a hundred dollars for an hour of work gets attention, especially in a dead-end town. It was the fact that they all stayed that threw her.

"For you, this is science. For them, it's survival," Helmi explained.

"Good thing for science," Louisa said, turning her attention to the assembled group.

"You will ingest a substance that scientists believe will induce a state of euphoria," she said.

One of the oldest made a puzzled face.

"Euphoria. A feeling of happiness. Each one of you will get a different amount of the substance. The purpose of the study is to test the dosage, meaning, how much is needed to induce the desired effect," Louisa said. "Any questions?"

"How long will we be high?" a nervous, fidgety young man with soft, dark teeth asked.

"You won't be high, not like anything you are familiar with, such as methamphetamine," she answered matter-of-factly. "It's more subtle than that. I expect it to last no more than thirty minutes."

One of them, or several of them — perhaps all of them, she realized — smelled of a deep, unholy body odor and she pushed back at the slight nausea forming.

"When will we get the money?" an older woman asked. She wore gray tattered sweatpants and a heavy plaid shirt worn through at the elbows.

"As soon as you are recovered enough to answer a few questions," Louisa said. "Any more questions? No one wants to know, for example, whether it's dangerous?"

"Um, is it dangerous?" a young woman asked timidly, unconsciously picking at a scab on her wrist.

"Very good. We don't think there is any danger," Louisa said. "I tested this first on myself. But you must sign a consent form to participate."

The form was really more for appearance's sake than anything real. She did not plan to track their future reactions and did not care if they understood the science. But old habits die hard.

The stink of sweat and cigarette smoke, affixed to the group as if lacquered with nicotine, kept building in the room like invisible, oily steam. Louisa pulled the large window open. A startled seagull flew off its edge as the cool, salty air swept out some of the stench.

Helmi looked at each person closely as she handed out forms fresh from the printer, wondering if any of her childhood friends or people her parents might know were in the group. The blonde girl with the knitted backpack seemed vaguely familiar. Each person signed without reading the form.

Yesterday, using Craigslist, Louisa posted an ad for volunteers for a paid research study. Within an hour, hundreds responded. She winnowed the applications down to an initial twenty, varying the acceptances for age, ethnicity and gender. Twenty was not statistically significant, but it would give her enough information to ascertain if her experience with the creature's blood had been unique, and to provide vital, basic data about the relationship between dosage and experience.

The unknown substance in the creature's blood was in short supply and she wanted to be sure not to waste any by overdosing her new test subjects.

Now, here in the cannery warehouse, just a floor above where the female had fallen into her daily comatose state, the twenty men and women were about to drink the distillate of the creature's blood. It had come to pass so quickly, Louisa thought. It felt good.

No one would die, she felt certain of that. At least not here in this room now. And this knowledge was crucial; the hastily created trial had to move forward, even if it was unusual in terms of its design.

From a scientific standpoint, the minimal, statistically suspect data stemming from this experiment might give her an idea of additional next steps. But that was not its primary purpose. She had to have this data if there was to be any hope of persuading Kingman to bankroll an emerging new direction for her research.

Next to the open window, she gratefully breathed in the clean sea air as Helmi completed the paperwork. A pair of crows grooming each other on a piling sticking up from a decaying jetty next to the warehouse caught her eye. Even from this distance, she could see a glint reflected in their steely dark eyes.

"We're ready," Helmi said crisply, hiding her own ethical uncertainty behind an efficient mask constructed from the tattered shreds of her few years of experience with research protocols.

The twenty men and women lined up behind Helmi like hopeful, nervous ducklings, following the cues of their mother. Helmi turned to face her brood, nodding to the first subject to come forward. The planks of the worn wooden floor squeaked beneath the movement.

Louisa strolled casually to the grubby crowd, her bearing causing them all to shrink back a little. Taking a black permanent marker from Helmi, Louisa slashed a number "1" on the female subject's right wrist. The ink bled slightly into the wrinkles like wet lipstick around the puckered lips of an old woman.

"You're lucky," Louisa said. "Number one. Maybe you'll go down in history."

"Yes, Doctor," mumbled the haggard woman.

"Weight?" Helmi asked.

"Ninety-five pounds, more or less," number one said quietly, with a scratchy voice.

"Age?"

"Forty-two. No, forty-four."

"When did you last eat?"

"Yesterday."

Helmi flinched, but the literature, and experience, showed that an empty stomach was an acceptable, if not ideal state, for almost any study. This controlled for unknown interactions, and less vomit to clean up. Later, with her cash, this woman, all of them, would be able to get a good meal. She'd send them all down to the Sauna, letting her dad know to give them a deep discount.

Louisa squirted a small measure of the unknown blood compound into a plastic cup of distilled water. She directed the first woman to drink all of it, looking into the cup to make sure it was empty.

The woman did as instructed without hesitation, and then looked at Louisa for approval, but Louisa had already turned her attention the second subject.

Helmi escorted the woman to a folding chair that was designated with her number, markered onto a scrap of paper.

After the nineteen others had cycled through the process, and were seated in their assigned chairs set in a half circle around the room, Louisa and Helmi watched and waited.

Louisa had not seen herself during her experience, so she had no idea what to expect, but the absolute stillness and silence was nowhere close to her prediction. So much had happened to her, and through her, after consuming the blood, but only in her mind, apparently. The gentle movement of their chests up and down was the only indication they were even alive.

Helmi wandered through the room, checking vitals and looking for signs of distress. The stink of them still hung heavily in the room, getting stronger, even with the open window.

"Are you killing them?" she asked.

"They are in the place, I think, the place it, she, calls the Meta."

Louisa was impatient, but knew there would be no hurrying through this part of the test.

After about thirty minutes, they began to stir, to open their eyes, but not sequentially in the same order they had consumed the blood. The dosage must have an impact on the experience, Louisa thought. As they wakened, each remained silently in their assigned chair, a stunned look on their face, eyes wider and sharper than before. A few smiled.

Helmi leaned over the man in the baseball cap. He was number three.

"Are you all right?" she asked.

"It was wonderful," he whispered. "Bless you. I'm not afraid anymore."

The man grasped Helmi's hand and smiled. Helmi was startled, and dropped the tray of cups she carried.

"Hurry, before they forget, we must videotape their responses, and please preface each interview with the subject's number," Louisa said to Helmi, then saying more loudly to the group, "Nobody leaves and nobody gets paid without first answering the questions."

All twenty looked at her and smiled in unison, and Louisa was taken aback by what seemed to be pity in their eyes. How could this bedraggled group pity her?

THIRTY-THREE

"That was pretty slick getting us out of there," Lenny said. "I thought that was gonna be my first and last egg cream. What did you really do in that restroom?"

"Took a piss," Tucker said.

"You mean you didn't call homeland security?" Lenny asked.

"Naw, I was just winging it," he said. "We got lucky."

After slipping out past the bewildered mailman, Tucker and Lenny sprinted down to the corner, splitting up for three blocks to lose the goons following them, agreeing to meet at the nearby tourist stand in ten minutes.

A little later, they were buying Yankees baseball caps, Empire State Building sweatshirts and fake Gucci sunglasses.

"A hundred bucks?" Tucker complained.

"Now ain't the best time to get all frugal," Lenny cautioned. "Don't forget, you're rich now."

"Oh yeah," Tucker said. "Here you go, pal, don't let anyone know you ever saw us." Tucker handed the young man behind the counter an extra hundred-dollar bill. "And I need a bag," he added, grabbing an oversized "I heart NY" bag from the stand and shoving in his cowboy hat and both their jackets.

Now in their tourist disguises, they hustled back to the diner and tried their best to hide, spy movie-style, behind opened copies of the *New York Daily News* across the street from The Red Flame.

Auscor paced in front of the restaurant talking angrily on his cell phone. A town car pulled up and he slammed into it like a guided missile.

"We need to follow that car," Tucker said. "Get us a cab."

"They ain't stopping," Lenny said, waving his arm madly as cab after cab drove by.

"Dammit, we're gonna lose them," Tucker said, growing frantic. "Why won't they stop for us? Ain't our money good enough?"

"Hey, country Joes," the doorman at the club behind them said. "If the light on top isn't lit, they already have a fare inside. They can't stop. Try that one," he said, whistling and waving his arm.

The cab stopped, eliciting a symphony of horns honking behind it. "Thanks, friend," Tucker said to the doorman, who shook his head as they jumped in.

"Where to?" the cabbie asked. He was an older man with a thick eastern-European accent, round old-fashioned spectacles and coarse white stubble on his leathery cheeks. His first name, according to the license, was Mateusz. His last name, made up mostly of vowels and z's, was faded and impossible to read.

"There's a big old black limo about three blocks ahead of us," Tucker said. "I will give you two thousand dollars if you keep us in sight of it."

"This is not an impractical joke?"

"We're serious as a heart attack," Tucker said.

"Let me see the money," the cabbie said.

Tucker dug into the money belt around his waist and pulled out a sheaf of hundreds and slapped them against the Plexiglas divider. "I don't even know how much this is, but you can count it later."

The man nodded. "I will. Hold on."

He surged the taxi forward and, honking madly, swerved into the intersection, racing the wrong way into oncoming traffic and nosing back in at the last minute, cutting off other cabs, almost hitting a biker and narrowly missing a garbage truck driven by a florid-faced man who flipped them off and honked back angrily.

"That is your car ahead, yes?"

"That's it, all right. Just stick with it."

"Like goulash on a top hat," the man muttered.

"I have no idea what that means."

"The silk, on the hat, it would stick," Mateusz said. "Goulash is very thick."

They followed the town car to JFK airport and watched helplessly as Auscor got out at the departure gate, flanked by two sinister-looking fellows who scanned the throngs of people with practiced caution.

"We'll never going to get close enough to figure out where he's going," Lenny said. "At least not without him recognizing us."

"Don't matter," Tucker said. "We have to go in there. We got no other choice."

"I see that man," Mateusz said. "You sit in cab, very still. Not to drive. For two more thousand, I will find out destination of flight."

"You got yourself a deal, old man," Tucker said.

They popped the trunk so it appeared Lenny was a fare, and Tucker slipped behind the wheel while Mateusz, his slouch hat pulled low, bustled inside.

"So how is it being a billionaire?" Lenny asked.

"I could get used to it," Tucker said. "I haven't had much time to enjoy it, and right now I'm too worried to think about anything other than finding Lizzie, but having a little extra money feels pretty good."

"And you're the good kind of rich," Lenny said. "You've done a lot of good things for the town already, that's for sure. The new library is going to be real nice."

"Lizzie is a big fan of libraries."

"Me too. And I understand you started a college fund for the entire FFA club in Travis's name."

"Yeah, seemed like the least I could do. And now that I found out he may still be alive, well that just makes it even more special."

"And giving Rose enough money to start up a vegan restaurant was real nice too," Lenny said.

"After what she went through out there in Plush, it only seemed right," Tucker said. "I feel responsible in a roundabout way for turning her off of meat."

"I don't think she's had a single, solitary customer yet," Lenny said.

"Don't matter," Tucker said. "We gave her the building. And there's enough money to last her for, well, ever, if she wants. For her, I'd probably even eat some of that tofu shit."

"Here he comes," Lenny said, watching Mateusz limp out across the pavement.

"Well?" Tucker asked, switching places.

"He is catching Delta flight 420 to Portland, Oregon, in one hour," Mateusz said.

"Lizzie must be there," Tucker said.

"Not Portland," Lenny groaned. "The last time we was there, things got a little hairy."

"We have to get there before him," Tucker said.

"Rurik's jet is fast, but not that fast," Lenny said.

Tucker reached up to push his hat back on his head to think, and found the Yankees cap instead. He switched hats so he could push the right hat back far enough to massage his brain. "I've got an idea," Tucker said. "Mat, how much for the glasses?"

"Two more thousand."

Tucker shrugged and held his hand out. "Put it on my tab. I'll be right back."

He pulled a flask out of his jacket pocket and splashed some whiskey on his cheeks like aftershave, swished a mouthful around, swallowed it and then walked into the terminal.

He pushed his way to the front of the line at the Delta counter, leaving behind a wake of angry people cursing and bristling and listening intently as he wobbled in front of the indignant service representative.

"Sir, you need to get in the back of the line."

"I don't want no ticket," he slurred. "I just want to give these eyeglasses back to your pilot. We was drinking like a couple of champs this morning and he forgot them. He'll need them for his flight to Portland, that's for goddamn sure."

"Sir, I don't think you…"

Tucker pushed the glasses onto the counter. "Just give these to Captain Chugs-a-lot, would you? I don't want him crashing Flight 420 on the way to Portland on account of he's too hungover to remember he's blind without these."

He pushed his way back through the onlookers, smiling as he heard the people in line grumbling and the customer service representative already on the phone.

He slumped back into the cab. "I think I bought us a little time, but they'll figure out I'm a liar real soon. Let's get our show on the road and fast. I'll call Wil and get a tail on him when he lands."

Mateusz, now without his glasses, honked and darted the cab out into traffic without even bothering to look.

THIRTY-FOUR

Resurrection, becoming one from the many, was always a brutal and dizzying process. Her mind raced as she became gradually aware of the boundaries of self, taking form in rushing motion as if falling from a great height — a mountain, or worse, a plane.

During the transition, at the moment the sun set, Lizzie slowly became conscious of thought, memory and images flying wildly from place to person and back again, unable to control the movement. The pattern revealed was a glimpse inside her own neural network, a reflection of the universal neural network, as the content of her mind ordered itself of its own accord, like a poem coming into being without a poet, or a song singing itself.

In this space between sleep and wakefulness, between life and death, the part of Lizzie that was her sense of self remained aloof but watchful, aware of her body but outside it, while simultaneously her mind traveled in the nightly prescribed free fall. Her body and mind, for this brief time, were at war of sorts, battling each other into mutual submission, into a mind-body reconciliation as time itself reordered into a single understandable stream.

She treasured this instant between breathing and death because images of her life — sometimes from the past, occasionally from the future — flashed through her thoughts, and a sense of certain purpose colored every event a deep and majestic purple.

"Are you coming?" her mother asked in the distance.

"Yes, yes, I'm on my way," Lazarus said from the bedroom above.

Lizzie glimpsed a memory of her mother standing impatiently at the base of a marble staircase, beautiful in a black cocktail dress with sheer stockings, a turquoise shawl draped around her shoulders. Lazarus descended, thin and devilishly handsome in his tuxedo.

He clasped her mother's hands, bringing them to his lips to kiss.

"You are lovely," he said, his eyes sparkling, but his voice flat.

Seeing them together, Lizzie sensed fragments of childish joy long ago shattered…but was this even real?

"You are safe, you will always be safe with me, I will not let them turn you," her mother whispered to Lizzie. She smelled like lilies, and her dangling earrings tickled Lizzie's neck. This was real.

Hours later, her mother returned alone, eyes red from crying. Silently, she began packing their belongings. They moved a few days later into a new apartment near the church with the hiding place in the catacombs. This too was real.

Lizzie's mind rushed past this moment, catching glimpses of what her mother's life must have been like all those years, protecting her child but living away from the man she loved (though Lazarus was not a man, she told herself). Her mother never saw Lazarus again; it was too dangerous. Lizzie herself would not put all the pieces together for another two decades.

The hunger clunked like an anchor dropping in her belly. This too was real. The natural resilience that would otherwise accelerate her healing was being rerouted, working overtime to keep Lizzie from shutting down completely. Protecting the child. Sparking the resurrection. All her cells, all her energy pushed her toward it. Without resurrection, Lizzie would cease to be. Without Lizzie, the child would cease to be.

Her mind melted into an image of Lazarus — fat, sad Lazarus years later — sliding into his nearly frigid dipping pool in New Mexico.

Her neck itched, her body ached — she was embodied again. This seemed less real.

I am not a vampire, she thought. Those memories are not real. Though her eyes itched and burned, she could see sun shining through the window at the foot of the bed. Vampires cannot be exposed to the sun. Ergo, I am not a vampire, she thought. Something came loose in my brain, in my memories.

But the headache was real, pounding like someone was hammering her skull from behind her eyes. Straining against her bonds and bending her neck, she could just touch her fingertips to her head. It was shaved. Her long blonde hair was gone.

"You cut off my hair?" she screamed. "You shaved my fucking head?" The world shimmered in anger and despair.

Her mother gave up everything for her, including love, to create a life in which Lizzie could experience what it was to be human. But it was a lie. Even if it was real, even if it was true, it was a lie. Her mother betrayed her. Life betrayed her. All of it was misery, whether a human or vampire existence.

Unless he was real.

If Tucker was real, it might all make sense. But she no longer knew. Were cowboys even real? Worse, she was not sure it mattered.

Without warning, she slipped uneasily, sloppily, back into death.

This was not how vampires died. Her mind flew to a rodeo, to a time before she had become this thing, this animal. A man with a cowboy hat falling from a horse into the mud, cursing. She could not see his face. The smell of fresh oats filled her mind and something, a sad-eyed dog maybe, was licking her hand furtively.

When she returned to her body, a girl was at her side, washing her hands with a warm cloth.

"I loosened your arm bindings," the girl said.

Lizzie leaned up with the girl's help, surveying her battered body, and then looked down at her feet. The pink nail polish had mostly chipped off except for a stubborn flash of shiny color on her right big toe.

"How are you feeling?" asked the girl.

"Terrible," Lizzie said, her voice thick. "You shaved my fucking head."

"It was for a test. We needed access to your…" Her voice trailed off.

"You shaved my head and drilled into my brain. This is not a hospital, it's a horror movie."

"You're going to be okay," Helmi said, voice shaking.

Lizzie shook her head, felt the starched pillowcase crinkling underneath. "I'm not doing so well. I need blood. A lot of it. We need blood," she said, nodding toward her stomach.

"I just put a new bag on the pole," Helmi said. "But what you really need is some good solid food to get you back to health. My dad is preparing a Finnish feast for you. It will be here soon."

"Are we in Finland?" Lizzie asked, squinting at the window.

"No, we are in Astoria."

"I don't know where that is."

"Oregon. On the coast. My family is from Finland and my dad is a very good cook. I will bring you pea soup and meatballs."

Lizzie laughed, a sound that felt out of place, and then coughed feebly. "That sounds delicious, but I don't need food. I need blood." She closed her eyes.

"What's your name?" Lizzie asked.

"Helmi," she said, touching Lizzie's arm. "Don't you remember me? We've talked before.

Lizzie looked at her blankly, and Helmi could see confusion behind her eyes.

"Are you going to help me get out of here, Helmi?" she asked.

"Your blood. It's like magic. All those people, they were so happy; they were blissful."

"Can you save me? Can you tell me if he is real?" Lizzie whispered.

"Who?"

"Tucker."

"Is Tucker your husband or something?" she asked.

"I think he is," Lizzie said. "It's all so blurry."

"Should I contact him for you?"

"Yes," Lizzie said, staring at the sun. She was silent for a long minute, and then turned her head toward Helmi. "I don't understand the sun, but I won't make it much longer. And the baby, she needs more than I can give her."

Helmi looked startled, staring at the video screen and the bright sunlight pouring out of it. It was night outside and they were tricking her, part of the therapy, Doctor Burkett said. "She won't let your baby suffer. She is brilliant, and you are different; not a vampire, just different. Together, you both will make something very important happen, I can feel it. I want to help."

Lizzie smiled weakly at her earnest sincerity.

"She is testing a theory to find out how to help you. What we are learning could help others too. Something happened to the people that took the samples. So happy. At least for a little while."

Lizzie seized Helmi's wrist so hard that the girl paled and wondered if the bones would fracture. "Did they become vampires?" Lizzie asked.

"No," Helmi said. "Please let go, you're hurting me."

Lizzie could feel the pulse of blood below the girl's skin and her hunger threatened to devour her reason. "Please tell me you didn't try it."

"Not yet."

"Don't," Lizzie said. "It's not safe."

The sliver of light that crept into the room as the door opened split into a rainbow of color, as if Lizzie was seeing the light through a prism inside her eyes.

"Helmi, you may leave now," Louisa said, entering behind the light. "Go home and get some sleep."

Helmi turned at the sound of the doctor's voice, startled and frightened. "I'd like to stay."

"I'll need you later. Run along."

Lizzie's throat tightened at the sight of Dr. Burkett. She felt so confused. Both women looked familiar, but she couldn't quite place them. Something was so wrong with her mind, as if the return trip from the Meta was incomplete and she was not quite anchored, not quite at home in her own time.

"How are you feeling?" Louisa asked after Helmi closed the door behind her.

"I think you already know the answer," Lizzie said.

"We have much to discuss," Louisa said, as she pulled a bottle from her bag. "Do you drink whiskey?"

THIRTY-FIVE

When Rurik resurrected, he was on his jet knifing through an ink-black night. Confidently, he let his senses stretch out past the confines of the coffin and felt the steady beating hearts of several humans, including one that tasted of worn leather and regret, and a canine. Tucker and his dog, then.

Returning to his body with the knowledge he had been at another's mercy for eight hours set Rurik on edge, though he knew the cowboy was trustworthy, at least to the extent any human could be. With their short lives and feeble minds, they were capable of treachery born of rapidly changing motives and emotions, neither of which they were able to control with any consistency.

Rurik was now certain Elizabeth was still alive. His experience of her as he left the Meta, weak and scattered, was definitive.

As he had every night since the attack on the truckstop, Rurik ran through the long list of likely enemies, trying to think of who could be behind this and why they had taken her.

Clearly it was not a rebellious faction of the Reptiles. Lizzie would be dead, those lowlife creatures would be crowing about their achievement and a civil war would have already begun.

Far more likely, one of the Royals had her and was using her blood to turn a legion of the faithful, arming themselves for a power grab. The undead, if anything, were predictable in their grandiose schemes for world domination.

Yet his carefully cultivated sources in each of the Royal houses could find no trace of her, and no whiff of maneuvering of that magnitude afoot. And why would they ally themselves with humans and expose such a devastating and terminal risk? If anything happened to Elizabeth, it would mean the end of them all.

He slipped out of his coffin, felt Elita stirring beside him, and left her stretching and fumbling for one of her foul clove cigarettes as he made his way forward.

Tucker was slumped in a seat in the near-deserted main cabin, his hat pulled low over his eyes and legs extended, his boots resting on the facing seat in front of him. His infernal dog was curled on the seat beside him, and across the aisle and two rows back, the other human, Lenny, was snoring soundly under a blanket.

At the sight of Rurik, Rex stirred and began to growl low in his throat — a hum of anger that woke Tucker, who pushed his hat back for a better view. "After all this time, he still don't like you much."

"A mutual feeling," Rurik said, nodding so that Tucker moved his feet and let the vampire sit across from him. "Or you, for that matter."

"And here I thought we were gonna be buddies for life, like the Lone Ranger and Tonto."

Rurik snapped his finger and a young woman with dark skin and short black hair strolled in from the rear cabin, a refugee of the sex trade who saw a year's worth of blood debt to a vampire as far more appealing than a short, squalid life in a shipping container brothel to be pawed, prodded and poked by leering men who smelled of cooked cabbage. Tucker arched his eyebrows at the sight of her.

"You object to my food source?" Rurik asked.

"Naw, it's just that she looks an awful lot like Virote," Tucker said.

"The flavor of the year," Rurik responded, casually.

The woman pulled up the sleeve of a loose silk dress, cinched tightly at her tiny waist. Rurik dragged a small blade across her forearm and clamped his mouth onto the wound. He fed slowly, thoroughly, noisily. Tucker watched the woman's eyes grow unfocused and then roll back in her head as she began to fade out of consciousness.

Rurik guided her body to the seat beside him and left her sprawled inelegantly, the coagulants in his saliva already stopping the flow from her arm.

"Where are we bound?" he asked, dabbing the blood from his lips with a handkerchief.

"Portland, Oregon."

"Why?"

"That rich guy, Auscor Kingman, kidnapped Lizzie and is trying to use her to cure aging."

Rurik shook his head. "A story as old as the vampire."

"He thinks there's something special about her blood," Tucker said.

"There is. She has the blood of the one true Royal running in her veins."

"Yeah, well, he thinks she has the blood of multi-vitamins in her veins. He thinks he can make a bundle off her if he can come up with a remedy for getting old."

"The last time a human tried to profit from vampire superiority was in the days of alchemy," Rurik said.

"Where are we going?" Elita asked, making her way up from the storage hold.

"Portland, Oregon," Tucker said.

She made a sour face. "That rain-soaked backwoods piss pot of mold and forced good cheer? Why in the world would *anyone* go there?"

"Lizzie's there, we think."

She looked down at the girl on the seat who was now stirring faintly, and Tucker thought he saw a shadow of sadness pass over her face, but it disappeared quickly.

Elita knelt down beside her and used her tongue to open the wound again, clamping her mouth on it and sending the girl back into dreamy oblivion as she fed.

Tucker averted his eyes at the sight. "The fellow that took her is using her blood to come up with a cure for aging, or some such bullshit. If he's hurt her, or the baby, pissed-off vampires will be the least of his worries."

"She's still alive," Elita said. "I could sense her just now. But unreachable. Who do I have to kill to get a drink around here?"

Rurik pressed an intercom button on the seat arm. "Vodka and...?" He looked at her.

"Champagne."

"And champagne." He looked at Tucker, who nodded. "And two beers and two whiskies."

A man with blond hair and blue eyes, wearing tight leather pants, brought the drinks back and set them on the table. Tucker watched Rurik as his eyes followed the servant, and arched his eyebrow when the vampire returned his focus.

"My taste in men differs," he said to Tucker.

"I have never been happier that I ain't a blonde," Tucker said.

Elita took the champagne bottle and grabbed the wrist of the young woman, who was gradually regaining her senses, and pulled her to her feet. "I'm bored," Elita said. "We'll be in the back. You boys play nice."

After she was gone, Tucker sipped the whiskey and petted Rex, who had only thrown up once on this flight. "Tell me something, Rurik, why'd you stick around?"

"To protect Elizabeth. I committed to that when the Nine signed the treaty. Remember?"

"I don't think that's the whole truth, is it? Something tells me you were waiting for everything to collapse so you could pick up the pieces."

"If you think I lingered in your little backwater town to pine away as a thwarted romantic rival for her affections, you are mistaken. I am simply caretaking the future of my people. Anything else is a reflection of your own insecurities."

"So you ain't going to admit you're a little sweet on my lady," Tucker asked.

Rurik laughed, which to Tucker's ears sounded like a train hitting flesh. "Human, even if I saw a place for me by her side, there is no need for me stand against you as a challenger for her favors. In the blink of an eye," he snapped his fingers for emphasis, "you will be dead and gone, moldering dust. I need only wait."

"That's your plan? To outlive me? That seems a little beneath you, being a brilliant war strategist and all."

Rurik leaned forward, his eyes flashing. "We are nothing alike."

"That's true," Tucker said. "Lizzie loves me. And I love her. And she's carrying my baby. Not yours."

Rurik sat back and tossed down a shot of vodka. "In the best case, what you call love lasts not one second longer than life, and usually dies much sooner than the flesh. With death, love — that mysterious derangement of the senses — becomes nothing but a tragic memory, a remembrance of things past. With the perspective of just a few hundred years, you would share my certainty that love, as you understand it, is nothing more than a pleasant cohabitation of emotions that can be as easily spun apart as held together."

"I have an alternate explanation," Tucker said quietly, sipping on his beer. "I don't think anyone has ever loved you. And I don't think anyone ever will. I'm willing to bet that if anyone ever took you out for any reason, if you ever disappeared, no one would give a flying crap."

"My people would find me," Rurik said confidently.

"If it was convenient maybe. But probably not. And I think that's the difference. Love makes you do things that ain't convenient, it makes you not selfish, because you don't have a choice."

"I am now risking my existence for your lover."

"Yeah, because Lizzie means something to you. Without her, you are all finished, eventually, all of your type. That's a pretty good reason. But there's something else, a glimmer of something in her that makes you think there's more to this blasted, empty un-life you lead," Tucker said.

The two men fell silent as the jet whispered through the night sky. Tucker stared down at his boots, thinking he was going to need to find some new duct tape, or maybe he'd just buy himself a brand new pair now that he had some money.

He mindlessly petted Rex while Rurik stared out the window at the blinking lights of a sleeping town below. From this distance, Rurik couldn't sense the sleeping bodies or sort through the good and evil for the most succulent, nourishing blood, but it passed the time to try from such a height.

The game soon lost its charm as the emptiness of prey availability left him cold and caused the bumping hearts of Tucker, Lenny and the other humans on the flight — one of them, the girl, weak — to loom larger in his hunger.

"She will live and you will die and any connection Lizzie and I have will be tested in the fullness of time," Rurik said at last. "And I am a patient man."

"Maybe I'll have her turn me into one of y'all," Tucker said. "Then I could just stay right by her side from now until Judgment Day."

Rurik smiled, revealing his teeth in the dim light of the cabin. "Obviously, I would have to kill you then."

"Lots of your kind have tried, and I'm still here."

"I haven't tried," Rurik said.

"When you do, no matter when it is or how you do it, you'll fail," Tucker said evenly.

In the blink of an eye, Rurik was up and clutching Tucker by the front of his jacket. It happened so fast, Rex barely had time to bark or even bare his teeth, and the sudden move caused Tucker to spill his beer onto the carpeted floor of the plane.

"You are slow," Rurik hissed, smiling widely. "I could open you now, bathe in your blood, toss you from the plane, and none would be the wiser."

"Why don't you, then?" Tucker said.

Rurik pushed him back onto the seat.

"I knew you had a thing for her," Tucker said, brushing off his shirt. "But you know the truth. She ain't gonna be with you, not even two hundred years from now, unless you can prove yourself to be more than just a blood-hungry hard-on. And you ain't never gonna be able to do that."

"I thought I said play nice," Elita said, strolling in from the back, her clothes and hair disheveled. "The spike in testosterone almost made me sick."

Rurik smiled and returned his gaze back to the window. "Challenge accepted," he said to Tucker.

THIRTY-SIX

"What are we celebrating?" Lizzie asked, looking at the bottle the doctor was holding. On the label, a skeleton squatted on a cask.

"Dead Guy," Louisa said. "I bought it just for the name." She popped the stopper on the artisanal whiskey. "I'm usually more of a vodka fan."

It had been twenty years since she felt so filled with promise, taken over by what she and her postdoc friends used to call the Holy Spirit of Science.

"I think it's time to lay my cards on the table. But first, damn, where's a glass?" she said, mostly to herself. Picking up a plastic specimen cup, Louisa laughed softly, sniffed and satisfied it contained no bodily fluids, filled it half full with the amber liquid. She swirled it around like a fine wine, then drank it down in one long, slow swallow.

"Again," she said, filling the glass and then holding it up to Lizzie. "Cheers. To scientific immortality, or maybe I should say to immorality. Amusing really, the power of a single letter," she said, downing the second cup. "My, that's strong." She dabbed the corner of her mouth with one finger and looked at Lizzie.

The events of the past few nights seemed to have taken a toll, and Louisa suspected the relentless pain had newly etched a map of furrows on the topography of Lizzie's face, her skin the color of spring corn — a fading, too-pale yellow. Jaundice, no doubt.

"What's your name?" Louisa asked. Had she pushed the creature too far?

"I know my name, and so do you," Lizzie said a little too quickly.

"When was the last time you saw me?"

Lizzie knew it was a trick question, and instinctively hid her uncertainty, but the truth was, she couldn't quite remember the woman and knew she should. And because of that, she sensed danger. She did not trust the fact that her memories were so shallow. Her skull ached.

Lizzie tried to sift back through more than just the recent minutes. Louisa took another swig of whiskey.

"Better slow down," Lizzie said. Her eyes itched fiercely. "What kind of doctor are you, drinking in front of a patient?"

A safe enough comment, she thought, at least until she could figure things out. Jesus, why is my head pounding, she wondered.

"A patient?" Louisa said, with a laugh. "I'm the very best kind of doctor, one who sees how things can be."

An image of an older woman with kind eyes, smiling, swept into Lizzie's mind. She felt a thud in her belly, and heard distant voices, but there was another sound too — a buzzing, like an insect, maybe a bee.

"My entire scientific life, I've been searching for proof of a theory of consciousness I developed when I was but a lowly grad student," Louisa said.

Lizzie moved her hand down to her belly, stroking the taut skin.

"Ah, yes, the baby," Louisa said. "A salvation of sorts. Children have a way of tying us to the present."

Lizzie shivered. A baby, yes, her baby. And Tucker. His baby. The doctor poured another shot of whiskey and Lizzie swallowed a wave of nausea caused by the sharp smell.

"Descartes was right, but for all the wrong reasons," Louisa said, talking to Lizzie but only passively. "The mind and the body are made of separate stuff. And you are proof of that."

Lizzie pulled quietly on her leg shackles and they held tight.

"Where are my manners?" Louisa said, stumbling a little over her words and an alcohol flush spreading across her cheeks. "A treat tonight, an extra bag of the concoction you call blood."

She put down the cup, opened the top drawer of the compact refrigerator next to the bed and pulled out a bag of blood. It really was blood — watered down and spiked with sedatives — but she told Lizzie again it was sugar water.

"Yum, yum," she said, holding it up, and then stood to hook the pouch onto the IV pole. She roughly swapped out the tubing into Lizzie's PICC line, and Lizzie winced at the pain.

Louisa sat down unsteadily. "Now we can both have a drink. *Salud!*" she said too loudly as she took a swallow of whiskey.

Lizzie turned her head to watch as the red liquid trailed its way down the clear tubing, not sure what it was, or why she felt suddenly so expectant. Everything was so confusing. Where was her mother?

"What are you giving me?" Lizzie asked. "Is that some kind of drug?"

"Truth is indeed stranger than fiction," Louisa said.

When the blood reached Lizzie's vein, the motherly image in her mind receded into a shadow as the doctor's sense of drunken elation mounted.

"You are going to prove my theory, and catapult me into the ranks of the greatest minds in human history," she said.

"You make no sense," Lizzie said. The blood flowed freely now down the plastic tubing.

"Darwin in his day struggled to articulate, eventually successfully, the greatest puzzle of the enlightenment age: the origin of the species. The greatest puzzle of our age is human consciousness and the origin of self," Louisa said.

She pulled a pack of cigarettes from her purse, slipped one out and held it up. "Do you mind?" she asked, kidding.

"I don't think you can smoke in hospitals," Lizzie said.

"They'll probably bend the rules for me," Louisa said.

"Then give me one," Lizzie said. "I think I smoke." An image of Tucker's disapproving face swam into her thoughts.

"Not in your condition," Louisa said, motioning at Lizzie's stomach and *tutting* disapprovingly. She rummaged around for matches, lit the cigarette and took a deep drag, turning her head slightly to exhale away from Lizzie out of instinct.

"It's the holy grail, and every neuroscientist worth their salt would admit, if they are honest, that this is what they are after," she said, taking another drag, and then pausing to watch the tendrils of smoke trail away. "We all have our pet theories, but mine is so out there, literally, that I kept it to myself."

"Tell me," Lizzie said, hoping to gain time.

"Okay," Louisa said, becoming drunkenly benevolent. "I believe the strictly material analysis of neurological data is too shallow, inadequate, and stems from a pre-conceived wish for consciousness to be proven as a purely biological function."

She caught herself and smiled. "It feels so odd, discussing this with a test subject. Suffice it to say this is, you are, the culminating shot in the age-old battle between religion and science that began a long time ago," she said.

Lizzie felt the baby kick, and suddenly, everything came back to her in an avalanche of certainty.

"Louisa," she said. "Louisa Burkett. Evil scientist from hell."

Louisa smiled and nodded. "You're back. Should I continue?"

"I'm not going anywhere. Yet."

"That's the spirit," Louisa said. "The centuries-old religious skirmish that Descartes tried to resolve with his clever mind-body dualism has, indirectly, framed even the questions asked by modern scientists, though we claim to be free of religion. Scientists are a tough crowd. We need facts, data, proof."

"And I'm your proof," Lizzie whispered, finally starting to understand.

"You are my proof of a theory of consciousness that is going to alter the course of human history and preserve my name in the halls of the scientific legends."

She dropped the cigarette, crushing it beneath a black heel. "Let's call it the third way. A bridge of sorts. Consciousness is not sent from heaven, nor is it strictly neurological. It's external and we have a receiver tuned in to the right channel. A new analytical framework for understanding human existence is about to open wide. I've opened the door. And you are the passageway."

Remnants of the Lizzie from long ago, the journalist desperate to win a Pulitzer for her writing, flooded her mind. She understood this woman, at least on some twisted, insecure level.

"I remember what it was like to sleep, the joy of no consciousness, of nothing," Lizzie said. The truth of nothingness, the beauty of an unperturbed death, she thought. "Be careful what you wish for; be careful what you seek to understand."

Louisa smiled, as if at a child, and shook her head. She fished the pendant from her pocket and draped it over the IV stand. "I don't expect a creature like you to understand anything, but for helping, here's a shiny little reward."

THIRTY-SEVEN

When she woke from a nap several hours later, Louisa was still tired and had a splitting whiskey headache. The brown spirits always did that to her.

She needed real sleep before Kingman arrived, but first she needed to ensure the weakest link in the chain was solid enough to hold for a few more days.

Rubbing her temples, she found Helmi, her back to the door, in the workroom. "She likes you," Louisa said.

Helmi brightened, but only by a few shades and still far below her normal resting state. "You think?" she asked without turning to look, but paused in her work — scanning consent forms.

Louisa studied her from behind, the girl's trim runner's body and annoying halo of optimism. "She likes you and we can use that."

"I'm not sure what you mean," Helmi said, slowly turning to face the doctor, her hopeful face framed by worry, and blonde bangs.

"Helmi, we need to talk," Louisa said. "I want to remind you about the nondisclosure form you signed when we hired you. Do you remember that?"

"Yes," Helmi said, her already uneasy smile wavering.

"Everything, EVERYTHING, that happens within these walls is covered by that form. You get that, right?"

Helmi nodded and darted her eyes past the doctor to the keycard-controlled door leading out onto the splintering dock. Her body betrayed her worry.

"The man I work for, the man you work for, is very powerful. Very wealthy," Louisa said, tapping the base of her ballpoint pen against her bottom teeth. "Do you know who Auscor Kingman is?"

Helmi shook her head.

"Not surprising. Astoria is a small town. Mr. Kingman is a billionaire with a singular, albeit newly acquired, focus — one might even say obsession — on monetizing a cure for aging. He stands to make a new, even bigger fortune, and we would all share in that, and in helping people enjoy a quality of life almost incomprehensible to us now. Does that make sense?"

"Yes, ma'am," Helmi said, mentally kicking herself in the brain. She hadn't called anyone ma'am since fourth grade. "But I really should be finishing up."

"The busywork can wait," Louisa said. "I need you to understand a few things. First, you should know that Mr. Kingman purchased the mortgage on the restaurant your parents own. If you do anything that breaks the sanctity of your nondisclosure agreement, he will close it down. Immediately. Do you understand?"

"That's all they have," Helmi said, growing a little sick to her stomach.

"Of course, which should underscore just how important your continued discretion is to this project. You are privileged to be part of this, I hope you realize that. The good we will do for so many is incalculable, but we are in a delicate phase and we need you, I need you, to stay focused. Can I count on you?"

Helmi felt her heart rate rising, and it was becoming increasingly hard to breathe in the warm room; hot even. Which was impossible given the damp, drafty conditions of the old cannery.

"Yes," she said, nervously.

"Good. The next thing is that I have tried, mostly unsuccessfully, to make both you and that creature think she is simply an intellectually disabled woman with a rare genetic disorder who thinks she is a vampire. She actually *is* a vampire."

Helmi started to say something, but Louisa raised her hand. "Let me cut you off for the sake of expediency. Yes, vampires exist. Yes, they feed on human blood. Yes, it's disconcerting to think such a significant species could exist alongside humans for so long, relatively undetected, but it's not impossible."

Helmi struggled to keep her breathing in check.

"All of those things are difficult to believe, but they are true, and we have been given an opportunity to make something huge and good with this knowledge. Now listen to me, because this is important. She is a vampire and that makes her a predator. A thing. An animal that we can use to change human life for the better. Are you with me so far?"

"I think so," Helmi said. "But she feels such pain. She is suffering. I don't care what she is, she's like us."

Louisa shook her head. "No, she is nothing like us. She sounds like us, and she looks like us, but she is not like us at all. She is not human."

Helmi looked at her directly. "Can you cure her?"

"You are not tracking. There is no cure for being a vampire. Just like there is no cure for being a rat, or a monkey. It's what she is."

"We could let her go then," Helmi said.

"No, this is a scientific bonanza," Louisa said. "It's highly likely we can find a cure, or at least a brake, for aging. Even better, her blood has a secret. It's a gateway to something huge, something bordering on the mystical. Only it's grounded completely in biology. Are you still listening? Because this is where it gets really good."

"Yes, ma'am," Helmi squeaked, mentally cursing herself again.

"When that thing dies every dawn — a full biologic death, and you've seen it happen — her consciousness literally leaves her body. I don't fully understand it yet, but I don't need to. I think she — it, I should say — might be living proof that consciousness is external, but shared. And not just for her species, for ours as well."

Louisa tried to smile reassuringly and failed. "I can't even begin to tell you what that could mean for the theory of self, the theory of mind, but I can tell you that after personally experiencing that alternate state of existence, what she calls the Meta, it is liberating and unnerving. And given how I feel right now, potentially addictive."

"I don't understand," Helmi said, growing paler.

"Think of it as a giant energy field, a battery filled with electricity, only the electricity is a million souls all tangled up together. When that things dies, the 'stuff' that is her ceases to reside in her body and resides instead somewhere else. And that's true for every other one of her kind."

"There are more like her?"

"Please, try to stay focused on the important part. We are on the precipice of a major discovery. I never really believed in all that near death experience business, but the literature is clear and my experience confirms it — even just a brush against this energy field has altered my perceptions. There's something to this. I will be discussing the possibilities with Mr. Kingman soon. In the meantime, to circle back to the beginning of this conversation, she likes you."

Helmi clutched the yellow legal pad she now held against her chest even tighter, eyes wide.

"Helmi, we need more from her. I need more from her. More information and more compliance. We need to move quickly and the procedures will not get easier. I need you to step up here and use your connection to get what we need."

"I'm not sure I'm comfortable with this anymore, Dr. Burkett," Helmi said.

"I know, and that's precisely why we are having this conversation. If you cannot commit, you need to leave immediately. Keep in mind that any breach of the secrecy around this project — not that anyone would believe you — will result in your prosecution and the impoundment of your parents' restaurant."

"And then what?"

"Mark can finish it off. I'm sure he won't mind the extra cash."

"And Lizzie?"

"Don't worry about it."

Helmi tried to slow her breathing and steady her shaking hands. She thought of her father and his stray dog, and the decision, though it wasn't easy, was made.

"You can count on me, Dr. Burkett," she said. "No question. I want to see this all the way through."

THIRTY-EIGHT

"After the shit from last time, I didn't figure I'd ever set foot in Portland again," Lenny said.

Tucker was wheeling a rented pickup and trailer through a row of clapboard houses with old washing machines and dilapidated, unusable swing sets in the yards. They were in a rougher part of town, a few miles east of the hustle and bustle, and police presence, of the more upscale downtown core with luxury condos looking out across the river.

"We didn't die, so we got that going for us," Tucker said, remembering their desperate search for Lenny's niece a few months back. "The thing I'm most worried about now is making it through this part of town without getting pulled over for driving under the influence of a rural upbringing."

"You do drive slower than my grandmother," Lenny said. "And she's dead."

"Sort of like the two in the back," Tucker said.

After the plane landed, and as dawn broke, Rurik and Elita climbed reluctantly into the coffins in the back of the rental trailer, none too happy with their continued dependence on Tucker. At least they were getting some rest, thought Tucker, who was feeling the effects of the cross-country flight, and at the moment, was envious even of Rex, curled up on the seat between the two men, snoring wheezily.

Tucker's cousin Wil had one of her contacts pick up Auscor at the airport and trail him to a town on the coast called Astoria. She also hooked them up with a guns dealer, although right now neither Lenny nor Tucker liked the looks of the address.

"This here's the place," Tucker said, pointing to a dilapidated house with a rusty, collapsing slide and an overturned kiddie pool in the front yard, and crooked, sagging blinds in the windows.

"No exits," Lenny said. "Seems like someone laid it out intentionally so that anyone walking up is exposed. Something smells funny."

Tucker looked down at the dog. "Sure it's not Rex?"

"It's a metaphor, Tucker," Lenny said. "Not the dog-fart kind of funny smell. A danger kind of funny smell."

"Lenny, we've faced vampire armies and CIA mercenaries together. I think we can handle a poor neighborhood and a few gun dealers. And besides, Wil vouched for them."

"Your cousin ain't here, and what if these city types find sport in shooting rednecks like us?"

"Speak for yourself, I ain't no redneck," Tucker said.

Lenny looked at Tucker like he was speaking another language. "You are my best friend, Tucker, but I've got news for you. You are like the king of rednecks."

Tucker put the truck in park and turned off the engine, eliciting a suspicious, one-eyed look from Rex. "We can continue this conversation another time. But you know as well as I do, Kingman's gonna have CMC muscle with him and we're gonna need our own hardware."

"I just wish we could've just swung by Wyoming on that cushy jet," Lenny said.

"No time," Tucker said. "And I know you've got something up your sleeve, or boot, or whatever. Right?"

Lenny nodded and pulled a black fiberglass dagger from inside his boot, and tucked it in his belt. "Got to get close for this to do much good, and it's not much of a defense against, you know, any kind of a gun or an actual knife. But I guess it's something."

The two men got out, leaving Rex blinking blearily, taking up his familiar sentry position behind the wheel. Two heavily muscled young men watched them warily from the porch.

"What do you want?" one asked. He was wearing a Trail Blazers baseball cap tipped to the side and a blindingly white tank shirt.

"We need to speak to Horace," Tucker said, tipping the rim of his cowboy hat in what he hoped looked like a friendly gesture.

"Ain't no Horace here," the other said, a gold front tooth glinting when he spoke. "Go on back to whatever hayride you fell off of."

"Wil Clarion sent us," Tucker said.

"Wil Clarion? Well shit, why didn't you say so?" he said, nodding and smiling, then let the smile fade. "There still ain't no Horace here. Now get your broke-ass back in your truck and haul your broke-ass trailer out of here before we have to stand up."

Lenny and Tucker heard the click of a gun being cocked. Lenny backed up a step, letting his hand drop to the plastic knife in his waistband. With a sigh, he moved forward a step.

"Fellas," Tucker said. "We really need to talk to Horace. He has some products that we are willing to pay top dollar for."

"Some meth?" baseball cap said. "You in the market for crystal?"

"No, no. Nothing like that."

"Maybe weed then?" gold tooth asked.

Tucker sighed. "We might be lost. We're looking for a specific product to help us catch up with some old friends, and Wil said Horace was the man to see about that. Sorry we've wasted your time."

"Hold on," baseball cap said, standing suddenly. "Just putting you through the wringer to be on the safe side. Wil said you were coming. Horace is expecting you."

They ushered Tucker and Lenny into the house, which was anything but run-down on the inside.

"Horace, Wil's friends are here."

Horace was sitting behind a desk staring at a spreadsheet on his Mac. "These two having a little fun with you?"

"A little," Tucker said.

"Get back out on watch, boys," Horace said, smiling.

"You part of some gang or something?" Lenny asked.

"No, we're independent," Horace said. "But we have to keep appearances. People see what they expect to see, and you can use that to your advantage. They want dead-end gangbangers; we give them that, and they confiscate a little dope and feel like they are doing their part."

"But in reality?"

"Let's just say I'm in the business of helping people, and sometimes small countries, solve problems," he said.

"Are we talking guns here?" Tucker asked. "Because sometimes I'm a little slow on the uptake."

Horace laughed. "Yeah, we're talking guns. In my experience, too many people use guns to solve their problems, but who am I to judge? I'm not saying it's the right way, I'm just saying it is a common way. There's money to be made when people take the path of least resistance."

"We need to start down that path," Tucker said. "Can you help?"

"Normally, we don't sell a damn thing out of this building," Horace said. "Too risky. It's more of a demo kind of a vibe. But I owe Wil one big-ass favor, and she's cashing in all her chips for you two."

Horace looked at Tucker and Lenny, who both, after the activities of the last few days, looked more like they'd recently become homeless than anyone who had such elite Portland arms connections. Horace shook his head, bewildered, and shrugged his shoulders.

Tucker grinned. "Lucky for me we don't get to choose our family."

"None of my business why," he said. "Come on down to the showroom."

Horace led them through the kitchen, which looked as if it had never been used, and opened the door to stairs leading down to the basement. A single bulb hanging from a cord illuminated the creaky steps, and in the cramped, musty room below, Horace grabbed the edge of a cluttered workbench and pulled it. The bench slid noiselessly forward, along with a section of Peg-Board wall behind, revealing a metal door with a keycard reader.

He slid his wallet over the reader and a tiny light turned green and the door popped open, leading to a deep, narrow room lined floor to ceiling with a staggering variety of guns.

Lenny's eyes glazed over at the sight of row after row of pistols, assault rifles and other accouterments of destruction. "Go nuts, fellas," Horace said. "But keep in mind, it ain't on the house. Just getting to shop here is the favor. And you have to tell Wil I treated you right and that we're all square."

"We'll tell her, for sure," Tucker said, looking askance at the endless array of modern weapons. "You wouldn't happen to have anything, I don't know..."

"Old-fashioned?" Horace said. "Something a little more John Wayne?"

"That sounds about right," Tucker said.

"I got just the thing," Horace said, moving aside a stack of ammo boxes to pull out a dusty and long-neglected Winchester lever action rifle. "This is some sort of fancy commemorative model 1894. Ended up with it in a, uhm, an estate situation. You can have it on the house because something tells me your friend is about to bust the bank."

Tucker ran his hand over the smooth wood stock and then held it to his shoulder, sighting it against the wall. "Now this is a real gun," he said.

"No, Tex, that's a real antique. But I'm glad it found a home in your Western-style road show."

THIRTY-NINE

"Are you really dead?" Helmi asked.

She was talking to herself, because Lizzie was stretched out, completely still and unresponsive, on the bed. She had been so pretty when she first got here, Helmi thought, and probably could be again. But the ordeal had drained her, leaving her feeble and pale. Her vitals showed no pulse; there was no blood pressure.

But when the sun sank, it always quickly changed.

Helmi placed her hand on Lizzie's belly as she had countless times since first joining this project, and felt the baby move. She pressed her stethoscope against the swell to confirm. Yes, a tiny heartbeat, but no heartbeat from the mother.

Could it possibly be true, she wondered. Vampires? Creatures of the night? She tried to let her rational mind tackle that question, but images of skulking, cape-swirling, scenery-chewing late-night horror movie characters mocked her efforts.

It seemed so implausible, so fantastic, so improbable.

Dr. Burkett's talk of a world beyond and outside the human experience, where some sort of throbbing life force swirled and waited and contained — what did it mean?

Everyone knew, at least those who thought about it, that the self was a simply a projection of the brain. Wasn't it?

No, it was all impossible, Helmi thought. She was a believer that truth could ultimately be found, if only the seeker knew enough to ask the right questions and had the right tools available to identify the right answers when revealed. Logic would guide her, even under these circumstances, when even that which seemed impossible was only the possible, the probable, even, not yet fully understood.

Logic and empathy.

The doctor was clearly mad as well, if a woman of science could so easily believe in the unbelievable. And Mark, while not mad, was blinded by greed.

This is not why I am in medicine, Helmi thought. To do the bidding of a damaged scientist, to inflict such pain for such nebulous ends.

And then she knew in a flood of unexpected certainty that she had seen enough and done enough harm to this poor woman. Her complicity in the torture of a deranged, pregnant woman would end on this day. She nodded in agreement with her inner conviction; she would save this poor wretch. She would find some way to return her to a semblance of life, or at the very least, to end her suffering and pain.

It would not be easy, though.

She checked her watch. Mark would arrive soon and there was no way he would let her take Lizzie out of here. Not that his resistance would much matter; the guards monitored everything, including the fake hospital room, and logged every entrance into and exit from the fortified building.

Helmi had an advantage though. She was born in Astoria and grew up exploring every building and jetty on the dock, and for miles on either side of the town. The daughter of a seagoing man who taught her early to rely on herself and to respect but never fear the currents of the Columbia River where they knifed into the ocean in one of the most treacherous bars in the world, she would not be boxed in by the cruel apathy of these drylanders.

She left Lizzie's room and peered through the fly-specked window overlooking the river, searching for a way out. Her gaze settled on the luxury hotel not far from the dilapidated cannery. She knew it well, working there as a maid during the summers of her college years to boost her income.

An idea came to her. The hotel had a car service, several restored classics made available to guests, and even though it was early, Walter would be around.

She fished out her cell phone and dialed the number from memory.

A pleasant-sounding woman working the front desk answered and Helmi said, "Hi, yes, I'm a guest and I went for a walk and I twisted my ankle. I hoped you could send a car over to bring me back."

"Of course," the woman said. "Should I call an ambulance?"

"No, I think I will be fine, thank you," Helmi said. "But I don't feel like hobbling all the way back. A ride would be greatly appreciated. I'm in the old cannery just down the way from you."

"Our driver is here working on the cars and I'll send him right down."

"Thank you so much," Helmi said. "I am just inside the front door out of the wind."

She broke the connection and went back into Lizzie's room. That took care of the diversion, but cameras were recording everything. Helmi avoided looking at them, finding out just how hard it is to not appear suspicious, as she traced the path of the cables back to the main computer. A faint smile of triumph was the only tell as she pretended to set her coffee cup on the edge of the table, acting surprised and clumsy when it tipped over and doused the router, which shorted out.

She darted back into the hospital room and quickly removed the IVs and monitoring equipment and, after checking the cavernous interior again, rolled Lizzie out and toward the back wall.

Helmi hid beside the gurney in the deepest shadows, watching the guards. Even from that distance she could tell immediately when the car pulled up by their anxious reactions. She imagined the sight of the gleaming silver 1938 Packard, belching smoke, rattling to a stop and the notoriously hard of hearing Walter stepping out in his uniform. That man should have given up his driver's license five years ago.

One guard went out to talk with — or rather, shout at — Walter while the other two watched nervously from the door, hands on their guns.

It had to be now.

Helmi pried open the emergency hatch covering the cargo slide that once led out onto the trucking dock and pushed Lizzie out into the sunlight and freedom.

And death.

The skin on the Lizzie's feet and calves darkened, sizzled and then burst into smoky flame. Helmi stood frozen, watching in disbelief until her instincts kicked in and she pulled Lizzie back into the sheltering darkness of the cannery and smothered the flames with her lab coat.

Heart racing and mind in turmoil, she looked at the charred skin, split and raw on the woman's legs. What the hell? Her once-comfortable world shattered in half.

She heard the dregs of a confused conversation and the old car pulling away and, running, pushed the bed back into the lab room and hooked Lizzie back to the monitoring devices.

She was rubbing antiseptic cream onto Lizzie's legs when Mark entered the room.

"Smells like bacon," he said. "What's going on with Sleeping Beauty?"

"I don't know," Helmi said. "Her legs are inflamed or infected or something."

"Let me see," he said, pushing her aside. He pushed the gown up and noted the pale, unblemished skin of her upper thighs.

"What have you done?" he asked savagely, catching Helmi by the shoulders.

"Nothing."

"Listen to me, you little simpleton. If you fuck this up for me somehow by growing a conscience now, I swear I will kill you."

"Mark, what we are doing here?"

"Good, lifesaving research. This thing here," he said, waving his hands to encompass the room, "all of this, if you haven't put it together yet, is our future."

"She's suffering," Helmi said. "She's in pain. She talks to us."

"Yeah, well do what I do. Put on your fucking headphones. She's not human, and we are about to do big things — big, moneymaking things. When they tell the story of your life, trust me when I say you will want to have bet on Dr. Burkett."

Helmi gathered her backpack and walked to the door. "I'm off the clock," she said.

"Yeah, go. Get your head on straight, blondie."

He watched her leave, and then turned to the corpse on the bed.

His cell phone beeped the arrival of a text message. It was Dr. Burkett.

Start the procedure. I'll be back in two hours.

He put his headphones on, turned the music up loud, and slid a tray of surgical instruments into place beside the body.

FORTY

Louisa stood on the pier next to the Maritime Museum. Three boys ran up the gangplank to the decommissioned coast guard ship docked there, the wet metal clanging beneath their dashing feet. Unlucky serviceman, thought Louisa, looking at the young man in his white starched suit attending to the flocks of children and tourists, a fake, distant smile plastered to his face like an unwilling contestant in a beauty pageant.

Oh well, she thought. Better than being posted in Afghanistan.

Seagulls, ever present and relentless in this coastal town, nervously shared century-old orphaned pier timbers poking up out of the water with shiny black cormorants. An orange coast guard chopper buzzed above, but the gulls were mostly unperturbed by the noise. Not so with the dozens of sea lions rolling around on the lower dock. Their annoying barks swelled to a crescendo as they argued futilely with the rotors slicing the wind.

She lit a cigarette and casually read a few lines on the placards describing the 1922 fire that wiped out the original stretch of docks in Astoria. Her phone vibrated with a text message.

Prepping now. Will keep you posted.

Three fishing boats chugged into the misty harbor, rods hanging off the sides like giant knitting needles. Farther upstream, four tankers were anchored in the widest, calmest part of the Columbia River. In the fog and steady drizzle, they looked like ghost ships stranded between life and death.

Before coming to Astoria, Louisa hadn't smoked for twenty years, feeling the specter of mortality, and the loss of precious minutes of life, with each puff. But today, she felt invincible. Science was coming to this place the creature called the Meta and she would be its carrier. Hmm, she thought, perhaps she'd need to come up with a better name for external consciousness. Later. Plenty of time for that later. She checked her watch and then flicked the cigarette hard, watching the embers arc into the waters beneath.

As she walked the two blocks to the restaurant, she again rehearsed what she would say to Kingman. The flock of seagulls flying above her seemed to screech their agreement.

At the restaurant, a town car was already parked outside. She opened the door and walked in, seeing him at a table on the far side of the dining room next to a wall of windows. The restaurant was on the corner of a rebuilt wooden pier jutting out into the water. As she sat down, she looked out of the windows and could see the far edge of the renovated cannery and dock where the lab was located. It looked deserted, as it should.

Auscor barely noted her arrival, focused instead on the menu. A plump waitress with red hair and a tattoo of a ponderosa pine on her wrist stood before them.

"I'm hungry and I don't want breakfast," he said. "My clock is all screwed up from traveling and what I want is dinner, and I am willing to pay well for it."

"Sure thing, man," the waitress said. "If you got the green, we'll make whatever you want."

"Good. I want a steak, rare, still bloody — like, it could be saved in skilled hands bloody — and a baked potato. If you have one left over from last night you can heat up. And a salad. And coffee. Be sure it's hot as Hades. What do you want?" he said to Louisa.

"Just a Bloody Mary," she said. Whiskey, vodka, cigarettes — what's next, she thought. Then she smiled. What was next would blow the lid off of civilization. She fingered the small vial of Lizzie's fractionated blood she carried in her pocket.

A massive tanker slid by, so close Louisa could see the sailors on deck. Dark-blue uniforms, dark-blue paint, flying under a Korean flag. She watched a man scramble up a rope ladder on the side of the mammoth ship.

"You have a situation on this river," Auscor said, pointing at the tanker as the waitress placed the drinks on the table.

"Oh, no worries, it's the bar pilot," she said.

"Hauling up liquor to the crew?" asked Auscor.

The waitress was hoping if she showed enough patience and solicitude, there would be a big tip from this strange, graying man in his expensive Gucci suit with a fancy car parked outside. She had already sized up Louisa and dismissed her, deciding anything other than a modest tip was unlikely from this woman in a white lab coat who reeked of cigarettes and booze.

"This area is known for its treacherous underwater topography, so only a few expert boat pilots are allowed to take ships over the Columbia River bar," she said. "Bar pilots. They get a ride out and then scramble up those ladders to get to the pilot room of the tanker."

"No shit?" Auscor said. "If the water's that rough, there must be lots of sunken treasure around here."

"I don't know about treasure, but there are more shipwrecks in this little stretch than any place in the world," she said, slipping into the flat, rehearsed voice reserved for tourists.

When the waitress said the word 'shipwrecks,' Auscor turned a steely eye toward Louisa, who was chewing on a celery stick salvaged from her drink.

"Thanks for that utterly useless but still entertaining bit of information, now leave us alone. But first, top me off?" he said, tapping on his coffee cup.

The waitress filled his cup and he took a sip, grimaced and then nodded. "Boiling hot, just how I like it."

The waitress smiled and then walked toward the swinging kitchen doors. Auscor watched her rear end, appreciating it's luscious swing, as she knew he would — the movement was rehearsed too.

The doctor's phone vibrated and she glanced down to see a text message from Mark.

Starting the procedure.

Auscor looked up at her expectantly from beneath long, delicate eyelashes, disdain mirrored in his hazel eyes. He had salon smooth skin and perfectly styled salt and pepper hair.

For an instant Louisa understood why he was, or had been, among the most powerful capitalists in the world. He was utterly boyishly charming and relentlessly forceful. In that moment, she would have done almost anything he asked.

He seemed to relish in the unexpected adoration, as if he knew exactly what she was thinking. They stared silently at the river for a few minutes, Auscor sipping his coffee and Louisa wondering what he was like in bed. Imperious, she thought, and controlling. She felt a throb between her legs.

"All right, Doctor, to business," he said at last. "Don't leave anything out. Convince me you're not wasting my money."

Her infatuation washed away like a morning tide, leaving nothing but gritty sand and bottom dwellers in its wake. She considered her next step and thought about the rehearsed words. There would be no turning back once she revealed everything to him. She didn't care so much about the money, although she wouldn't turn it down, of course.

"Data collection to assess the biological mechanism that is responsible for the creature's longevity is complete," she said.

"Wonderful. Our own little fountain of youth," Auscor said. "What did you find out?"

"We have four hypotheses and it will take several months to structure the tests to ascertain which one is correct. My best hunch is that we are looking at a genetic mechanism, but we won't know until we can complete the sequencing."

"Months? I don't want to wait that long."

She drew in her breath and prepared to answer, but the waitress returned and put his meal on the table, smiling.

"Thanks, you're a peach," he said.

Steam poured out of the baked potato as he slit it neatly from top to bottom and then slathered it in butter. He traded his dinner knife for a serrated steak knife with a wooden handle and sawed carefully, methodically at the steak. Watery red fluid escaped from the meat and puddled in the bottom of the plate, coloring the rubble of the pristine white potato a light shade of pink. He speared the piece of meat, put it in his mouth, and chewed.

"My mother taught me to chew each bite twenty times," he said, shoving a second piece into his mouth. Louisa admired the exquisite perfection of his straight, gleaming white teeth; too perfect, she thought. The best money could buy.

"I wonder what was in the cargo hold," Auscor said, tilting his head at the retreating memory of the ship. "Probably drugs or stolen technology covered up by a ton of moldy wheat. What a great opportunity to smuggle shit. I'm in the wrong business." He speared another piece of meat and pushed it into his mouth. "Note to self: get in that business."

"Don't forget, twenty chews," Louisa said quietly.

"Continue," Auscor said, coldly.

"We are in the analytical phase. After we narrow it down so we know what we're focused on, it will take a considerable amount of time, likely years, to synthesize, test and ultimately mass-produce a compound that could, in the best possible outcome, mimic the genetic behavior of the creature and stave off the effects of aging."

Auscor sawed at and then roughly stabbed another piece of meat and chewed it angrily. Louisa resisted the temptation to reach out and wipe off the rivulet of watery steak juice dripping down his chin.

He watched a second tanker slide past the wall of windows, moving steadily frame by frame as if part of a silent movie, now in slow motion.

An array of insect remains splattered on the left side of the window caught Louisa's eye. She couldn't identify the species; they had been pasted on the glass too long and all distinctive features now were reduced to a pasty, filmy sameness.

"You were never quite this specific before in your prior calculations of the time involved," he said. "Will it be worth it?"

She nodded her head. "The potential is huge, as long as we are able to continue to work outside of the formal reach of regulations, but do so in a way that the end result can still be integrated into the workings of major research labs, including pharma. I am confident you will be very happy with the results. We could have a pill that cures aging," she said.

"Could? I hate ambiguity," he said. "What actual data do you have for me?"

"Reams of it, back at the lab."

"I require access to the documentation, and assurances you are the man — pardon me, the woman — to get this job done. I have two others eager to take your place."

Louisa knew there were very few people in the world with the combination of expertise and willingness to work outside the boundaries of peer review and, to be honest, the law. But there were a few. The threat was real.

It's now or never, she thought.

"I have discovered something else," she said. "It is of great scientific importance; it will change the course of human history. You may want to shift, or at least postpone, the focus of your investment. Just for the short term."

"I am suspicious of mission creep, and melodrama," he said. "But you've got my attention for about three minutes, which is how long it will take for this coffee to cool down to the point it's no longer drinkable."

Louisa told him how, in the process of trying to find the source of immortality in the vampire's biology, she discovered neural cells in Lizzie's blood that functioned like a drug, a gateway to all the beauty of a near death experience without the specter of death itself.

She told him about the effect of Lizzie's blood and the results of the impromptu clinical trial. She told him they had a hallucinogen without addiction or health risks and that, if her instincts were right, it could give people instant meaning in an otherwise sad and lonely existence. That seemed worth a billion or two, and would give Auscor an economic foundation to continue funding the research that would cure aging.

"I've named them necrotopes," she said. "They trigger a biological reaction in humans that is a gateway into a collective field of consciousness."

Auscor took a sip of coffee. "It's cold," he said.

She stopped talking. The green tanker disappeared from their window movie screen, continuing upriver toward Portland.

"Why is that so earth-shattering?" Auscor asked. "And that's a boring name, by the way. Why not name them after a person?"

She paused, unsure which question to answer. She chose the first one.

"It proves my theory. Human consciousness is neither heaven-sent nor biological. It is something else entirely."

A red flush appeared around his neck. He sipped more of the cold coffee. Louisa was afraid things were about to go sideways. Finally, he spoke.

"I'm not the National Institutes of Health," he said at last. "And I require a more immediate return on my investments. I don't care about adding to the body of research for future generations. LSD already exists and the market has not indicated a pent up demand for a new synthesized psychedelic. Why would anyone want to trip out on Dracula juice?"

Here was her moment; she had set him up for this, now finish the deal, she thought.

"It's not that simple," Louisa said. "I'm not talking about altering perceptions, I'm literally talking about offering insight into a new plane of human existence, another way of being."

"Again, I ask you, how is this of any use to me?" His voice was cold. Louisa could see the rage building in his eyes. Had she tragically miscalculated?

The waitress slipped next to Auscor to clear his plate. She fumbled it, spilling the potato skin and giggling quietly. He could smell a hint of pot smoke beneath her patchouli and waited, irritated, for her to clean the mess. After she left, he turned back to Louisa.

"Well?"

"The demand for mind-altering substances is always high," she said.

"As our waitress just proved," he said.

"People need to escape. And I can attest that this experience leaves one…altered. More centered. With a sense of meaning. And that's just the raw necrotopes. We could strengthen the effects."

"Anybody want desert?" the waitress asked. Auscor glared into her red, glassy eyes and she mistook it for interest.

"Another Bloody Mary," Louisa said, glad for the diversion.

"Whiskey. Neat. A double," Auscor said.

As the waitress left to get their drinks, Auscor looked out over the river. Louisa followed his gaze to the seagulls battling each other to grab a crumb or two from the slices of bread tossed by a group of tourists.

"Is it just her blood or all of them?" he asked.

"Unknown. We need more subjects."

He drummed his fingers on the table. "Let me think this through," Auscor said. "If I understand you correctly, you're saying we could develop a fairly inexpensive hallucinogenic in the short term and invest the profits into a cure for aging?"

"Yes," she said.

"That could work," he said.

"There is just one small problem," Louisa said. "The necrotopes from this creature are inactive at night."

"You can only get high during the day?" Auscor laughed. "Well, that won't do. End of discussion."

"I think I have it worked out, but will need a little more time," Louisa said.

"How?"

"The fetus doesn't die during the day. Necrotopes coaxed from these embryonic stem cells are likely to be stable, and limitless."

He narrowed his eyes. "What are you waiting for?" he asked.

"Nothing," she said, swirling her second Bloody Mary with the swizzle stick, then extracting the celery spear and taking a triumphant bite. "My assistant is extracting stem cells as we speak."

Her phone beeped with an incoming text message.

There's a problem.

FORTY-ONE

"You know, I've never seen the ocean," Tucker said. He was leaning on the railing of a pier looking out over a small fleet of commercial fishing boats along the edge of the Columbia River. A barge loaded with old tires cruised by noiselessly, pushed by a stubby tug boat, and the floating pier beneath them was filled, fin to flabby shoulder, with grunting, barking, groaning sea lions.

"Really?" Lenny asked.

"Yeah. I mean, I've seen it on the TV, of course," Tucker said.

"That doesn't count," Lenny said. "I do believe if you look due west, you'll see the Pacific out there in the distance."

Tucker looked out toward the ocean, but it all looked like river to him, so he returned his attention to his dog, tugging on Rex's collar. "Easy, boy, don't let them old walruses get you riled up."

Confounded by the massive beasts, Rex was straining against Tucker's hold, growling and barking at them, skittering backward whenever one of them blew out an especially ferocious and snotty roar. Lenny was also entranced, watching the graceless hulks transform into aquatic acrobats the second they slipped into the water.

"I think they're sea lions," Lenny said.

"You ever been to the ocean?" Tucker asked.

Lenny nodded. "The army used to move me around a lot. I was in Cambodia for a while. Hawaii too, and Thailand once. And June and I spent some time in Baja, Mexico, when we was younger, on a lark, before I got shipped out."

"I did not know that," Tucker said. "I feel decidedly untraveled at the moment." He watched the sea lions, and tugged on the leash again to rein in Rex's barking. Rex felt the pull and looked up at Tucker as if he had violated one of the Ten Commandments.

"What?" Tucker said. "You can't be running around here, all right? They'll put you in the pound. Real towns have rules about pets," he said, trying to explain why he was yanking on Rex's neck with what he knew Rex realized was a simple twist of baling twine. Rex was therefore complicit with the fact that he could dart off and pull loose of the twine at any moment, but he didn't actually want to tangle with the strange fishy creatures below them.

"Lizzie always said I spent way too much time in Wyoming," Tucker said. "That I needed to see the world. I guess we was close to the ocean in New York, but something about that city feels bigger than the entire sea," he said. "I always wanted to feel the sand between my toes just once in my life."

"You will," Lenny said. "When we get Lizzie back, you got plenty of money for a little getaway to any beach you want. Permanent-like, if that's what you prefer."

"Not sure I could ever get LonePine out of my blood," Tucker said. "And besides, I don't think it would be quite the same for Lizzie anymore. Beaches are kind of a sunshine thing."

Lenny quietly sipped a soy chai latte, and not because he was lactose intolerant. He was convinced hormones in the milk supply were introduced by the government to ensure a less aggressive populace for the impending overthrow of the country by the Chinese, the UN and a secret military arm of the Vatican. "I'm betting moonlight walks on a tropical beach are pretty damn romantic."

"Nothing feels especially romantic right now," Tucker said, turning his jacket collar up against the cold. "And I'm pretty sure these Ore-y-gon beaches are not particularly tropical, even in the middle of summer."

He checked his watch and then jerked his thumb back at the trailer with the coffins, easy to overlook in a parking lot filled with rust-damaged trucks and boat trailers. "It'll be a while before sundown when evil and eviler join us. Let's poke around a little and figure out what we're dealing with. Come on, Rex," he said.

With one last befuddled *woof*, Rex left the sea lions to their raucous grumbling.

Tucker hopped into the back of the trailer with the coffins and scribbled a note on the back of a napkin — *Astoria. It's in Oregon. Lizzie is here somewhere. Call when you ain't dead* — and stuck it in Elita's rigid hand.

The sight of Elita — cold and stiff — called up memories of Lizzie, always looking so beautiful in death, beside him every morning, and he clenched his jaw.

After jumping down and closing the trailer, he looked north toward the main part of town and the old houses lining the wooded hills. "Seems like a real nice town. Where do you think Kingman might be hiding a secret lab?"

"If I learned anything from watching Perry Mason," Lenny said, "it's that drunks and nosy old ladies always know what's going on in small towns." He adjusted the matching shoulder holsters, well-hidden under his baggy fatigue jacket, holding a pair of Colt Combat Commanders with extended clips.

"I believe Perry Mason learned that from LonePine," Tucker said. "So where do we find them?"

"Drunks are at bars, on park benches or selling cars. And nosy old ladies, and some gents too, are just close enough to any of them three places to be constantly offended, but far enough away so's they don't have to actually talk to them."

"There's a brewery down the way here," Tucker said. "Let's start there and work our way toward town."

The brewery was a bust. The staff was nice, but had no information. The waitress asked the cook and he brought the brewer out, but none of them knew anything about Auscor Kingman, a secret research facility or anything particularly suspicious. They did give Tucker a dog biscuit made from distilled grains and bone meal for Rex, who was peering through the open door wide-eyed and hopeful.

The morning progressed in similar fashion in other bars, with very little information, but a great many dog biscuits, to be had. Rex was growing fonder of Astoria by the minute.

They stopped to talk to all the daytime drinkers they could find, including three old men nursing bottles in brown paper bags and sitting on the park bench at the memorial for fallen sailors. No dog biscuits there. And even less information.

They struck gold, however, at the Desdemona Club. Tucker was sitting at the bar drinking his ninth ginger ale of the day after getting the same answers from the bartender to the now-familiar questions.

Lenny, who had overdone it on the ginger ale as well, came out of the restroom and caught his arm. "We've been asking the wrong questions," he said.

"What do you mean?"

"It just hit me. No one is going to notice nothing about research equipment because that'll be brought in at night and hidden, but they will damn sure know if some place around town is being guarded. And we know Auscor will be guarding the shit out of his investment. That's what we should have been asking."

"Dammit, that makes perfect sense. Why weren't we asking that all along? Hey, buddy," he said, catching the bartender's attention. "Forget all that other stuff I was asking about. Do you know if anybody has been hiring for new security guard gigs?"

The bartender, a heavyset man with a tattoo on his forearm of a mermaid, faded by age into a fish-tailed blob, thought for a moment as he wiped water spots from beer mugs. "Come to think of it, I did hear something about that. From Frank down there." He gestured at an older man down the bar from them, his head in his hands and his arms resting on the counter.

"Hey, Frank, didn't you say you was trying to get hired on as a guard somewhere?"

Frank looked up, bleary-eyed. "Goddamn right." He turned on his stool and slapped his leg. "All I had to do was sit and watch a goddamned video screen for two weeks while they brought the machines in. But they said they couldn't hire me on account of my bum leg. Bunch of pissants with their goddamn uniforms and their goddamn rules and their goddamn good pay though."

"Where was the job?" Tucker asked, his voice cracking with growing excitement.

"I don't know," Frank said, dismissing the whole conversation with a wave of both hands.

He turned his wobbling attention back to his beer glass and drained the last flat, warm remnants before roaring back to life.

"Down there at that old cannery I guess is where it was. You know the one. The old Sea Bitchy place. All falling to shit now. Better days, but who hasn't?" he cackled.

"Some rich guy's gonna put a casino in or some such bullshit. Had some slot machines trucked in and was paying top dollar for round-the-clock watchers and why wouldn't that be me? Hells bells, I used to work there when they was squirting salmon in them cans."

Exhausted, he returned his attention to mourning his empty glass.

Tucker turned to look at the bartender expectantly. "Just follow the trolley tracks down about a half mile," the man said. "Can't miss it. Says Sea Beauty on the side."

"Thank you," Tucker said. He fished two hundreds out of his wallet and dropped them on the bar. "I want you to buy Frank's next twenty drinks. The rest is for you."

Tucker and Lenny hurried outside and the bartender watched them go. "Hey, want a biscuit for your dog?" he called, but only Rex heard him.

FORTY-TWO

The sun sank into the ocean like a sword slipping into a scabbard, and once again night began to claim the sleepy coastal town of Astoria. Up the river, the big ships were anchored tight.

Tucker crouched in the shadows next to the truck, clutching his stomach and vomiting over the pilings into the water below.

Lenny held Tucker's hat worriedly. "I told you not to eat those buffalo burger sliders," he said. "How many times have I told you, never trust food unless it's local? Do you see any buffalo in Astoria?"

Tucker waved him away and vomited again over the pier into the river water below, retching repeatedly and watching the chunks float downstream. His face was flushed and his heart was hammering at double speed. Sweat stood out in beads on his forehead. He straightened up, paused, and then doubled over to throw up again, but this time there was nothing there, nothing but spit and bile and blood.

"It's not the food," he managed to choke out.

"Do I need to take you to a hospital?" Lenny asked.

"No hospital," Tucker responded, his breath still short. A darkness spread across his heart and a chill rippled down his spine as echoes of pain and confusion tore through him.

"Are you okay?" Lenny asked. "What's going on?"

"I don't know," Tucker said. "Something just hit me hard. But I'll be fine."

"You'll need to be more than fine," Lenny said, turning his attention back to the old cannery, studying it through a pair of binoculars purchased earlier at a bird-watchers' store.

"He brought plenty of muscle," he said, watching a pair of armed men in dark uniforms positioned outside the main door of the factory that, in its dilapidated state, faded easily into the backdrop of the murky gray waters of the Columbia.

The guards, just a few of many, were on high alert and scanning their surroundings, fingers on the triggers of ominous assault rifles hanging on slings.

An armored SUV, empty, was parked by the main door. Another SUV, this one with two men listening to the police scanner and ready to deal with interlopers, was angled across the narrow access road leading from the main pier into the old factory. The roadway, perched on rickety-looking pilings, was effectively blocked.

"How do we always seem to find ourselves in these spots?" Tucker asked, pale and shaky. "Minutes away from almost certain death."

"It may have a little something to do with you dating a vampire," Lenny said. "On the plus side, ever since this whole thing started I've learned that death isn't really all that certain. I mean, it would be for us, of course."

Tucker leaned against the hood of the rental truck, parked, along with the trailer full of coffins and vampires, in the farthest, darkest corner of the parking lot of the nearby luxury hotel, giving them some protection from curious eyes and a clear view of the old cannery.

As the sun tipped fully past the horizon, they heard banging around in the trailer — Elita and Rurik were re-inhabiting their bodies and crawling out of their coffins. Rex, napping in the front seat of the car, sat up, awakened to action, as always, by the flow of returning undead energy.

The door to the trailer crashed open and Rurik leapt out, followed by a less animated but no less dramatic Elita. She had changed into a vintage Iron Maiden concert T-shirt, the sleeves cut out and the neck ripped open to reveal too much of a jarringly delicate pearl-gray bra; jeans shredded at the knees; a pair of cobalt-blue combat boots; and a vintage studded denim jacket with a stencil of the Cramps on back.

"Something is wrong with Lizzie," Elita said.

FORTY-THREE

The awareness of self was wrong. That was her first thought, and the thought itself was a clue to the tragedy. Thoughts did not exist here, only a vague sense of unity and love and long-ago memories.

Lizzie had only been conscious in the Meta in this embodied way twice before. Once when she turned Dad and once when she failed to turn Virote. Both times had disastrous consequences. This time would be no different.

But then the sense of tragedy paused and she was floating, enveloped in softness, as if moving through a large, cottony cloud on a summer day, wrapped in the coolness of a quiet joy that seemed inevitable in both purpose and fleetingness.

In the distance was Dad. She could not make out his discrete appearance, but saw the tips of his familiar muddy cowboy boots, heard his voice clearly and felt the warmth of his smile.

"Marion! We miss you so much," Lizzie said. "I never got the chance to thank you for what you did for me, for us. I owe my life to you."

Lazarus came into view. He looked like every childhood painting she had ever seen of Jesus — long, flowing hair, robe, sandals — except he was a hundred pounds fatter and his toenails were painted purple.

Lizzie giggled at the sight of him and was about to speak when she saw her mother's face hovering behind Dad and Lazarus.

"Wow, I've hit the happiness jackpot," Lizzie said. "What's going on?"

She followed their gazes as they all looked down the baby cradled in Dad's arms.

"It's a boy," Dad said. "I told you. A beautiful baby boy. He'll always be here, with us, and with you."

"I was so sure my baby was a girl," Lizzie said, laughing now, her hands setting lightly on her abdomen.

"Whatever you do, don't name him after my boy," Dad said, his rough and cracked hands gently stroking the soft peach fuzz covering the fragile head of the infant. "Tucker has just about used that name up."

"His name is Jacob," Lizzie whispered. "Jacob. My sweet Jacob."

"This is going to be real hard for you," Dad said. "But don't give up."

"I don't understand," she started to say, but then Lizzie was resurrected with a force that slammed her back into the bed like a giant magnet dropping against a metal anvil, knocking her head hard against the bars of the bed's headboard. Her breath came quick. Panting, she opened her eyes, ready to do battle.

The human girl Helmi stood before her, her face wet with tears.

"Why are you crying?" Lizzie asked, but she knew the answer before the words even left her mouth.

"Jacob," Lizzie whispered. "Jacob."

Helmi reached forward and touched the gauze wrapped loosely around Lizzie's belly. Lizzie curled up on herself, feeling the absence of mass and life within her, and let out a low, raw wail, an animal howl drawn deep from within the ripped flesh and blood of her wounded body.

The tragedy told her who she was, and in it there could be no more confusion, no more uncertainty: a mother forced to endure the unimaginable.

"It was supposed to be a simple stem cell extraction," Helmi said, crying freely. "He botched it. Mark botched it."

Lizzie pulled her legs into her belly more tightly. The sheets were stained with widening patches of dark blood still seeping from between her legs.

"My God, I'm so sorry I left you," Helmi said, as Lizzie's wail trailed off into silent weeping. "I'm getting you out of here."

Louisa cracked open the door, looking around the room calculatingly. Finally satisfied, she walked in and stood staring, detached and observant, as if looking at a priceless Renaissance oil painting of the pietà hanging in an ancient stone museum.

For an instant, the shame she felt colored and burned her face and trembled her motion, but she fought against it and in a flash, regained composure. If Louisa doubted herself or her actions, she could never show it, not now, not ever. To do so, she knew, was to show a degree of weakness that would be fatal to the scientific outcome, along with her life, she surmised, given the size of Auscor's investment.

Lizzie straightened, swallowed her sobs long enough to look directly at Louisa through a fog of pain. "You are a dead woman," she said quietly.

"You are a threat only to yourself," Louisa said.

"I will drain you and leave you alive only enough to be conscious of the wharf rats feeding on your eyes as you die," Lizzie said.

Helmi backed away from the bed, moving against the wall. Louisa glanced quickly at Lizzie's ankles to be sure she was still chained.

"None of this matters to you now," Louisa said. "I have uncovered the truth of what you carry in your blood and what this can do for humanity. In a way, I am grateful, but I don't expect you to understand."

She turned to Helmi, checking her watch. "I need you to assist me in the lab immediately with the additional analysis of the secondary subject," Louisa said.

Lizzie roared at the words. "Bitch, leave my child alone, leave him alone!" She pulled violently, helplessly at her chains.

Louisa looked at Lizzie through the cold logical lens of a research protocol coming to a close. Her need for Lizzie, for the nonhuman test subject, was ending. For the time being, she needed her blood, of course, and would for some time, but she would find a way to replicate it soon enough, rendering Lizzie herself dispensable, disposable. Someone else would pick up these pieces of the subject's life, and make decisions about how — or if — to continue using her.

One thing was clear: it was time to move on and the charade could end.

"Helmi, get this cleaned up and change the bedding. Don't throw anything away that has blood on it. Put it in a sterilized bag. And get a collecting basin beneath the vaginal area. I want every drop of blood preserved."

"I can't...," Helmi said.

"You are complicit now," Louisa snapped at her. "Do as I say." The door swung shut behind her as she left the room, muffling the echo of her heels striking the floor.

Helmi moved to Lizzie's side. "Let me help you. Please. Is there someone I can call?" Helmi asked, but Lizzie was unreachable, curling into grief, inconsolable.

Helmi stroked her head quietly. Lizzie's bruised and scabbed skull was covered by a fragile, gauzy layer of downy blonde hair just growing back.

In her pain, Lizzie flashed back to her childhood, lying on the blanket in the warm sand near Cape Cod, with her head in her mother's lap. As the ocean waves broke in metronomic splashes, her mother stroked her head, telling her how much she loved her.

Lizzie's shattered heart fell into the memory, like a glass of champagne thrown into a dark sewer hole, but even in this moment of despair, her rational mind was thinking about a bloody revenge.

FORTY-FOUR

"What do you mean something is wrong with Lizzie?" Tucker asked. Color was slowly returning to his face, hastened by anger and worry.

"I felt something in the Meta," Elita said. "Something bad. Something tremendously painful." She looked at Rurik, rattled. "Did you?"

The Russian nodded. "She is suffering."

"I felt something too, but didn't want to think the worst," Tucker said, his face twisted in anguish.

"Impossible," Rurik said. "You have no access to the Meta on your own."

"He felt something, all right," Lenny said, "And then shared it all over the boardwalk. I was standing right beside him."

"All that matters is she's alive," Tucker said, taking strength from that certainty.

"For the time being at least," Rurik said. "What do we know? Where are we?"

"We think Lizzie is down there in that old factory," Lenny said, pointing. "Auscor is in there. That's his car. And he brought plenty of goons with him."

"I love goons," Elita said, dusting stray silk coffin threads from her jacket. "They taste cheap and expendable. Like fast food."

"We must go now," Rurik said, but Tucker caught him by the arm.

"Hold on a minute, we need a plan," he said. "We can't just go strolling up to the front door."

Rurik shook Tucker's hand free and swelled with indignation. "The woman you claim to love is suffering, perhaps dying, and you wish to dally?"

"What I wish is to get her out of there alive, not just storm the gates and get shot to shit," Tucker said, his voice as flat and certain as a shovel blade.

"Dispensing with humans," Rurik said, "is not particularly challenging for our kind and certainly requires little strategy."

"Them old boys down there are from CMC," Tucker said, motioning toward the factory. "They know all they need to know about vampires from our recent escapades. You can bet they won't make the same mistakes again."

"It's true," Lenny said. "They got the place pretty well covered and the only way in is blocked."

"That means they also have the only way out blocked as well," Elita said with a cruel smile.

"I like the way you're thinking," Lenny said. "But the question is how we get inside the building without getting perforated by whatever combination of machine guns and crossbows and wood-encased claymore mines are standing between us and Lizzie?"

The four stood silent, looking at the old factory and listening to the guttural call of foghorns as long, painful seconds passed.

"I think we're gonna have to get our feet wet," Tucker said finally.

Ten minutes later, they were waist deep in the frigid Columbia River, guiding a coffin out into the water. Rurik carried the heavy wooden box, pulled from the trailer, down to the riverbank in his arms as easily as a picnic basket.

Rex and an assortment of weapons were stowed inside the impromptu raft. Rex was sitting wide-eyed on the silk cushions watching suspiciously as they held on and let the flow of the river catch them.

The current was strong and immediately sought to pull them farther out into the channel, but the two vampires were strong as well, swimming with all their might to keep the coffin, and the two men holding on to the handles for dear life, close to the shore as they guided it downriver toward the old cannery.

Silently, they pushed the coffin between the splintered pilings and more-recently-reengineered modern support beams on the vulnerable waterside of the building, until they were able to stand on the rocky, muddy river bottom and look up into the crisscross of light streaming through the floor and spackling the cold, gray water.

Tucker and Lenny shivered, but made no sound, only looked at each other for an instant recognizing the peculiarity of the situation, as they helped lift a coffin now serving as an armaments raft onto a pier that once welcomed fishing boats loaded down with salmon.

Rex hopped onto the weathered wooden dock gratefully and watched as the four pulled themselves up onto the platform. Elita let her senses wash out around her and held her hand up to caution them that someone was approaching.

Within seconds, they heard the heavy footfalls of a guard making his way around the exterior of the building. Elita motioned the others back into the shadows.

The man turned the corner, his gun at the ready, but he was completely unprepared for the sight of a wet coffin and a dry dog on the edge of the dock. "Hey, fella, what are you doing here?" he asked, confused.

"Watching you die," Elita whispered, falling on him from the shadows and twisting his neck savagely before he had time to cry out.

Bones crackled and she held her hand over his mouth, biting into the side of his throat, letting his blood surge into her. He struggled and tried to pull the trigger on his machine gun to signal the others, but Rurik was on him as well, swatting the gun from his hands and sinking his teeth into the man's wrist hard enough to nearly sever his hand as he fed at the wound.

The man thrashed and kicked feebly, his heels clunking and slipping on the wet planking. With a final groan, he spasmed and died, pinned between the two vampires. Elita, her eyes wild and mouth ringed with red, threw her head back, panting, and then toppled the body into the river. They all watched as the black water swallowed it up in seconds.

"He was delicious," Elita said. "So perfectly amoral."

"Pace yourself," Tucker said. "There's a whole passel of bad guys out there."

She smiled. "I don't have to feed on every one of them. Sometimes, killing is reward enough."

"This is a weird world we live in now," Lenny said, teeth chattering.

FORTY-FIVE

"Does it always smell this bad?" Auscor asked.

"Usually worse," Louisa said. "I'll be washing the fish smell out of my hair for years."

"Your patient looks like hell," Auscor said, peering at the pale, emaciated woman chained to the bed.

"Test subject, not patient," Louisa said. "And the last few days have not been easy on it."

"She," Helmi said quietly. She was standing next to the bed holding Lizzie's hand.

"Excuse me?" Auscor said.

"She's a 'she,' not an 'it,'" Helmi said.

Auscor looked puzzled and turned to Louisa. "Which one is this again?"

"This is Helmi, our own little conscience throughout the proceedings."

"I see." He turned to face her. "Helmi, I'm Auscor Kingman. Your employer."

"Nice to meet your, sir," she said.

He raised his hand to cut her off. "I don't like it when employees talk to me out of turn. Or ever, really. Refrain from it in the future or leave now."

Helmi bit her lip and fought the urge to throw a pair of scissors at him.

"Dr. Burkett, let's talk about the data in the office." He paused at the sight of Mark standing just outside the room in the shadows, showing just the right amount of deference. "Which one is this?"

"Mark. While clearly lacking in a few fundamental skills, such as extracting stem cells without causing a miscarriage, he has been helpful, and should join us," Louisa said.

"Fine. Come with us."

"Yes sir, Mr. Kingman," Mark said, smiling over his shoulder at Helmi.

She watched them leave and became gradually aware of increasing pressure on her hand.

"I think you are a good person," Lizzie said. Her blue eyes were ringed with red and pooled with tears. "But you are in a bad place."

"I don't belong here," Helmi said, voice cracking.

"Neither do I," Lizzie said.

Helmi looked around at the equipment and the bloody gauze.

"I'm a vampire," Lizzie said.

"I know," Helmi said. "I didn't believe it, but earlier I tried to get you outside, you were dead, and the sunlight caused your legs to burn. They caught on fire."

Lizzie nodded. "Could I have some water?"

Helmi let go of her hand and got her a cup of water.

"When did you take me outside?" Lizzie asked.

"Yesterday morning."

Lizzie thought about that. "My baby died," she said at last, and Helmi choked back a sob. "They killed him."

"It's my fault," Helmi said. "I tried to take you away, but I didn't know what to do. You caught on fire. I shouldn't have brought you back."

Lizzie drained the cup and held it out again. "May I have more?"

Helmi returned with a fresh cup.

"I am glad you tried, at least," Lizzie said.

"I don't have the keys to your shackles," Helmi said. "I've looked all over. But I think you are too weak to run even if I could let you go."

Lizzie motioned feebly toward the blood bag on the IV pole. "I don't think it's really blood."

"It's not," Helmi said. "It's mostly sugar water with just enough blood to keep you from dying for good."

"I need real blood to regain my strength."

"How much?" Helmi asked quietly.

Lizzie looked at her closely. "I don't know. A lot, but probably not all of it."

"So it wouldn't it kill me?"

"I have a memory of using my cowboy's blood each night to survive," Lizzie said. "I think it's real. The memory. I can't make much sense of things right now."

"I want you to live," Helmi said. "I need you to live. This is not who I am. This is not who I was raised to be. I want to help people."

"I'm going to do bad things to them if you let me go."

"They have cameras in the room," Helmi said. "I can't shut them off. If I do, they will make me leave and you will be on your own."

"Then you have to be careful," Lizzie said, breathing heavily from the exertion of even just these few words.

Helmi looked at the cameras, tracking the best angle for a partial blind spot. If she stood over Lizzie on the left side of the bed, her back to the third camera, it would appear she was adjusting the bedding or taking a reading.

"Okay," she said at last. "Where from?"

"The wrist, I guess," Lizzie said. "The most blood quickly."

Lizzie could feel the heartbeat of the young woman accelerating, felt a flood of fear coursing through her, and found herself trembling at the thought of sustenance and revenge.

"I don't know if I can do it," Helmi said.

Lizzie squeezed her eyes shut, frustrated. She no longer cared about living, only surviving to avenge Jacob.

Helmi held her hands to her forehead, struggling to will herself into action and possibly into her own demise.

She grabbed a set of sheets from the cabinet and unwrapped them, shaking them out. The billowing fabric created a natural diversion and as the sheets temporarily blocked the bed from the camera, she slipped open the narrow top drawer and pulled out a scalpel. Bundled in the sheet, she pulled the knife out of the blue sterile wrapping and palmed it, feeling the knick of the tip against her palm.

An idea jumped into her mind as if placed there like a nugget of gold by a benevolent god and she slipped the scalpel, point up, into the pocket of her scrubs.

"Get ready," she said, but Lizzie was not listening. She was too weak, too confused.

Helmi thought of her parents, pictured them smiling in her mind, and wished there was some way to tell them good-bye, because she was not sure she would emerge from this mess alive. Texting them was too risky; it would implicate them. Instead, she silently hoped she had led the kind of life that would make her parents always assume the best about her, even in the midst of this terrible situation.

She thought again of her father protecting the stray dog, thought of her mother taking meals they could not afford to give away to the homeless shelter, and nodded. Yes, she thought, they would understand, and both would do the same thing.

She took a deep breath and then said a silent prayer. "Get ready," she said again, shaking Lizzie slightly. "Get really ready."

Lizzie stirred and opened her eyes.

"In a minute I am going to place my hand over your mouth," Helmi said. "There will be a gash in my palm. There won't be much time. At first, it will seem as if I am simply washing you, but quickly enough it will be clear something else is going on. They will come running soon after that."

"I will try my best to keep you safe," Lizzie said.

"I don't have a key," Helmi said. "I can't free you from the restraints."

"You won't need to," Lizzie said.

In full view of the cameras, Helmi grabbed a container of antiseptic wipes and appeared to struggle opening them, quietly cursing, hoping the guards would notice what appeared to be her extreme irritation. Loudly, she said, "I hate this job."

She pulled out a wipe and turned back around to face Lizzie, her face now obscured. Gently, she wiped Lizzie's head with her right hand.

"Here we go," she whispered. Lizzie was motionless, but her eyes were open, expectant.

Helmi pushed her left hand deep in her pocket over the point of the blade and winced at the pain as skin, flesh and a first layer of muscle gave way. She pulled her hand out and blood was already gushing out of the deep wound. She pressed her palm neatly over Lizzie's mouth and, with her other hand, continued to wipe Lizzie's face and neck.

At first, Lizzie could barely respond as the warm, sticky blood seeped into her mouth. But as the liquid slid down her throat, she began to recover her hunger and pushed her tongue into the wound, probing and pressing so that the trickle became a stream.

In her half-starved state, she began to choke and sputter, but kept her mouth pressed tight and sucked harder, ravenous. Helmi was growing weak as Lizzie, her eyes newly ablaze, pulled life out of Helmi's hand and into her body.

Helmi watched, woozy and bewildered and amazed, as Lizzie's skin turned from a wan yellow tone to a healthy glowing color. Suddenly, what had been parched, flaking skin plumped out as if water was being directly injected into her face. As Lizzie continued to drink, Helmi watched the sores and scabs on her scalp start to heal over.

"How can this be?" Helmi said, even as her own vision blurred around the edges.

Lizzie looked at her with grateful, flashing eyes. She broke the seal between her mouth and Helmi's hand for a second. "Almost done."

Helmi marveled at the unfamiliar melody of this voice, soft and velvety, and felt as if the person before her was totally new.

"What the fuck?" one of the guards said to himself as he looked at the bank of video monitors in the corridor outside the hastily constructed lab. "Is she trying to smother her?" he said to himself. He tapped the audio on his headset. "Clarence, get into the room. Find out what that nurse is up to."

He looked again at the video feed, his alarm growing. Where the fuck is Clarence, he thought.

As he watched the feed, the nurse collapsed and fell to the floor, and then Lizzie was suddenly standing upright next to the bed, naked and unchained, the snapped restraints dangling from her wrists, the pendant from her mother in one hand.

She looked fiercely at the cameras, extended both arms and thrust out her middle fingers.

"Fuck all of you," she mouthed.

"Oh shit," the guard said, tapping the audio channel again. "All hands, all hands, alpha alert status. Repeat, alpha alert."

In the lab, Auscor watched Louisa peer through a microscope. She had gathered the stem cells from the umbilical cord in one tube, but the pluripotent ones in the placenta were the real treasure, preserved in the glass box next to the microscope. In a third container, blood from the infant's circulatory system had been collected. There was one more bundle, wrapped in plastic on the table, next to the equipment.

Louisa looked up, startled, when she heard alarms ringing and saw emergency lights flashing.

Auscor turned to Mark and asked, "What the hell does alpha alert mean?"

Even as the words left his mouth, a muffled explosion shook the frame of the entire building, and two guards burst into the room, gas masks in place and their weapons — beefy assault rifles — held waist high and poised to shoot.

"Let's go," one of them shouted. "Outside now."

FORTY-SIX

Minutes earlier, Tucker whispered to Lenny, "We need a distraction."

They were crouched beside an old, frayed conveyor belt leading up to a shuttered window. The night had hardened around them and only the lap of waves and the roar of traffic from the bridge connecting Oregon to Washington could be heard.

"We don't have much time," Lenny said. "Those guys are pros. You can bet they have a check-in protocol. When the floater don't call in," he said, gesturing toward the river that had recently claimed the body, "things'll heat up."

Tucker worked the lever action of the 30-30 to seat a round and dropped a handful of the shiny cartridges into his jacket pocket. "Then we'd better get moving."

Lenny looked askance at the rifle Tucker was holding. "You sure you don't want something a little more, I don't know…"

"Modern?" Elita said, finishing the sentence for him. "Or perhaps effective? Or deadlier?"

"There's something to be said for the classics," Tucker said. He had his .454 revolver at his hip in a leather holster with a row of cartridges in the belt loops. "Besides, I'd just as soon leave the killing to the pros."

Lenny had no such qualms, and bristled with high-tech weapons like a tactical hedgehog. "My goal is to not be killed by the pros," he said. "Y'all want some extra firepower?" he asked, looking at Elita and Rurik.

"Nope," Elita said. She held up a pair of shiny hatchets, sharpened to a razor edge.

"I find those more disturbing than any machine gun," Lenny said.

"You should," she said. "And thank you. I take that as a compliment."

"What about you, Rurik?"

Rurik sniffed. "I do not require the tools of humans to destroy humans."

"Nothing is just ever 'yes' or 'no' with you, is it?" Tucker said.

"No," Rurik said, flashing a satisfied smile in the half-light. "Would you ask a wolf if he wanted antlers to hunt deer?"

"Probably not," Tucker said. "But I doubt many wolves would turn down the chance at a couple of Uzis."

"Quiet, children," Elita said sharply. "Something is happening. Adrenaline and blood and power, together. The taste of it is palpable."

Rurik felt it as well, a part of him ashamed at devoting even a fraction of his attention on the human cowboy. "No more waiting," he roared. "The queen returns to herself."

Rurik threw himself against the back wall, hammering his fists into the corrugated metal. Crumpled tin and moldy timber exploded inward, opening the building to the night.

In the shadows of the cavernous building, bodies moved against distant lights and voices shouted in confusion as a pair of floodlights blazed on and bathed the breach in high-watt discovery.

"I guess we're the distraction, then," Lenny said.

Tucker watched Elita, momentarily lit up like a rock star on a stage of old crates, wheel the hatchets gleefully and then dart into the building. Rurik was gone already, and Tucker could hear small arms fire and saw crossbow bolts *thunk* into the planking around him as he raced for the shadows.

He snapped the rifle to his shoulder and fired a quick round into the first light, levered in another cartridge and took out the second light.

Darkness returned to the buildings as shards of glass rained down. Tucker bent to shield Rex, and motioned for Lenny to stay put as bullets whined around them and more crossbow bolts plunked into the wall and hummed by out into the night, splashing into the river.

Within seconds, the screaming started and the bullets and bolts began to wane.

Two shadows streaked through the old warehouse dealing death and destruction.

Tucker reloaded his rifle and then moved forward carefully, heart racing, his vision narrowed to filter out everything except threats. Rex stayed close on his boot heels. When Tucker turned to check on Lenny, his friend motioned that he would stay behind and watch the breach in the wall for rearguard protection.

Even as Lenny settled in behind a dusty old generator, a guard poked his head through the wreckage of the wall. Lenny sent a stream of bullets in his direction, every fifth a tracer so that it looked like he was aiming a fiery laser at the man. The guard swore and retreated under the withering fire.

Tucker put his trust in Lenny to watch his back and kept moving cautiously forward.

Somewhere close by, in the smoke and shadows and confusion, he heard a wet clump, and then a head rolled past them, the mouth still trying to make sense of its lack of body.

The farther into the warehouse he and Rex advanced, the more body parts he saw — hands, arms, feet. The floor was slick with blood.

Rex crept along, his belly close to the floor, scared and watching Tucker with big, serious eyes. There was motion behind him and Tucker spun, rifle ready, only to see Elita — crazed from the killing — drop down to the floor from the walkway above.

Her hatchets were covered in gore and brains and hair, and he was afraid for a moment she wouldn't be able to control herself, but her eyes softened at the sight of him.

"Rurik and I are almost done here. She's up ahead," Elita said, out of breath. "There's one person with her, but I think Lizzie is killing her. This is fun," she said. "We should do stuff like this more often."

Then she was gone.

Across the warehouse near the front door, Tucker saw Auscor hustling toward the exit along with a woman in a white coat. They were flanked by two mercenaries, one of them dripping blood from a gash in his back.

Tucker drew a bead on the back of Auscor's head and felt his finger tightening around the trigger.

It wasn't an easy shot, fifty yards and a moving target, but he knew he could make it; he'd made tougher shots all his life. A quarter inch of motion and a lead slug would pierce the brainpan of the bastard who started all of this madness.

But Tucker wasn't an executioner, and he knew from experience that it was too hard to recover from the urge to kill, once acted upon.

He lowered the gun to aim for the legs of the fleeing man — wounding him certainly felt appropriate — but in the corner of his eye he saw Rurik a split second away from dying.

The Russian had pinned a guard against the wall with one hand while clawing at his throat with the other, pulling loose a cravat of flesh and bone and blood. Unbeknownst to him, another mercenary was kneeling on the floor behind him, bleeding from the mouth and ears but steadying a crossbow leveled at the vampire's back. Without hesitating, Tucker snapped a shot in his direction and, before even looking at the result, levered in another round and fired at Auscor.

But it was too late. Auscor scurried out the front door and disappeared as the slug pierced the door frame at knee level.

With a curse, Tucker looked back to see crossbow man toppling slowly forward and Rurik, still holding the other dying man tightly against the wall, looking at a crossbow bolt buried in the wall inches from his cheek.

He turned his head slowly and looked at Tucker, their eyes locking across the chaos. Tucker swore to himself. I should have let him die, he thought, and Rurik smiled as if agreeing with him, and released his grip on the corpse, letting the body slide to the floor.

"They're pulling out," Lenny shouted, running up from behind. "I'll cover you. Find Lizzie."

Tucker nodded and looked down at Rex. "Come on boy," he said. "Find Lizzie."

Rex, taking his charge seriously, darted forward through the chaos, barking.

He led Tucker to the door of a closed room and scratched at it anxiously. Tucker drew his foot back and kicked out savagely, the heel of his boot connecting squarely above the handle. The door flew open and Lizzie, naked and her head shaved down to stubble, was standing over the body of a young woman.

She was confused to see the tall cowboy standing in the doorway, a rifle in his hand and his eyes filled with pain and relief.

"Are you real?" she asked at last, voice wavering. "Are you really real?"

He dropped the gun clattering to the floor and moved across the room to catch her in his arms. "Yeah, darling. I'm just as real as the day is long."

She collapsed into his embrace. Rex, barking joyfully, entered the room and leapt up at her, wiggling in midair in each jump as he tried to lick her face.

"Even Rex is real," she said, smiling, but it didn't last long. "They did things to me, Tucker," she whispered. "Nothing made sense."

She looked down at the raw scar on her belly, grabbed his hand and placed it over her wound. "They killed our baby." Tears dripped from her eyes. "I couldn't stop them."

His jaw hardened. "It's going to be okay," he said.

"I don't think so," Lizzie said. "I don't think it will ever be okay again."

He slipped off his denim jacket and put it around her as Rurik and Elita arrived.

"My queen," Rurik said, bowing slightly.

Elita moved beside Tucker and caught Lizzie's arm, offering her balance. "We must get you out of here."

"Even my crazy fantasies are real," she whispered, looking at Elita and Rurik curiously.

"Cops are on the way," Lenny shouted, poking his head through the door. "Lizzie, glad to see you," he said.

"Head for the back," Tucker said.

"She saved my life," Lizzie said, gesturing toward Helmi, unconscious on the floor. "We have to bring her."

Rurik scooped her up and tossed her over his shoulder like a sack of potatoes. They made their way toward the back of the cannery, Lizzie clinging to Tucker and Elita. Lenny stayed behind, watching for any security people that hadn't yet been butchered.

At the hole in the wall, Lizzie paused, feeling life nearby — cowardly, craven life. Mark.

Eyes glazed with fury, she pushed herself free from Tucker and Elita and reached into the shadows under a heavy desk and pulled him out with a squeak.

"Wait, wait," he begged, crying and dripping fearful snot. "I was following orders."

"You killed our baby," she said, voice flat.

"It was an accident," he said.

"This is not," Lizzie said, slapping him so hard his jaw ripped free in a shower of blood and splintered teeth. He tried to scream but couldn't make a sound through his ruined mouth. She shoved him through the opening in the wall, where he fell backward into the empty coffin.

He tried to sit up, gurgling bloody bubbles from his shattered face, but she was on him too fast, snapping his arms like twigs and stuffing him back inside.

"Remember me," she hissed, pressing her face close to his, then slammed the lid. With a fearsome shove of her foot, she sent the coffin shooting out into the river so hard it skipped twice on the surface before slowly turning into the current and drifting toward the ocean.

"The cops are out front," Lenny said. "There's an old rowboat just down at the end of the pier, it ought to get us far enough away to avoid spending the rest of our life in an Astoria prison."

Lizzie snatched a flare from Lenny's tactical vest and turned to go back into the building.

Tucker caught her by the arm. "Lizzie, honey, we have to go."

"Let go of me," she said, angrily, shaking free and pushing past him.

Tucker started to follow her, but Elita held him back. "Let her do what she has to," she said.

Lizzie returned a few minutes later, tightly holding a tiny, tragic bundle. "Now we leave."

They crowded into the boat, dangerously overloaded and already taking on water, and Rurik grabbed the oars and began to propel them away from the shore. Strobes of red and blue lights from police cars washed across the old cannery even as flames flickered in the darkness from the fire Lizzie started.

FORTY-SEVEN

The sun gleamed through the floor-to-ceiling front window of the Finnish Sauna and bounced off the spotless floor. Lenny sat in a booth at the front of the restaurant, squinting in the sunlight and keeping a direct line of sight to the truck and trailer parked out front.

The restaurant was empty and the Closed sign turned. Beneath it, a handwritten note was taped to the glass: *Private Event*.

Lenny took off his baseball cap, the Leatherman logo faded by years of grime and grease, to wipe the sweat beading on his forehead. Helmi sat across from him.

"I know this ain't a real sauna anymore, but it kind of feels like one now," Lenny said.

"Give it a minute, the sun will move behind a cloud," Helmi said.

A seagull hopped down the sidewalk, investigating a white speck on the curb. Helmi watched as the bird pushed at what turned out to be a piece of wet cotton and, realizing there was no sustenance, took flight, flapping hard four times before soaring out of sight.

"When I was little, I wished I could fly," Helmi said.

"I think every kid wants to fly," Lenny said, stirring nondairy creamer into his coffee. "I still want to."

"I always knew it was a fantasy, though," Helmi said. "And there was a certain kind of security in that."

"We actually can fly," Lenny said. "People do it every day on airplanes."

"Not like birds, though," she said.

Lenny looked at her quizzically. Helmi rested her bandaged hand quietly in her lap. She was pale and worn. She ripped open a pink packet of fake sugar with her teeth, and stirred it into her tea with one hand, the clinking of the spoon taking the place of conversation for a few seconds.

"Was it very hard to have your entire reality turned upside down?" she asked. "You know, when you first found out about the vampires?"

"Sort of," Lenny said. "I'm still a little upside down, and finding out new stuff all the time. I'm not sure it will ever get much easier. But I keep telling myself there are only a few things that matter in this world — love and friendship, and doing the right thing. Nothing changes that, not even when nightmares come true."

"Maybe you and Tucker are just tougher than I am."

Lenny smiled. "I don't know much about you, but I know you helped someone when you didn't have to. And you put your own life at risk to do it. In my book, that makes you pretty tough. In his book," he said, jerking his thumb toward the trailer, "you are nothing less than an angel."

"Where is she now?" Helmi asked. "I'm worried about her."

"He's sitting inside there with her, in the dark. I'd be surprised if he ever leaves her side again," Lenny said.

"Is she dead again?" Helmi asked.

"For the time being. But I think you know all too well that it's only temporary."

"And the others?" Helmi asked. "The Russian?"

"Rurik finally slowed down long enough for his protectors to catch up to him," Lenny said. "They took him someplace safe."

He leaned back and adjusted his cap again. He had dark circles under his eyes, like obsidian crescent moons, and his body was an advertisement for exhaustion. He sipped the coffee and sighed.

"Is he nearby?" she asked.

"I don't exactly know, but I guess so. He's got his handlers watching our U-Haul like hawks. And us too."

"And the woman? The scary, beautiful one."

"Elita. She's a piece of work, isn't she?" Lenny said. "She's in the back of the trailer too. She's got a lot riding on Lizzie staying alive."

Helmi glanced up at her father standing nearby, and he nodded at her as he wiped the bar clean for perhaps the hundredth time. She knew it was just busywork to keep an eye on her and a hand close to the shotgun under the counter.

"You got a fine girl here," Lenny said to her dad. "You ought to be proud of her. She did the right thing when she didn't have to."

"I am indeed proud of her," Oley said. "But I would expect nothing less from my daughter. I'm also a little nervous now. Can you tell us what is going on, what we should expect?"

"I'll tell you everything I can, everything I know," Lenny said. "But I think I may need something a mite stronger than this coffee." He nodded at the bottles behind the bar.

Helmi's father pulled out a bottle of whiskey and filled three glasses and then joined them at the table, scooting Helmi over.

"Here's to you both," Lenny said, and they clinked shot glasses and tossed back the whiskey. "It's a little early," Lenny said with a shiver, "but that hit the spot." He wiped his mouth with the sleeve of his denim shirt.

"How did they meet?" Helmi asked.

"It was on account of him being the last cowboy in Wyoming," Lenny said. "She was a reporter in her first life, her real life, and she met him on assignment. It never should have worked, even before she was, you know, turned into a vampire. And definitely not after. But somehow it did."

Oley poured another shot and Lenny told them about the cowboy and the vampire, the clash of undead species and the special blood in Lizzie's veins.

When he finished, Helmi said, "I thought I understood this world, a little a bit at least." She looked out across the parking lot at the trailer. Her father was silent, unsure what to say next.

Inside the trailer, Tucker sat crouched down in the corner next to the door, his hand resting on her coffin. There had not been enough time to talk, to say the things he wanted to say before the night gave way to day, but all he really needed to know was conveyed by her emaciated appearance, anguish and incoherence.

Her words still echoed in his mind. *Are you real*? Then she put his hand on her hollow belly and broke into sobs.

He wasn't sure he would ever recover from that moment, from the pain that knifed into his heart.

She was safe now, at least for the time being. Tucker swore to himself that he'd beef up security tenfold. That little impromptu marriage in an unsecured truckstop, that kind of foolishness was over. With help from Lenny and Rurik, they would turn LonePine into a goddamn fortress. No other way out of this, he thought.

LonePine. If they started driving now they'd nearly be there by the time the sun went down. He knew in his soul she would start feeling better when she was someplace familiar, someplace that felt like home.

It was time to go.

He stood and opened up the back door of the U-Haul and looked cautiously around the parking lot. There was a black, heavily armored SUV in the back of the lot. One man was in the driver's seat. Another stood outside by the passenger door and Tucker saw the bulge of fire-power under his coat. A third, the tallest, was simply standing forty feet away watching the trailer and not even trying to hide his interest. He nodded at Tucker.

Rurik's men, Tucker thought.

Inside, Lenny noticed the movement and excused himself, then went outside to meet him.

"I want to get going," Tucker said. "Now."

Lenny looked around and saw the SUV. "They ain't the enemy, that's Rurik's people," Lenny said.

"I don't care about them one way or the other," Tucker said. "I just want to get her home."

"You sure LonePine is her home?"

Tucker looked up at the misty clouds swirling in from the river and thought back to better days when Lizzie and he lay together in the pasture behind the barn and found funny faces in the sky. He sighed. "I don't know where else to go," Tucker said.

"That's as good a reason as any, and I am sure missing my June," Lenny said. "Let's get going."

"I got some thanking to do first," Tucker said. "Would you...?"

"I'll watch over her," Lenny said.

Tucker entered the restaurant and Oley met him at the door.

"Your friend left before he got to the important part," Oley said. "How much danger is my little girl in?"

"You ain't in danger from her kind," Tucker said. "There ain't no reason to be afraid of them."

"By them you mean vampires?"

"Yeah, you got nothing they want, other than blood, and they can get that anywhere," Tucker said. "But you may be in danger from those other people, the rich bastard behind all this business."

Helmi looked up at her father with sad eyes. "Daddy, I'm so sorry. They told me they would ruin you."

"That's not going to happen," Tucker said, looking at Helmi and then taking both her hands into his own. "They might be pissed about what transpired, so you might want to get away for a little while, all of you; shut the bar down and just go."

"I'm too old to live on the run," Oley said. "I'll take my chances here."

"Fair enough," Tucker said. "Just keep your eyes open and a gun handy. If I get my 'druthers, the people who done this won't be around for too much longer."

"The bar, can they take it?" Helmi asked.

"Nope," Tucker said. "I paid off the note on this place. It's yours free and clear now. And I set up an account in your name down at the local bank and put some money in there. A lot of money."

"I can't accept that," Helmi said. "We can't."

"You can do whatever you want with the money. Throw it in the ocean. Give it to charity. I don't care. You done something for me and Lizzie that I can't ever repay, but this is a start."

Lenny knocked lightly on the window, looking at his watch. Tucker nodded at him and turned back to Helmi. "You got a friend for life in Wyoming. You need anything, you just call me."

"No time to say good-bye to her?" Helmi said, touching her palm.

Tucker shook his head. "I'll tell her, I promise." He hugged Helmi and walked out the door.

FORTY-EIGHT

Sheets of rain and hail blew sideways in front of the headlights of the truck, driven by strong winds uncoiling inside a spring storm sweeping through the valley. Throughout the afternoon, Tucker watched the angry clouds building over the mountains as he dug down into the hard soil. The squall started just before the sun went down, which was why Rex was watching, dry and warm, from the front seat.

He was used to hard labor, of course, so the shovel felt natural in hands as he dug, but it was painful work for his heart, digging such a small, square, deep hole. He bought a plot next to his mom and dad, and spent the afternoon attacking the hard, rocky earth.

Aaron Purvis, the caretaker at the cemetery, said he'd take care of it for free, begged Tucker to let him help, but somehow it felt more appropriate to do it himself. After all, he kept telling himself, it was his fault, his failure to protect Lizzie.

She didn't believe that, of course, and told him so, but her words could not reach the part of him able to hear or understand. Not that had she tried very hard; they had been back in LonePine for two days and her grief left her almost mute.

The cemetery was deserted as night fell, though the transition was hidden by the darkness of the storm. There were two coffins in the back of his truck under a frayed blue tarp diverting the rain. One was full-size and held the body of Lizzie; she would resurrect in a few minutes. The other was barely two feet long and held the body of their son. Aaron gave him the coffin, top-of-the-line, free of charge. When Tucker saw the tiny, ornate box, he cried and almost collapsed, and Aaron had to hold him steady.

Now, hours later, his emotions had curdled into anger and he was too numb to feel anything else. He was soaked through, the rain dripping from the brim of his hat as he looked down into the hole, now gathering water and mud.

He leaned on the shovel and watched the water trickling in, then speared the shovel savagely into the muddy mound beside the undersized grave.

"Goddamn it to hell," he said. "Can't even have a proper fucking funeral."

There was a clap of lightning and a peal of thunder, and then Lizzie was standing beside him and he jumped.

She looked worried and sad and angry, catching his hand in hers. "Are you all right?" she asked.

"No," he said. "Are you?"

She shook her head. "Not really. But you know, when I die and come back, it's like he's still alive. All the promise and joy and potential. It's not fair to you, and I shouldn't even tell you about it, but it's kind of amazing for just a split second in the in-between place."

He squeezed her hand. "I'm glad one of us can take something good from all this."

"It's not good," she said flatly. "It's just not quite as terrible for a heartbeat."

"Maybe that's enough," Tucker said with a shrug.

"I don't think so," she said.

"It's time," he said, and Lizzie nodded, silently, following his lead. They carried the tiny casket to the grave and bent to lower it in carefully, then stood quietly as the rain swirled around them.

"Should we do anything?" Tucker asked, watching water bead up on the lacquered wood.

"Like what?" Lizzie asked.

"I don't know," Tucker said. "Maybe say a prayer or something?"

Lizzie shook her head. "There are no gods, Tucker. No vampire gods, no human gods. No animal gods. And certainly no gods of little babies who didn't do anything wrong at all except try to be born to parents like us."

He took her hand. "You can't think of it like that," Tucker said.

She looked deep into his eyes and he saw a terrible loneliness and emptiness reflected there. "There's no other way to think of it," she said.

"We can try again."

"Yeah," she said, acid in her voice, "I'll just magically make myself human again and then we'll try again."

"We could adopt," Tucker said.

"Right, that's a great plan. We'll bring some poor kids into this crazy fucking world of ours, of mine, kids I might need to feed on in a pinch."

It was grief making her angry, he knew that, but that didn't make it any easier to stomach. Rain was pouring down her face, and her hair — barely grown back in — was plastered to her skull.

"Then maybe we could buy a fucking orphanage somewhere," Tucker said. "I don't know, Lizzie, I'm just trying to come up with…"

"Practical solutions," she said. "I know, and that's what I love about you. Always trying to fix things. But I don't think we can fix this. I don't think anything will ever set it right again."

"What are you saying?" he asked.

"Nothing. Something, but I don't know what yet," Lizzie said, her voice ragged with regret. "But I know this. A normal mother would have been alive to fight them off. A normal mother wouldn't leave her baby trapped in a dead womb to be off floating around the Meta while bad people poked syringes into me."

"You can't blame yourself for this," Tucker said. "I'm the one who let you get taken. I'm the one who couldn't find you."

She shook her head. "Stop. We can't do this. It won't help. Let's just try to get through the next few days."

"Fair enough," he said. "But I do have a few things to say."

He took his hat off and stood, head bowed, next to the grave. "Jacob, I never got to meet you. I reckon I will, just for a second anyway, when I finally die, and I'm looking forward to that." He wiped the rain and tears from his eyes. "I'm real sorry about how everything turned out, but you have to know your mom and I loved you and we wanted something real different for you and for us."

There was a flash of lightning — a long, endlessly bifurcating line of electric dendrites that scorched a nearby hillside, followed by a rolling bellow of thunder that caused them both to flinch.

Tucker glared up into the heavens as if begging anyone up there defy him. "Anyway, I don't really understand how all this afterlife or underlife business works, but I know my mom and dad — your grandpa and grandma — are there looking out for you, and Lizzie's mom too. I want you to take it easy on them, and not run them ragged chasing after you."

"It doesn't work like that," Lizzie said quietly.

He looked at her sharply. "Does it matter? Does it really fucking matter how it works if that's how I want to think about it?"

She shook her head, chastened by his anger. "No, sorry. Of course not."

He returned his attention to the tiny coffin. "Be a good boy. I guess that's all I have to say," Tucker said, reaching for the shovel.

"Wait," Lizzie said. She pulled her mother's pendant from her neck and dropped it on top of the coffin. "I'm truly sorry, Jacob," she said, voice breaking.

She nodded, and Tucker began slinging shovelfuls of muddy earth into the hole. Lizzie stood silently beside him until he was finished. He carefully smoothed out the mound of dirt with the back of the shovel, again and again, back and forth, unwilling to let even this last physical link to the boy end.

Finally, without saying a word, he tossed the shovel into the back of the truck and they rode back to the trailer in silence. Rex curled his head onto Lizzie's lap as she watched the windshield wipers battling and losing against the rain.

FORTY-NINE

"This is completely unacceptable," Auscor said, sipping champagne fortified with a heavy splash of brandy and staring sullenly out into the New York night. His vision, clouded with anger, barely registered Gramercy Park below and the flow of traffic along nearby Park Avenue.

Louisa was with him in his suite, though she was staying in a 'regular' room two floors below, which was opulent beyond her experience, with a mahogany ceiling, expensive antiques appointing the room and commanding artwork on the walls.

"It doesn't have to be over yet," Louisa said, distracted by the luxury.

He refilled his glass, careful not to let the champagne bubbles build to overflowing.

"We were driven out of that wet pee-slit of a town by a drunken cowboy and two shuffling creatures of the night. We have nothing to take to market, no data to hook pharma, and therefore no hope of monetizing the research I've already paid for before we end up on the wrong end of the financial spectrum."

"That's not exactly true," Louisa said. "We know a few things. We know the creature's blood is laden with physiological secrets that might cure aging, someday, but in the meantime, the necrotopes in her raw blood are powerful enough to immediately trigger a chemical reaction that opens a doorway to a spiritual dimension — with life-changing consequences. We also know the baby was from a human and a vampire."

"A half-breed," he said, then sipped his champagne. "So what?"

"A hybrid," she said. "We determined the stem cells are useless in terms of harvesting necrotopes. That leads us to two possible conclusions useful for the immediate goal of monetizing the psychotropic experience. Either the blood of all full vampires contains necrotopes or only her blood contains the necrotopes."

"Great," Auscor said. "Because we also know there is a pissed-off cowboy guarding her and her blood very carefully, and at least two pissed-off vampires looking for revenge." He eyed the door, glad CMC muscle was posted outside. Eager to redeem their growing catalog of missteps, CMC was overcompensating with extravagantly large men carrying extravagantly large weapons. He smiled at the predictability of human psychology.

"If, and that's a big if, I continue down this path, the smart money is to get her back, thereby covering both eventualities. We can find out about other vampires at our leisure, or maybe at the same time if we can grab one or two more of them in the process."

"My thinking exactly," she said. "Can we afford a retrieval operation?"

"We? We, my dear doctor?" Auscor asked. He held his hand up. "Rhetorical question. I need to work the angles for a second, a cost-benefit calculation given this new wrinkle. Let me think. Please be quiet and gawk at the photos, curated by the ever-annoying Julian Schnabel. Or perhaps marvel over the fireplace there, designed by Stanford White in between diddling teenyboppers all those years ago."

She stood, rebuked, and moved to the bar to pour herself a cognac, then admired the fireplace, though she hated herself for following his suggestion.

A few minutes later, he grunted and stirred himself from his reveries. "I think I've got the glimmer of something, but I need to experience it first. The trip, I mean. You brought samples?"

She nodded and retrieved a vial of the blood from the room's mini-fridge.

"I'm quite happy being me," he said. "This won't make me a philanthropist or anything, will it?"

"We've had time for only limited testing. As you can imagine, it's hard to be thorough under the circumstances. But based on my experience, and on the experience reported by the sample group, the effects are subtle and powerful, but not long lasting," Louisa said.

"It's safe then?"

"It's a derivative of vampire blood, Auscor," she said, exasperated, but then stopped, embarrassed when she saw him recoil slightly at the familiarity. "I mean, Mr. Kingman, sorry. We don't have data on blood-borne diseases associated with the undead. Until a few months ago, I didn't even know they existed."

"Fair enough," he said. "Nothing ventured, nothing gained."

With a shrug, he popped open the sample tube and downed the contents with a flick of his wrist, grimaced, and then picked up the bottle and drained the champagne to chase the bitter blood.

Scowling at the combined taste, he stared at his watch. "It's not working," he said impatiently, but he was speaking only to himself because the second hand on the clock froze, the room split apart into reflective shards, and he was gone from himself, floating supine on a river of velvet and shadows.

Gliding along, he felt time rearranging itself around him, breaking down into a series of video screens — tiles really — that swirled like sparrows, then like a tornado, assembling themselves into a tunnel of activity around him, inviting and propelling him forward and backward and onward. Each screen showed some scene from his life, things that were and things that might have been.

Energy crackled from his fingertips in lavender bolts of lightning, stretching out into a web of potential and power that reached across time and space and joined them together into one thing and pushed them apart into everything.

The collection of regrets and triumphs that was Auscor Kingman throbbed and swirled and pulsed toward a circle of light in the distance that grew more intense until the shielding of his sadness from it became all-encompassing. Just as he felt his beliefs and doubts brush against the very horizon of eternity, felt the pull of a permanent dissolution into disembodied certainty, the light flickered and dimmed and he was falling, careening down, gaining weight and dimensions, tumbling in a blur until he landed in his own body with a jolt.

He was surprised to find himself on his hands and knees on the floor, panting, and also surprised to find that at some point, he had ejaculated.

Louisa was bent over him, worried.

"Whoa," he said, looking up at her.

"Intense, isn't it? Are you okay?" she asked.

He had to think about the answer. "I'm not sure." His vision was still all fireworks, and he had a fleeting sense that there was a much, much deeper meaning to life than his grubby efforts to concentrate wealth. But as he waited for his heart to slow down, the old pedestrian thoughts of economic dominance began to creep back in.

"Hmm, I stand corrected. This is more than a simple narcotic, as I originally thought," he said, not caring that the front of his pants was clearly damp. "A drug that gives you temporary access to a deeper sense of meaning? Yeah, I think we can make some money off this."

Louisa helped him stand. He smiled cruelly and popped open another bottle of champagne. "Imagine a nation, a planet even, full of dead-end worker bees slaving away in dead-end jobs to earn a paycheck that will never, ever keep up with the cost of living. And with no hope of advancement, no hope of breaking the cycle, mired in debt and servitude until the day they drop from old age and exhaustion only to be replaced by their children."

"That sounds a lot like the world we live in now," she said, confused.

"Yes, it does," he said, smiling broadly. "Now imagine if every one of those disposable sets of ambulatory skills had access to a drug that convinced them life had some deeper, secret meaning."

He let the words sink in as Louisa wrestled with the implications.

"Yes, think it through," he said, twirling his finger in the air like he was running an old-fashioned video camera. "The drones would pay us for the privilege of medicating away their doubts and dignity while they work themselves into an early grave."

He cackled manically, and then caught himself before lurching into stereotype. "Seriously though, we can turn a profit while ensuring that the makers, the doers of this country, this planet, have a ready supply of human resources, the fucking takers, mindlessly trudging to and from whatever job they have, convinced they are part of something special."

"The drugs make an unbearable situation seem bearable, thus prolonging it indefinitely, and big business benefits?" she asked, seeking clarification.

"Exactly. There will be distribution challenges, of course. We can't exactly get FDA approval. We may have to powder this shit and mix it into an energy drink or something. Sell it through head shops." He licked his lips. "We have to get that bitch back."

"I have some new tests in mind, and ideas on how to keep her blood flowing until we can synthesize the necrotopes," Louisa said, already growing excited by the scientific possibilities of delving back into her theory of consciousness, abandoning thoughts of anything else.

Auscor stood, excited, and pulled out his phone, dialing his money man in New York.

"Don't talk, just listen," he said. "I need more. Five million. I'm on to something that could change things forever. No, forget about aging. We can figure that out later. I'm talking about something bigger than immortality. I'm talking about capitalism on steroids."

FIFTY

Tucker watched Rurik light Lizzie's cigarette. Her hand trembled and Rurik reached out to steady it, touching her wrist gently, as she leaned in to catch the flame of his lighter. Tucker's heart skipped a beat, waiting to see what would happen next. He was relieved to see her turn coldly from Rurik and look up at the moon as she exhaled. But his relief gave way to anxiety as he realized Lizzie was not looking for him either.

Rurik moved closer to Lizzie, but she was intent only on smoking her cigarette. Lenny fidgeted uncomfortably on the deck, a semiautomatic rifle leaning easily against his thigh, as he whispered into a cell phone to June.

"I'll be home as soon as I can," Lenny said, with a furtive glance at Tucker. "And go ahead and make up that extra room, okay honey? I think Rose might ought to stay with us in the bunker for the next few nights. Tell her I'll even eat some of that homemade vegan chili."

Elita stood next to Tucker. She was wearing a man's oversized Western shirt with the sleeves cut out as a dress and a rogue Western belt held tight around her tiny waist and fastened by an ornate silver buckle. The sides of her breasts peeked out of the loose armholes when she moved and her feet were bare except for a turquoise ring on her left pinky toe.

"Finally," she said mostly to herself. "Tragedy has molded a real queen. It gives me hope for our future."

Tucker looked at her, realized it was his shirt she had turned into a fashion piece, and was poised to throw out a retort, but the words got caught in his throat and a sheet of pain slipped across his face.

She sensed a flush of anger and despair and sought out the source, surprised it was coming from Tucker. She thought again of the frailty of humans, but then an image of Virote slipped into her thoughts and she could almost understand. Her shoulders sagged. This moment must be torture to him.

"You will owe me," she said quietly to Tucker as she walked over to Rurik, shaking one of her clove cigarettes free. She clasped her hand around his, urging him to flick a flame to life, then held it to the tip of her cigarette and drew in hard.

"I'm bored," she said, exhaling a cloud of sweet smoke. "I wish to leave this town immediately or find a way to be less bored."

"I intend to leave tomorrow night," Rurik said. "You may come with me. I will take you wherever you wish."

"That's not soon enough to relieve my boredom," Elita said.

"Do you have any suggestions?" Rurik asked.

"Feeding on a human is always diverting," she said. Faster than the eye could follow, she had her arms around the neck of one of Rurik's human guards. The startled man dropped the shotgun as she pulled his quickly blanching face close to her own. "This one will do nicely," she said.

"Leave him be, Elita" Rurik said. "He is under my protection."

Elita released him her hold on the man and hissed theatrically, causing him to lurch backward in fear and stumble off the deck. "Then you must entertain me," she said, petulantly.

"You are like a cartoon vampire," Rurik said.

She slid her arms around his waist and nipped at his neck. "Can a cartoon do this?"

"I can still smell our lovely Virote on you," Rurik whispered. Elita's breath caught slightly at the sound of her dead lover's name.

"Did you know how much she loved chamomile tea at night?" Rurik asked. "The last thing I gave her each night was a cup of hot tea. So like a child, and yet so very much not like a child in other ways."

"Perhaps she needed the tea to wash the taste of you out of her mouth," Elita said.

Rurik smiled slightly before answering. "It matters little now because she is dead and gone and you are alone again as you and your cold-blooded kind always shall be. No tribe, no connections."

Lizzie listened passively to the conversation, growing tenser by the second. She took one last drag from the cigarette and crushed the butt beneath her shoe.

Tucker watched her movement so intently that it became painful to her, oppressive. He crossed the rough pine deck to stand by her side.

Lizzie met his eyes as he approached, then quietly took his hand in hers. Tucker felt the entire universe existing between the touch of their entwined fingers, and when she slid her hand farther down his wrist, touching the inside of his palm with their secret signal, he felt as if he would faint with desire for her.

"Let's get out of here," she said.

He nodded, clasped her hand firmly, and led her off the deck. Rex followed behind, his toenails *clickety-clacking* against the wood planks of the deck, happy in the knowledge that the three of them were leaving, and that perhaps there would be a more regular supply of kibble in his future.

"One more night," Rurik said to their retreating backs. "Elizabeth, I give you one more night. It is time for you to behave like an adult, a leader."

Tucker turned around abruptly, his face flushed. And there it all was, unable to be contained. The bottled-up rage about everything — the death, the evil, the things he had done for love, and for what, he now wondered. For what? All of it burst from him like a homemade bomb, ragged and unpredictable.

"Go to fucking hell you bastard!" he yelled. "You assholes have ruined our lives, and you ain't taking one more thing; you ain't taking my Lizzie. She's mine. Mine!"

Tucker was gripped in the vise of a blind rage unlike anything he'd ever experienced, not even when Travis disappeared. It was a tortured emotional mix of passion, anger and despair that culminated in his singular wish that Rurik would die tonight, forever and by his hand.

Rational thought fled and, powered by instinct, he dove headlong at a surprised Rurik, hitting him low on the legs and toppling him to the ground.

He punched Rurik on the chin and, from across the deck, Lenny thought he heard bone crack; that would not be on the vampire, he thought.

In the heated exchange, small details stood out to Lenny like the dancing light of Elita's eyes as violence flared up, and just how sculpted Rurik's chin really was, like a marbled statue in a Greek art museum. He noticed all of it calmly as he readied the thermite grenade in his jacket pocket and slipped the safety off his machine gun, pointing it — and the stream of wood-tipped bullets it could unleash — directly at Rurik.

Tucker pushed Rurik's shoulder down, and placed his knee against his neck. Elita flew across the deck and pinned two of Rurik's guards against the railing, her hands poised to tear out the veins now pulsing in fear in their necks. Tucker drew his gun, pushed the barrel against Rurik's forehead, and cocked the hammer.

"You know I could kill each of you now, correct?" Rurik said calmly from his prone position.

"We'll all go into that Meta thing together," Lenny said, brandishing the grenade with his thumb holding the spoon down, looking at Tucker. "This ain't how I planned to go out," Lenny said, "but at least I'll take a Russian asshole with me."

Tucker pushed his knee even harder against Rurik's neck and willed his finger to pull the trigger, imagining the heavy slug tearing through the undead skull.

Rex growled and snapped at the vampire, but Rurik lay perfectly still, except for his eyes. He sought out Lizzie and saw sadness and clarity in her face when their eyes met. He nodded slightly.

She turned toward Elita, who was holding the two guards and hoping blood would be forthcoming. "Elita, let them go. Everyone stand down. Please."

No one moved. Rex whined softly.

"Please, Tucker, get off of him," she said. She walked over, pushed the gun away, and steadied Tucker to his feet. "Lenny, go home. Elita, find your food and entertainment elsewhere."

"Don't be so sure you could have taken me, you undead asshole," Tucker said.

"Come on, Tucker," Lizzie said. "You cracked your knuckle. Let's get it taken care of." Her heart felt heavy, and the fact they seemed destined to skate forever on the razor edge of violence saddened her beyond belief.

She led him up the steps of the trailer and he paused. "Anybody comes through this door tonight, I'm shooting a stake through their innards," Tucker said, slamming the door. Rex, stuck outside, looked confused and barked.

Tucker opened the door and let him in. "Except for Rex, of course. But nobody else."

FIFTY-ONE

Tucker sat on the bed, his back against the trailer wall. Rubbing his aching hand, he listened to the clanging of ice ricocheting against metal and muffled voices from the other room.

"This should do the trick," Jenkins was saying. "I venture a bit of this as well."

"Think I should take him to the ER or something?" Lizzie asked.

"That would be some distance from here. I believe for minor injuries, up to and including the loss of a limb, cowboys prefer going to the local large animal vet," Jenkins responded dryly.

Tucker winced, but knew it was true, thinking back to the time Dr. Near patched him up after his first run-in with the undead. Lizzie walked into the bedroom holding a metal bowl full of ice cubes in one hand and a bottle of whiskey in the other.

At the sight of the bottle, silently, Tucker forgave Jenkins for the vet crack.

"This is for your hand," she said, setting the bowl down next to him.

"I'm fine," he said, thrusting his left hand into the ice. "Damn, that's cold."

"And this is for your head," she said, handing him the bottle. Tucker popped a piece of ice into his mouth, crunched on it twice, pulled out the bottle stopper and poured a shot into his mouth.

He handed the bottle to Lizzie and pushed his injured hand deeper into the ice. Lizzie took a long swig and then dabbed her lips, put the bottle on the nightstand, and then stretched out beside him on the bed.

"I just remembered, I really don't like whiskey," she said. "How's the hand? Do you need more ice?"

"What I need is for you to stop taking care of me; I don't need mothering and you got enough on your mind," Tucker said, already feeling ashamed of his outburst, and awkward, but he was damn tired of that Russian slinking around leering at Lizzie.

She smiled, a thin effort. "I like taking care of you. It makes me feel human. It's really all I have left."

Tucker took a deep breath, hoping maybe it would help stem the growing fear that his strength was slowly being sucked out of him, like a tire with a pinprick leak, now finally getting close to flat. By his reckoning, loss and sadness had piled up nearly as high as the love between them, and the dead-even weight of passion and tragedy teetered now in an uncertain balance.

Lizzie rolled over across the bed toward him, reaching out and stroking Tucker's face gently, her fingers running over three days of stubble. Her hand was shaking slightly and she looked at him with hungry, searching eyes.

"You are still Lizzie," he said. "And we are going to make this work."

"You keep on saying that, but I don't really think you believe it anymore," she whispered.

For a moment, neither of them spoke. Finally, she forced a smile and sat up. "I think it's time," she said.

He wasn't sure exactly what she meant and felt words catching in his throat as she pulled his hand from the ice, water dripping onto his jeans.

"Oh my God, your hand is frozen," she said, holding it between her hands.

"It is pretty cold," Tucker said.

"Let me warm it up," she said, slipping his hand under her shirt. They both sighed as he timidly cupped her breast.

It had been many weeks since they last made love. It was on their wedding night, which seemed a hundred years and a million tragedies ago. The lovemaking was awkward, because of her swollen belly, but enthusiastic. The last good memory before the attack on their wedding.

After returning to LonePine, neither made overtures for sex, waiting for some sign from the other that it was time and that they were ready. Instead, Tucker bathed and bandaged her tenderly after each sunset and again before every dawn. The minor wounds were healed, and her hair was growing back, but the deeper scars were slow to repair.

She curled in close and her hand slipped under the waistband of his jeans, the heat from her palm warming a passion in him.

"Are you sure?" he asked. He was struggling to control a wave of need, and felt if they could just do this, just break through, it would be enough to, not erase, but maybe rebalance the joy in favor of the loss.

She nuzzled his ear, and then sat up and pulled her blouse over her head. Tucker's heart stopped at the beauty of her still-full breasts, but his heart also broke a little, seeing remnants of needle marks scarring her belly and arms. He leaned in to kiss the narrow valley between her breasts, pulling her gently back down to him.

But as he looked into her eyes, he knew he'd got the signs wrong. She wasn't just making love, she was saying good-bye to the life she wanted, the life that could never be. He had to try to stop her.

"I love you so much," he whispered.

"Me too," she said. "I always will, and only you. Don't ever forget that. From the moment I first laid eyes on you back at that rodeo. You were so handsome then."

"Then? You saying I ain't handsome no more?" he asked, breathing in the honey scent of her.

"Ain't is not a word," she said, smiling.

"That *ain't* an answer to my question," he said, pressing his lips against hers. He felt his entire soul spill into Lizzie and also a sense of finality. It fueled his passion with desperation. Lizzie felt it too, and kissed him back deeply. A flush spread across her cheeks as she fumbled for his belt and unzipped his jeans.

He moved on top of her, pushing her skirt up around her waist, and when he entered her, they gasped at the power of their union, the sheer physical joy and the naïve hopefulness arising from the fact that there in the darkness of their current existence, they could still become one.

Tucker pushed deeper, and Lizzie felt her skin come alive, her breath quicken; she wanted to crawl inside Tucker, to see the world through his eyes. She wrapped her legs around his waist, pulling him closer, as they moved together and she looked into his eyes.

His eyes sparkled with tears, some mixture of relief and anger and pleasure, and she was crying too. Her heart opened up, grief spilled out and light flooded in behind. At that instant, they climaxed together, and for a moment, forgot everything of the past and believed only that their future together was possible, even inevitable.

Not wanting to let go of the feeling, they clung to each other, holding on to emotion with the stillness of their bodies. Slowly, their breathing returned to normal, and Lizzie reluctantly unwound their limbs and snuggled next to Tucker, resting her head on his chest.

As the minutes ticked by, Tucker fought to keep his eyes open, an effort not lost on Lizzie.

"It's okay," she said softly. "You sleep."

"I don't want to lose even a single minute with you," he said drowsily.

"Tucker, it's nearly two in the morning," she said. "You haven't slept in days, with your relentless watching over me. Sleep for a little while. You are merely human, after all."

The hint of humor gave Tucker a tiny ray of hope and a glimmer of confidence that maybe things would turn out okay, that their life together could be normal, after all. What was it all those psychologists said? If you act like you are happy, you will be happy. Why not act normal, he thought. We're just like any other cowboy and vampire who have suffered tragedy after tragedy.

"Maybe I'll just rest my eyes for a minute," he said. "I am pretty damn tired."

He leaned over and pushed the button underneath the table by the bed.

"Alerting security?"

"I'm never gonna let you down again," he said. "The perimeter is one thousand percent secure. Lenny saw to that. We beefed it all up these last few days. This is our new normal."

He opened the drawer in the table, pulled out the Casull, laid it on top of his chest, and shut his eyes. "Just for a minute or two, okay?" he murmured.

"I'll wake you up, I promise," she said.

"Do you need to drink first?" he asked, pointing to the bandage on his inner arm.

"I can wait," she said.

Within minutes, Tucker was softly snoring. Lizzie pulled on her blouse and skirt, slipped out of bed, and walked quietly to the bedroom dresser.

She pulled out two oversized books from the top drawer, the vampire bible and the ledger, placing them both on top of the dresser. She delicately fingered first one then the other, appreciating them for their beauty and history, even as she despised them for the dark history recorded in their pages.

The bible contained the vampire mythology, all the way back to the era of Lazarus, the first of their kind, raised from the dead by the hand of Jesus. In what she had come to think of as the evil twin of Jesus, the story of Malthus was also told in this bible, the prophet who rescued the vampire gene from the reptilian line and bestowed on a chosen few the power to turn humans with the latent genes into vampires. He also charged them to fulfill their destiny of consuming evil to give room for human good to triumph.

She shuddered at the memory of when she first learned all this, months ago, bound and gagged at the feet of Julius and a much different Elita.

Lizzie managed to push the buried image from her mind but there was no hiding from the fact that the bible contained the prophecy that put all this insanity into motion.

With the loss of her son, there was no clear answer to the prophecy of a new savior. As predicted, she had turned a full human, but that was when she was still pregnant, and she wondered if the power existed in her, or in her unborn son?

The nine tribes would insist on an answer, of course. The respite Tucker and Lizzie felt tonight would be short-lived. What human would become the test case for her powers this time?

Perhaps a stranger. Or perhaps the tribes would engineer a situation in which she would be forced to test her power by turning Tucker. Or Lenny. Or even June. Whoever it was, there was no guarantee she could turn them. She had failed before.

Rurik was right. It was time to make a decision, but for different reasons than he thought. She would not continue to put Tucker and everyone around him in jeopardy. LonePine, a place that against all odds now felt like home, would require constant protection, relentless fortification. Once, she idealistically assumed her existence would ensure the town's survival, but it seemed the opposite was true. Perhaps she was ensuring its eventual destruction.

Lizzie closed the bible and turned her attention to the ledger, leafing through the now-familiar pages carefully. The ledger contained thousands of years of vampire history. While the earliest pages were covered with scripts she did not recognize, about two-thirds of the way through, familiar names and events from the parallel human history appeared, including some mind-swimming secrets about humans who collaborated through the years with the species, along with vampires who passed as prominent humans.

The last time she opened the ledger, she glued her mother's letter into it. Lizzie touched it now tenderly, brushing her fingers over the familiar handwriting. She sighed. It was time for a new entry.

Lizzie knew her own future was uncertain. Yet she wanted the world, even if it was only the vampire world, to know about their son. He existed. Jacob was real. In the human world, he was merely a shallow grave in a remote Wyoming cemetery. There, he would soon be forgotten, in a decade or even a century. This could not happen. If she had to rely on a vampire legacy to embrace and celebrate his existence, that would have to do.

Silently, she told Jacob she loved him, and would always love him. She felt a throb in her breasts as they contracted again, drawing the sustenance for a now-ghostly child back into her cells. Lizzie put both books inside a backpack.

"Why are you packing up those two vampire books?" Tucker asked quietly from the bed.

"Jenkins needs to protect them, and I want to add Jacob to the ledger."

"You don't know he was a vampire."

The silence was heavy, and then Tucker realized what she was really doing. She was packing. Running. He stood, naked, and wrapped his arms around Lizzie from behind, speaking softly.

"You're planning on leaving me, ain't you?"

"I'm thinking about it."

"Why? It don't make no sense. Not now."

"The perimeter will never really be secure," she said out loud. Unless I leave, she finished in her thoughts, leaning against him and drinking in the warmth of his body. She felt her hunger rising, triggered by the nearness of his blood.

"I let you down," Tucker said. "I can see why you'd stop loving me."

"It has nothing to do with that," she said. "You did not let me down. If anything, I let you down. Not just once, but over and over again. And it's hard to see how any life with me wouldn't be more of the same."

Lizzie allowed herself a moment of imagining what Tucker's life would be like if she left. It would take a while, but eventually, he'd find someone else. A rich, handsome cowboy, he'd have his pick, she thought. Maybe Melissa Braver.

"I'll never love anyone else again, so don't comfort yourself with that notion," he said, reading her thoughts.

"We have nothing holding us together now," she said. "No baby, no future. We're not the same people we once were."

"That's true, we're different, but that don't mean bad," Tucker said. "I'm begging you, don't do nothing hasty. We've got all the time in the world. We can talk things through. Figure things out."

Lizzie wriggled out of his embrace. "I'm just tired," she said. "Tired and disappointed. But mostly tired. Of all this."

Tucker caught her by the arms to look into her eyes. "You should be tired. We've been through a lot, and that likely won't change, but that's the deal. Sometimes when you love someone, you have to be willing to sacrifice. I know what I've signed up for here," he said.

"How much should you sacrifice for the person you love?" Lizzie asked. She looked at him with a quiet sense of desperation.

"Everything," Tucker said. "You have to be willing to sacrifice everything."

She nodded, lost in thought. "Maybe I'm not the woman you thought you knew," she said. "I used to be a regular person with regular worries, and do you know what I am thinking about right now? As the man who loves me is trying to help me? I'm thinking about how I'm going to kill her, that doctor, and how I can make him suffer forever."

He choked out a laugh. "Don't think vampires are the only ones with a bad side. I've been thinking about killing Auscor and his entourage since the day I found out he was behind all this," Tucker said. "I just wanted to make sure you were safe before I thought too much more about it. We are of the same mind."

"What have we become?" she asked, her voice burdened with sadness.

"People pushed too far," he said. "That's all."

He pulled on his jeans and reached for a shirt. Despite her sadness and fear about their future, her breath caught in her throat at the sight of his naked body; somehow the recent scars and bruises made him even more attractive, as if each one was a peculiar witness to their love. "We can be on the East Coast by the time you come back to life tomorrow night," he said. "Rex is getting real good at traveling."

Rex perked up at the mention of his name but, with no movement or treat forthcoming, settled back into sleep, soon snoring gently the way only old dogs can.

"We don't need to leave LonePine," she said. "I have a plan."

FIFTY-TWO

Lizzie watched over Jenkins's shoulder as he navigated the website.

"Is this the correct amount to allocate to the new fund?" he asked. "Transferring such a large amount makes me quite nervous."

"Will it cover what's needed?" she asked.

"By my calculations, under almost any imaginable circumstance, including another great depression, the income generated on this endowment will be more than adequate."

"Good," she said, the furrow between her eyebrows deepening. "The agreement must be ironclad. Ironclad. Do you understand me?"

"I've registered a business expressly for this purpose," he said. "Those who agree to participate will be rewarded handsomely," Jenkins added. "How long should the agreement be in effect?"

Lizzie looked at Tucker, who was bent over another laptop while Lenny talked quietly into a cell phone.

"Best-case scenario, make it ninety," Tucker said. "You never know what miracles modern medicine might come up with."

"It'll be a miracle if he makes it a year," Lenny said, cupping the phone.

Jenkins finalized the transfers and set up the accounts with a few more attentive taps on the keyboard.

Lizzie paced nervously across the living room of the double-wide. Rex followed her every step like a canine moon trapped in her orbit. Every minute or so, she leaned down to scratch him around his ears, and whisper what a good dog he was.

Tucker's affection for Rex surged and he promised himself that after all this they'd take him up to Widow Woman Creek for a good long dog vacation.

"If and when circumstances change, we can figure out a way to divert the money to some worthy cause. Maybe one of those microloan things. Set one up here in LonePine," she said. "Or give it to the county vet."

Rex shuddered and gave a nervous *woof*.

"Don't worry, Rexie, I'm not taking you to the vet," she said, with a tentative laugh. It sounded foreign to Tucker, and harsh, like it was coming from a place in her he had never visited.

"A microloan program in the dying West. Now that's a good idea," Lenny said, taking his turn to pet Rex as Lizzie paced by with him in tow. "Folks around here sure could use that. A save-the-endangered-cowboy nonprofit."

"Are you done with your part?" Lizzie asked.

"Just about," Lenny said. "I got a few more calls to make to some old friends, but you should have the people in place by tomorrow night."

"In perpetuity?"

"Forever is a long time, but as long as the money's there, the work will be done. Turns out he's kind of hated.

Didn't take much arm-twisting to get folks to sign up."

"Beating him at his own game," Tucker said. "The ultimate revenge."

Lizzie smiled and, despite the circumstances — plotting someone's ruin and what felt like a new and dangerous distance growing between them — Tucker's heart swelled at seeing her happy, no matter the reason. He wrestled down the tiny voices warning him that they were both running close to an irreversible red line.

"What about her?" Jenkins asked. "The doctor?" He managed to make the word sound about the same as 'rotten turd.'

"I have something else in mind for her," Lizzie said. "You ready, Lenny?"

"Yep," he said, hitting the 'connect' button on his phone. He waited a beat, and then spoke quickly.

"Starting tomorrow, they'll be staying at the Grote Airfield House outside LonePine," Lenny said. "The money better be there. Like I said, twenty grand. And they don't want any more violence. They just want to talk. Bring the doctor." He disconnected and dropped the phone on the table.

"You realize he would have given you significantly more for the information?" Jenkins said.

"Sure I do," Lenny said. "But that lowball ask was more in keeping with their misperceptions of us redneck types. I was playing to character to get them here faster."

"That's a wrap," Lizzie said. She felt her legs grow weak, her thoughts scattered, as the sun threatened to peek past the horizon.

Tucker followed her into the room, holding her hand as she lay down on the bed, preparing for her daily death. She stared deeply into his eyes as the wave crept up from inside, and with a surge of energy that flared behind her eyes, she was gone.

Tucker knew he should be used to watching her die each morning by this time, but it still froze his heart a little, watching Lizzie go. There was always a nagging worry that each death was the last one, and he couldn't help but wonder if she'd come back to him at sundown.

He moved to the small windows in the double-wide, checking the blackout curtains to be sure not a single ray of light could sneak in.

As she swirled away, Lizzie could see him watching over her, but was pulled by the pinprick of light far in the distance. She felt the light, and heard it too, and smelled the sweet cleanliness as it moved closer to her. She left Tucker, the cords of his love still palpable, but thinning, as they always did, with her ascent.

At the border of life and death, as her consciousness raced to enter the Meta, she sensed the threads of Jacob's identity in that soft light before her, a faint but distinct presence. Even consumed by sadness, she felt him reach out to her, and encircle her with compassion, and a new wisdom descended on Lizzie, a truce of sorts with the pain of her existence.

As Lizzie moved fully into the Meta, Jacob's light dimmed, and two final truths pushed their way into her dissolving sense of self: Jacob had been human, like his father. And Tucker, the man she would love eternally, was also the man she now had to leave behind forever.

FIFTY-THREE

The phalanx of armed former soldiers moved cautiously through the sagebrush, some of the fragrant plants as tall as their shoulders. In lockstep, the group of highly trained professionals, each man adrift and abandoned by a native country that once formally sanctioned their violent talent, now scanned the darkness with silent intensity. They continually checked their weapons, keeping their fingers on triggers.

Even though she was scared, Louisa — who was at the center of the knot of soldiers, along with Auscor — couldn't help but marvel at the gaudy arc of stars splashed overhead, the smell of the sage and the depth of the rich, soft soil they passed over. In some places, her feet sank down into the loamy earth as if it had recently been plowed.

With three dozen highly trained professional soldiers around them, each armed to the teeth with high-powered assault rifles, crossbows and thermite grenades, Louisa felt silly for being scared at all, but images of the aftermath in the cannery were still fresh.

The destruction of his property was explained away as the result of a meth lab explosion. It seemed a group of well-armed white supremacists, explaining the presence of so many, many assault rifles, were squatting in the abandoned factory to pursue their illicit activities. They were all killed in the blast and burned beyond any hope of recognition.

The locals were shocked, of course, but not shocked enough to prevent themselves from contributing quotes to the local paper about the scourge of drugs in the coastal town of Astoria.

The truth, of course, was much worse, and Louisa and Auscor watched the grainy video footage capturing the horror, and their own well-timed escape, together over several glasses of Oregon Pinot gulped down to calm their nerves.

The vampires were animals — incredibly strong, fast, smart animals — that left a charnel house of twisted limbs and drained husks in their vicious wake. Blood flowed like ink, gleaming in the black-and-white video, and she knew the picture of Mark, begging for his life with his lower jaw missing, would haunt her for the rest of her days.

If they survived the night.

"You know this is a trap, right?" she whispered to Auscor, as they slipped quietly through the sagebrush.

Auscor was unexpectedly scared too, but the strain was compensating for the fear with a crazy kind of energy and he looked at her through wide, red-rimmed eyes. "It's not a trap if you know it's a trap," he said, with harsh bravado.

The CMC mercenary next to him held his gloved finger to his lips to shush them. He and his crew were eager to exact revenge on the cowboy and his undead allies for their unprecedented assault on the Controlled

Marketing Corporation office, making fools of them in New York, destroying the cannery and, it was presumed, having something to do with the an entire missing team. But they were professionals, all veterans of active combat, holding to a credo that under fire, discipline equals salvation — even from vampires.

The group advanced cautiously and in a loose square formation, unconsciously modeling their movement on a brutally efficient strategy perfected by Greek warriors of days gone by. On each corner, a soldier with finely calibrated motion-sensitive goggles scanned the Wyoming flats with a focus bordering on manic. Any motion — they learned the hard way that vampires had no body heat to register — would be instantly translated into a splash of color and warrant a hail of bullets, arrows and flames. But so far, nothing.

"We should have just flown in," Auscor said. "It is an old airport after all."

The captain sighed. "We've been over this," he whispered. "They would be expecting that. A plane or chopper is an easy target. Now please be quiet until we get there. We never should have brought you along at all on a seek-and-destroy mission."

"I keep telling you, it's not a seek-and-destroy mission," Auscor said. "It's a seek-and-secure mission. Possibly a seek-and-secure-and-maim-a-little mission. But they wouldn't let you get close without me along."

The night was cloudless and the moon made it easy to see the target ahead. The cluster of old buildings was hard to miss.

In the earliest, heady days of air flight, the US Department of Commerce built a network of landing fields, many carved into the flat, open spaces of the West, in case commercial aircraft flying along airways between major cities ever had to land in an emergency. One of those, the Grote Airfield, as it was known, was in LonePine.

It was decommissioned in the 1960s, and the old buildings, rough towers and slowly narrowing stretch of field were all that remained after that distant Washington, D.C. decision — shadows of history, comfortable in its slow, lonesome decay.

The degrading buildings hosted a series of transient ranch families through the years, each turnover marked by a fresh coat of paint on the buildings and towers — once orange, then bright blue and finally faded red, the colors now mixed in the splintered hue of decades of hard winters and brutal summers.

When Auscor received the call from Lenny, two CMC surveillance experts who had been hiding out in The Westerner Motor Lodge, one of two hotels in LonePine, motel for weeks as part of the contingency plan were immediately deployed to watch the old airport buildings.

They spent the next two days camouflaged in tan ghillie suits to blend in with the patchwork of grasslands and farmed fields, spying from the top of a distant plateau through spotting scopes. They watched as Lizzie and Tucker arrived, and then stayed. Only the cowboy and the target were inside, they reported. And a mangy dog.

In the call, Lenny told Auscor that Tucker and Lizzie wanted to avoid more violence. But Auscor didn't believe them. You don't succeed in business by trusting anyone. He made them wait an extra two nights and days to give his men time to observe. But no one — not even Lenny, the paramilitary nut job who started the whole thing, or the slutty vampire who seemed to pose in front of the lab cameras as she chopped his men to ribbons of flesh and splinters of bone — had come or gone in the days or nights since. Maybe they were serious.

The group paused at the edge of the runway, hidden in the rough hedge of sagebrush, and trained their weapons on the house, where inside a flickering light cast two shadows against the flimsy window shades.

Two men and a woman from CMC quickly assembled a mortar, calibrated it and stood ready to level the house at the slightest provocation. Another fired up a shoulder-launched surface-to-air missile, just in case they brought in reinforcements from above.

Inside the house, Tucker peered nervously through the window shade. "Think they are out there?"

"Yes," Lizzie said, simply and without doubt. "I can feel them."

"I guess he didn't come alone like we asked?"

"No. There are many of them," Lizzie said. "But we knew he wouldn't come alone."

"Think he's gonna just blow this place up? That would really put a crimp in things for us."

She smiled, but the kind that lacked all humor. "They are here for me. They think my blood will help them make drugs so people can live forever."

"They are kind of right," Tucker said. He had the lever action 30-30 on the table and his dad's .454 Casull in a leather holster around his waist. The weight of the cartridges in the bullet loops caused it to ride down low on his bony hips.

"Not in the way they think," she said. She looked at her toenails, freshly painted pink, then at Rex, who was curled up on a doggie bed in the corner. He waggled his haunches when he realized she was looking his way.

"How are we going to play this?" Tucker asked.

"We need Kingman and Burkett in this room," she said. "Nothing else, and no one else, matters."

Outside, a flare came arcing into the yard from the shadows. It lit the buildings up in a synthetic, blinding, flickering glare. "Hello the house," a voice called.

"This is it, then," Tucker said, with one last look back at Lizzie. She nodded, and he leaned the rifle against the wall just inside the door and cracked it open. "Don't shoot," he said. "No one here but us."

"Yeah, we know," Auscor said, impatient and jittery from adrenaline.

"Come on in," Tucker said. "We need to talk to you and the doctor."

"We'll talk, all right," Auscor whispered under his breath. "How do we know you won't just kill us?" he shouted.

"Unless you are stupid, I'm guessing you got too many guns out there for that," Tucker yelled back. "And I know you and your hired muscle have been watching us," he said. "No one has come in or out since we got here." He looked down at his phone, which showed no service. "And you've been blocking our cell phones, so you know we can't call the cavalry."

Lizzie listened to the back-and-forth, feeling her anger rising, and thinking that if she were a good person, a good mate, she'd let Tucker play this out as he saw fit; she would trust that together they would be better at solving this than either one of them acting alone.

But when she heard Auscor's voice, and imagined Louisa next to him, her filters evaporated. Be damned, she thought. It will all be damned, I'll be damned, but I will have my victory.

Lizzie pushed Tucker to the side and snatched the door open. "Kingman, stop fucking around out there," she said. "I know you want my blood. You aren't going to kill us. Now come in and let's talk. Negotiate. You are supposed to be some kind of a big-shot businessman. I've got the commodity you want, so let's hash out a compromise. I don't want to spend the rest of my time being hunted by you. No one else has to get hurt. We can make a deal."

"Yeah," Auscor snorted under his breath. "The deal is, you will be the headwaters of my fortune, the cowboy will be dead and this Podunk town will never know what happened to you." He rubbed his hands together. "Right. A deal. Okay, I'm coming in."

"Bring the doctor. This may get a little technical," Lizzie said.

"I'm bringing a bodyguard with me too. And trust me when I say, they have orders to blow this unwiped shit-hole of a building down if anything goes wrong. And they'll drop a nuke on LonePine. They'll blame it on terrorists, of course, but it'll be your fault."

"Got it. Nuclear bomb," Lizzie said, looking at Tucker wistfully. "You really will do anything for money, won't you?"

"It's the only reason to do anything," Auscor shouted. "I'll be on the radio the entire time," he said, tapping his earpiece. "No funny business."

He nodded at the captain, who, with his machine gun up, advanced out across the yard and stopped at the door. When nothing happened, he nodded and Auscor and Louisa scurried across to join him.

The captain led the way in, his gun trained on Tucker, then on Lizzie, who sat impassively behind a dusty table. Rex began to growl low in this throat.

"Sit, please," Lizzie said. Auscor raised a single eyebrow, and grinned.

"Fuck the sitting. Let's end the charade here," Auscor said. "We have you surrounded. The only way your cowboy lives is if you come along with us willingly. We need you alive to keep your blood flowing, and the point of negotiation is how comfortable you will be until we can synthesize the, um, whatchamacallits."

"Necrotopes," Louisa whispered, staring at Lizzie, mesmerized.

Even though her hair was still cropped short and her frame thin, the female creature was healthy and filled with energy, a far cry from the weak, emaciated thing she had last seen.

Lizzie looked into her eyes with smoldering hatred. "You killed our child," she said, and Louisa blanched.

"An unfortunate accident," Auscor said. "Certainly not our intent. You can make more."

"It doesn't work that way," Tucker said.

"Fine," Auscor said. "A tragedy then. But let's not allow a little accident to come between us and what has to happen now."

"Yes, by all means, let's talk about what happens next." Lizzie said. "Atonement, and a settling of scores."

The temperature in the room dipped.

"Don't be foolish, you're surrounded," Auscor said.

"Actually, you're surrounded," Lizzie said. During the conversation, she let her senses wander out across the night to the slaughter taking place. Adrenaline spilled out into the edges of the Meta, hearts labored and stopped, vampires glutted on blood and rejoiced. Not a single shot was fired.

"In fact, it's already over," she said. "I don't know why you thought I would ever be alone; I have an entire army of vampires at my command."

Auscor and his bodyguard were fixated on Lizzie's regal, impassive face as she spoke. The ratcheting of metal on metal brought them back to their senses. It was the hammer on the Casull being cocked. The big gun was in Tucker's hand and pointed at the mercenary. "Ease that gun down, son. No one else has to get hurt."

But someone did have to get hurt. Tucker could read it in the man's eyes. The soldier tried to swivel the machine gun up and around, but Tucker was ready and pulled the trigger. The gun bucked in his hand and roared in the confines of the old airport house, causing Auscor and Louisa to flinch, and causing Rex to leap forward, anxious and whining.

The bullet caught the man in the chest. His body armor kept the bullet from punching a hole through his spine, but the force briefly stopped his heart, cracked four ribs, and knocked him unconscious into the wall.

No one moved in the ringing silence.

Tucker slipped the pistol back into his holster.

"How did you…?" Auscor said.

"My blood is more important to the vampires than it could ever be to you," Lizzie said. "Without me, they cease to exist. Your petty schemes almost resulted in a mass extinction. Rurik and a dozen of his tribe have been buried in shallow graves around this property since before we called you. Content to lie in wait in the dirt, hungry and pissed, until you arrived. Elita too."

As if on cue, the door swung open and Elita dropped a pile of bloody, twisted rifles on the floor. "They never fired a shot," she said cheerfully. "All dead. We'll be waiting outside."

She was wearing a prim and proper pink dress and sweater ensemble that would have been at home in the 1950s, with a matching Jackie-O style pink pillbox hat and satin gloves, the fingers shredded and bloody. She was covered with dirt and spattered hair and bone fragments. She picked the unconscious mercenary up from the floor with one hand and dragged him outside. "I've got one more," she said happily.

"Please don't kill me," Louisa squeaked.

Lizzie smiled. "I'm not going to kill you, Dr. Burkett," Lizzie said. "Quite the opposite. I'm going to run a little test of my own. I need to know if the power to turn is in me, or if it was in my child you killed."

"Our child," Tucker whispered.

Lizzie tipped the table over as she walked to the woman, catching her by the neck and driving her back against the wall. She pinned the doctor there, terrified, and then curled her fingers around the woman's windpipe.

"Sometimes, the quest for knowledge requires certain sacrifices," Lizzie said, echoing Louisa's own words from the lab. "I wouldn't expect you to understand."

Even as Louisa tried to find the words to beg, Lizzie opened the woman's throat with a savage yank. A shower of blood sprayed out as Louisa gurgled her protests and began to slump into death.

She bit deeply into her own palm and opened the flesh, then pushed her hand into the woman's wound. Louisa grew pale, twitching and shaking. Lizzie focused her thoughts and flared the necrotopes to life, willing them to bond with the dying woman's blood.

There was a crimson swirl of disembodiment as they were both transported to the Meta. Lizzie's anger transformed the experience into a murky, pain-tinged nightmare of dark, roiling clouds and sickly, jaundiced lightning. She towered over the life force of the woman, now cowering and shrinking and trying to hide from the moment.

"You cannot escape me," Lizzie said. "This is your existence now." She focused her thoughts, willing a flash of light into the darkness.

Louisa moaned in terror.

"Now return to your new life," Lizzie said.

She waved her thoughts and sent them both crashing back into their bodies. Tucker was holding Lizzie and watching a horrified Auscor.

When Louisa opened her eyes, Lizzie glared at her. "You wanted to study a vampire so badly?" Lizzie whispered savagely. "Practice on yourself. Now leave this place, or I will stake you in the sun."

Louisa held her hands over the gash in her throat, feeling it already knitting together, and tried to shriek, managing only a wet gurgle instead. She ran outside on unsteady legs past a highly amused Elita.

"They'll let just anyone be a vampire these days," Elita said.

Tucker slammed the door shut behind her and he and Lizzie turned their attention to Auscor, who shrugged, resigned to dying.

"That's pretty horrific," Auscor said. "And kind of fitting, I guess. Am I next?" he asked, already thinking how he could use it to his advantage in the business world.

Lizzie shook her head. "No. Nothing like that for you," she said.

"Pity. Will you just kill me, then?"

"I wanted to," Tucker said quickly. "I still think we should. But Lizzie has something worse in mind."

"What? Torture? Pain? I'm at the end of my rope here, I've got nothing to lose."

"You killed our baby, you threatened the world, and all for money," Lizzie said. "It's a fate worse than death for you."

"What could possibly be worse than death?" Auscor asked, with a growing sense of panic.

"What you don't know about me is that I have more wealth at my control than you can possibly imagine."

"I doubt that," Auscor said. "I can imagine a lot. That's why I wanted to, you know, use your blood."

"Even your dreams of wealth are impotent and feeble," Lizzie said. "I could have given you what you wanted a hundred times over just to leave us alone, and never even missed it. I would have given everything to you in exchange for the life of Jacob. But you didn't even ask, you just ruined everything."

"I don't get where this is going," Auscor said. "Are you trying to make me jealous?"

"She's trying to say she owns you now, you dumb fucker," Tucker said.

"I bought your debt," Lizzie said. "I bought your money men, and your mad men. I bought your identity. I bought everything about you. You are ruined and gone, a ghost, and nothing more. I will live forever, and you are no more."

"You can't keep me down," Auscor said, still not comprehending. "I'll be back."

"There's no 'you' to come back," Lizzie said. "You have disappeared."

"How can you make me disappear? I'm famous."

"You're a sniveling asshat," Tucker said.

"You are already gone," Lizzie said. "Starting today. Apparently, you died in that explosion in Astoria. You must have been checking the property, or maybe you were there for the meth, we'll never know. They found all the evidence they need. You dropped off the radar right after that. No one has seen you since. Even though someone has been using your card, booking rooms in New York and flying around."

"But Dr. Burkett…"

"Is no longer a reliable ally."

"What about CMC?"

"They've gotten their asses handed to them every time we cross paths," Tucker said. "It's not like they are anxious to keep this little chapter alive. Besides, we bought them too."

"Those unfortunate men and women out there took your contract to the grave with them. Everyone knows you've been going a little crazy these last few years," Lizzie said. "And you've been off the grid for a week now. It was easy making you disappear. The life you knew is over."

"I don't believe you; it's impossible," he said.

"Leave this place. Find a job as a dishwasher. Or a greeter at the Buy More. Or live on the streets. You were willing to sacrifice everything, including your morals, for profit. You lost. Now live with the consequences."

"I'll rebuild."

"No, you won't," Lizzie said. "You're not getting me. You'll never have a credit card again, never have a bank account, never have a Facebook page, never own a phone, never sign a rental agreement for a shitty little apartment next to the bus station. We hired someone, several someones, to do nothing but track you and destroy anything you try to do. You are persona non grata until the day you finally decide to end it all and steal a gun and blow your brains out and return to the Meta knowing your life was nothing but a failure."

"Now get," Tucker said. "Get on out of here before I come to my senses and put a bullet in your spine for good measure."

He jerked the door open and Auscor walked out into the yard where a group of pale, ghastly vampires stood silently, watching him, their faces smeared with blood.

"Let him pass," Lizzie said, and Rurik bowed in her direction, leering sideways at Tucker.

FIFTY-FOUR

"I have to tell you something," Lizzie said. They were driving back to the trailer in Tucker's truck. The back was filled with dirty, blood-splattered vampires, including Elita and Rurik. "I've never liked country music."

"That's, uhm, random," Tucker said, reaching down to turn off the radio. "And okay, I guess."

"I've had enough of all this," Lizzie said. She was trying hard to stay focused on what she knew had to happen next.

"We can listen to anything you want," Tucker said. "I mean, only a couple stations come in, but…"

"That's not what I'm talking about, and you know it," she said. "This life, it will never work. The violence, the death. I've had enough."

"Be careful what you say here," Tucker said.

A sad, empty ache was growing in the pit of his stomach and spreading out into shallow breaths and cold, sweaty palms. "We always said we could make it through anything, as long as we had each other."

"Yeah, well, we were wrong," Lizzie said.

Her heart was breaking like a piece of obsidian dropped from a great height as she lied to him. Her mind was made up though. Tucker had been right that night in the trailer — it seemed so long ago now —

though it would kill him to know his words had given her the strength and conviction she needed.

Sometimes when you loved someone, truly loved them, you had to be willing to sacrifice everything. And she would sacrifice everything for him now. It would be easier for him if he believed she no longer loved him.

"Darling," he said. "We've been through a tough few months. This last week alone would've killed most people."

"I'm already dead," she said. "I just think my mind finally just caught up to my body. I'm dead and there's no room in an undead life for a cowboy."

Tucker gritted his teeth and stared straight ahead. "I know you don't believe that," he said.

She looked out the window, trying to hide the tears flowing around the edges of her lies. "There's nothing left. The best part of us died in Astoria." That part, at least, was true.

"I can't believe that," Tucker said. "I won't believe it. Something good was taken from us, no question, but we can get through it. We can make this work."

"A cowboy and a vampire?" she scoffed. "We've got the whole world stacked against us."

"We've ridden down a lot of rough trails, Lizzie, but this shouldn't be the end, this can't be the end."

"It is," she said, her voice as cold and flat as a toppled gravestone. To keep him alive, to protect him, she had to make it convincing, but the effort was immense. Watching him watch her kill their love, seeing the hurt and pain dim his eyes, was like a red hot cleaver through her heart.

He pulled the truck to a stop outside the trailer, and took her hand in his. "You once told me you thought only weak people could be happy, and that you wanted to be complicated," Tucker said. "This is complicated, this love we have, this life we have. And it makes us both happy. Don't throw us away."

That almost did it. His words almost wrecked her resolve. She wanted to throw herself into his arms and beg him to hold her and never let go, to find herself resurrecting every night beside him and together to dare the world, dare the vampires, to try and come between something so real, so powerful, so truly immortal.

But she knew it was selfish, a little girl fantasy. If she stayed, he would die, caught up in some undead intrigue or another mad scientist horror movie. She loved him, and in the real world, love meant making sacrifices. And he could never know the sacrifice she was making.

She squeezed his hand gently, looked deeply into his eyes, and leaned over to kiss him. "I loved you Tucker. I truly did."

"Then why are you doing this?" he asked.

"Because our love is dead, just like me. And you are alive." She squeezed his hand again, this time hard enough to make him wince. "It's the right thing, and you know it."

Rex was whining softly, picking up on the momentous swirl of emotions.

"That is not true," Tucker said. "It's exactly the wrong thing."

"You always were stubborn," she said.

"That ain't true neither."

"Ain't is not a word," she said, choking back a sob. "Be safe, and think of me fondly," she said. "And take good care of Rex." She petted him softly and he let out a small, nervous bark.

Lizzie jerked the door open and climbed out of the passenger side. "Rurik, I want to be in the air by dawn."

The Russian leapt to the ground and dusted soil from his lapels. "I do not understand."

"I am leaving," she said. "To Russia for now. My life here, this life, is over."

"Don't do this," Tucker said, stepping out of the truck. "Please."

"Stay out of affairs that do not concern you," Rurik said, a sticky, gloating triumph sliding into his words.

Tucker drew his pistol in a smooth, practiced motion, aimed it at Rurik's face, and cocked the hammer. "Keep talking, you commie son of a whore."

"My people will kill you before the bullet even strikes my face."

"You seem to think I care," Tucker said.

Elita leapt to the ground and snarled up at the Russian vampires, who were already starting to stand in the back of the truck and making ready to kill the human. "Whoever touches the blood bag dies in pieces," she said.

"Tucker, put the gun away," Lizzie said, stepping between him and his intended target so that the barrel was aimed right at her heart. She gently pushed the gun down. "This is not a shooting thing."

"It feels exactly like a shooting thing to me."

"It is time for us to stop pretending," she said. "I need to be with my own kind; I need to be protected. I need to stop hiding and finally assume the role destiny has shackled me with. And I need you to let me go, to forget about me and get on with your life."

"Those are two different things," Tucker said. "You may leave me, but I guarantee I won't ever forget you, and I won't ever quit waiting for you. We belong together."

She pecked him on the cheek and traced her fingers through the stubble along his jaw, then spun and walked toward Rurik's car.

"Jenkins," she called over her shoulder to the elderly butler standing bewildered on the porch. "Please take care of my belongings and join me at your earliest convenience. Elita, you're with me."

Elita looked at Tucker with wide-eyed incredulity. She felt a pang of something unfamiliar. Pity. For a human. The words snaked out before she could even stop them, and felt dirty and strange in her mouth. "I'm sorry, Tex," she whispered as Lizzie opened the back door of the car.

Rex, assuming another trip was in order, followed along and hopped into the backseat and fell over slowly as Lizzie tried to pull him out, petting him again and burying her face in his fur.

"Watch over her," Tucker said to Elita. "If she ever needs anything, you know where to find me."

"Yeah, Shithole, Wyoming," Elita said.

"Rex, get your ass over here," Tucker called out, rage flooding in to fill the cavernous heartbreak of grief. "She's done with us."

Rex jumped down, looking back and forth between Tucker and Lizzie, confused, until she slammed the car door closed.

Rurik pulled away in a roar of tires and gravel. Lizzie watched through the back tinted window, tears streaming down her cheeks, as Tucker walked stiffly up to the trailer and went inside without once looking at the convoy of luxury sedans speeding off down the dirt road toward the airport.

FIFTY-FIVE

Tucker sat on the front porch of the trailer in one of the rocking chairs they'd bought together. He'd thrown the other one out into the yard. Rex was curled up at his feet.

A cup of strong coffee in a blue enamel mug was steaming on the railing, and he poured a healthy splash of whiskey into it. Rex looked up at him in dismay.

"Yeah, I know it's too early for booze," he said, "but right now, I need to think less."

Rex, unsatisfied with that answer, flopped his head down onto his crossed front legs and continued watching the road, waiting for Lizzie to return.

As the sun tipped up over the edge of horizon, Tucker imagined Lizzie, now cold and dead, on the private jet — no doubt next to Rurik, that bastard — on a flight to Russia. He allowed himself the pleasure of letting one hot tear escape from the tangle of crow's feet at the corner of his eye, and then tamped the sadness back into the hole in his heart and buried it, but only shallowly.

"It's for the best anyway," he said, not for a second believing it. "I always did like the sunrise."

His cell phone rang and he snatched it up, sure she'd changed her mind. But it was Lenny.

"Hey, Tucker," he said. "I heard they cleared some flights out of the airport. Did the Russian go back?"

"Yep," Tucker said. "And took Lizzie with him."

There was a long silence while Lenny tried to make sense of it. "Did you try to stop him?"

"Wasn't no reason to," Tucker said. "She wanted to go. She left me. Said she didn't have no life here anymore."

"Clearly she wasn't thinking straight," Lenny said.

"Seemed pretty damn straight and clearheaded to me," he said. "She said get on with my life and forget her."

"So what are you going to do?" Lenny asked.

"I bought myself thirty bottles of whiskey," he said. "I'm gonna drink one every day for the next month, and if that don't kill me, then I am going to do exactly what she said — get on with the rest of my life."

"And forget about her?" Lenny asked dubiously.

"I never said that."

"All that other business get sorted out?"

"Yep," Tucker said. "It was a long, ugly night."

He paused as a trail of billowing dust indicated someone turning onto his road from the highway. His heart surged at the sight, but as the vehicle drew closer, he could see it was a rental car — a sky-blue economy two-door — with two passengers. Maybe three.

"I have to go. Someone's coming."

"You need backup?" Lenny asked.

"Naw, I think those days might be over." He broke the connection and stood, letting his hand brush against the butt of his pistol instinctively. The car was driving too fast for the gravel road. The person in the back, he realized, was actually a dog. A big dog.

Rex started barking, unsure of the visitors, but his tone took on something verging on excitement as the car slid to a stop in the front yard, kicking up gravel and dust. A young woman hopped out. She was lean and confident, and stretched slowly to unkink hours on the road. She nodded in his direction. "Howdy, cuz. Long time no see."

"Wil," he said, "What the hell are you doing here?"

"Sake, do your business," Wil said, and a regal, somber Akita leapt out of the car and loped toward the house, then circled around it on a security check.

Rex scrambled up to his feet and chased after her, stumbling and yipping and trying to keep up. Sake tried her best to ignore him, completing a circuit and, after finding no sign of trouble, returning to Wil's side. She bent down to pet her.

"You ought to try checking your messages once in a while," Wil said. "I've been calling for three days."

"My phone was on the fritz," he said, thinking about the jammer at the air field.

"That made it kind of hard to tell you about my little surprise," Wil said. "I've got someone who wants to hi."

The passenger door opened and a man stepped out. Even with all the years passed, eyes dulled by injury, and loneliness and extra weight from institutional eating, there was no mistaking Travis.

"My brother," he said, smiling broadly.

"Good goddamn," Tucker said, stunned. "Travis." He stumbled down the steps and caught his brother around the neck, hugging him tight.

Tucker felt the stirrings of joy, but also a cascading overload of confusion and mistrust that any feeling of happiness could penetrate his heavy heart. He struggled to push everything aside, every minute of the last few months, to let this miracle in. Travis was recovered. Nothing would take away from that — not now, at least. Tucker held Travis even tighter.

"I knew you would find me," Travis said, smiling inside Tucker's embrace. "I knew you wouldn't leave me there forever."

"Ahem," Wil said, clearing her throat. "Travis, what did we talk about in the car? Like, the *only* thing we talked about in the car for three days. I was the one who found you. Me. Your cousin, Wil."

Tucker broke his embrace long enough to catch Wil around the waist and hoist her up in the air. Sake growled and tried to insert herself between them, tripping over Rex in the process. She bared her teeth and snapped at him savagely and he yipped and retreated, but not far.

"I owe you, Wil," Tucker said. "Big-time."

"It was my pleasure, Tucker. Best use of my particular skill set in quite some time," she said. "Now put me down before my dog kills that mutt of yours. And if he gives her fleas, I swear I'll never forgive you."

She looked around the desolate landscape. "Speaking of communicable diseases, where's this lady of yours I've been hearing about?"

"That's a long story, Wil," Tucker said. "The most important part is the ending. Come on in, I'll fix you a little breakfast and tell you about it." He looked at Travis. "That sound okay?"

"I like pancakes," Travis said, his face deeply serious.

EPILOGUE

Two months later

Portland, Oregon

Auscor sat on the sidewalk holding a cardboard sign that read 'Trying to rebuild my life. Anything helps. Seriously, anything.'

He was talking to himself, a new habit that fit in well with his general low opinion of others, and muttering and laughing too. But it was not the kind of laughter provoked by happy things.

A wispy beard lined his sunken cheeks, like mold on a desiccated apple, and he stank so badly he offended his own sensibilities almost as much as those of passersby, who provided a wide berth.

He watched any approaching person like a coyote watching a mouse or a prospector sizing up a stream.

There was gold ahead — a family of tourists hurried down the sidewalk in his direction, trying to get to their nearby hotel without having to talk to him or any of the other street people staking out their corners.

As the parents marched their brood past, herding them forward and shielding them, at least temporarily, from the realities of life, the youngest child — a girl with a fuzzy monkey backpack — veered from the group to talk to the homeless man.

"What's your job?" she asked him.

He looked at her expectantly, trying to ascertain if she might have any money. "My job, right now, is to borrow money from investors like you," he said.

"What do you want the money for?" she asked, fishing a wrinkled dollar out of her monkey's pouch.

"Do you know what venture capital is?" he asked.

She shook her head no.

"It's money I can use to start a business, and then pay you back twice what you gave me, or more."

She pursed her lips in concentration.

"You would be the third investor of the day," he said. "If I can find five thousand more of you, I know I can turn this around."

The girl's mother realized her youngest charge was lagging and swooped in like a protective hawk, clutching her by the arm. "Don't bother the man," she snapped.

"I'm not bothering him," the girl said indignantly.

"She really isn't," Auscor said. "She's helping me. Any chance you could add to her investment?"

"No," she said. "Amy, keep your money."

"But mommy," the little girl said. "I want to be an investor. Can't we help him?"

He looked at the family pleadingly. "Yeah, Mom, can you help a man out?"

"So you can blow it on booze?" the father said, coming back to grab the tail of the monkey backpack and tug his daughter, protesting, farther along the sidewalk.

Auscor sighed and watched them leave.

Things had not gone well for him since staggering out into the Wyoming night. He thought about that moment often and was coming to the realization that maybe, just maybe, that bitch and her inbred cowboy had outsmarted him.

With no money, no credit cards that worked, no friends, no spouse, he found himself quickly disappearing from the world. That first night, he managed to hitch a ride all the way to Salt Lake City. Along the way, he borrowed ten dollars and used it at an Internet café where he found all his e-mail accounts deleted and his bank accounts locked out.

He borrowed a phone after pleading with the owner and called Tommee, his former assistant.

Tommee, who had been warned, ostensibly by someone from the FBI, that impostors would try to play on Auscor's good name, was not having any of it. A coroner's report, he said, made it clear his former boss — who'd apparently left him $1 million in his will — was killed in Astoria. *Don't call me again*, Tommee said.

Auscor opened a new e-mail account and wrote to every address he could remember. He spent the night sleeping behind a Laundromat. When he logged in the next morning, the account was disabled. That was the moment he knew he had underestimated his opponents.

Things got worse after that. A lot worse.

Now he was sitting on a sidewalk in Portland with an abscessed tooth, spiking high blood pressure and less than two dollars to his name. His only hope, rapidly dimming, was to make it back to the East Coast to prove his existence in person to Tommee before life on the street made him disappear completely.

On the plus side, he knew from firsthand experience that, if he failed, the Meta would not be so awful when his time finally ran out.

He put his cap upside down on the street in front of his cardboard sign, dropped the change he had collected into it in hopes of attracting more, and watched as a skateboarder whizzed by and snatched it up, hat and all.

He picked himself up and then pushed his cart toward the shelter, hoping for a bed and a cup of scalding hot coffee.

LonePine, Wyoming
"Dammit, Travis, stop laughing at me."

Tucker picked himself up out of the mud, ears ringing and spitting out dirt and manure from the fall he took.

They were at the local jackpot roping where his degraded skills were all too evident, but the fact that they were even there at all meant the darkest days had passed. Thirty bottles of whiskey were sacrificed on the altar of his pain, the empties lined up like soldiers around the edge of the dump and blown to pieces with Dad's .454 Casull. Now he was back to just regular maintenance drinking, the hurt and heartache balled up and stuffed into the furthest reaches of his heart.

Wil and Sake stayed for the first few days, until his self-destructive behavior and crazy stories forced her to head back to Portland, leaving Lenny to look after him.

This roping was his first human activity in months, and it was not going well.

He fell because he was riding a new horse, a handsome, solid Appaloosa named Oklahoma Joe on paper, but Tucker called him Cocoa because of the splash of white and brown dappling his hindquarters.

Cocoa took cowboying seriously and responded almost before Tucker could give him a cue, which is why it was the third time Tucker had been unseated and the third time the calf, the intended target of his rope, was running free.

Cocoa was the only thing Tucker used the vampire money on since Lizzie left him. Correction: Cocoa and a new folding knife, because his had disappeared.

Travis was adjusting to being home, with pancakes every morning and his own room with a TV. He was sitting on the fence, laughing uproariously at his brother and slapping his knee, asking Rex if he saw Tucker fall.

In two months, Tucker had seen only one vampire — Elita. She stopped by to check on Rex, she said, to see if he needed a new home. Tucker was touched, but would never say it. They drank together for three straight nights and neither mentioned Lizzie once. She disappeared like a ghost, along with a local teen arrested on child pornography charges but out on bail.

He stood and dusted off his chaps and let his gaze travel out of the arena, across Travis and Rex and then past the meadow and the sagebrush and the foothills and all the way to the mountains lighting up as the sun started to sink.

Rather be miserable here than anywhere else, he thought. Even though he hurt something fierce, at least the view was nice.

Near Gdov, Russia

I hate this place, Lizzie thought. She was looking out over the still and dark waters of the lake. Rurik's summer home was both luxurious and heavily fortified on the banks of Lake Peipus. Centuries ago in another life, it was where Rurik waged war against the German Teutonic Knights on the ice, eventually turning the invaders back. His reward was eternal life, eternal hunger.

The outlines of Rurik's story were in the ledger Jenkins brought with him after closing Lizzie's affairs in LonePine and joining her in Russia. She was sure Jenkins understood her motivation; understood, but did not condone. He had nothing to say about Tucker's mental state, only that he seemed pleased his brother was alive and home.

Rurik filled in more details about the savage battle in bits and pieces as they sat together on moonlit nights drinking silently. He clearly wanted more from her, this she knew, but the trauma, pain and grief had transformed her. She was here for Tucker, not herself, and certainly not for Rurik.

In seemingly securing the favor of the queen against the rest of the tribes, and how could he know she only accompanied him to preserve the safety of the man she loved, he had grown smaller in her eyes. He appeared to understand this, and did not press himself on her, even though his desire had become close to all consuming.

She felt it, his constancy and the undercurrent of lust. If she had anywhere else to go, she would leave.

Any of the tribes would take her in, of course, but the issue would remain. And disappearing from their world of ancient intrigues altogether would unleash an avalanche of frantic vampires sweeping into LonePine to seek her, and Tucker might not be up to that challenge.

The only way out, she feared, was a permanent and highly visible death. Solar suicide. At the present, she was far too sad and lazy to kill herself. So for the time being, she was stuck.

At least the accommodations were lovely. And Russia, with its vast, open spaces and rough-and-ready inhabitants reminded her a bit of Wyoming. She thought of Widow Woman Creek, high in the mountains, and the time she and Tucker went skinny-dipping. How she'd pleaded with Rex until he reluctantly joined them, regally putting up with the cold water and splashing and laughing, and then shook himself off and lay down on Tucker's clothes.

The thought of Tucker's naked body, his thin waist and bony hips, the heavy muscles of his shoulders and chest, his gentle hands, sent a pang of longing through her shattered heart. She told herself, again, that the fact he was alive was more important than being with him, more important than her own selfish desires. And lately, her desires were growing more intense. She lit a cigarette and refilled her glass with the last of a dusty bottle of Madeira carefully preserved from the Napoleonic wars.

A knock at the door caused her to jump and she started to fling away the cigarette, but caught herself. Only Tucker cared about the smoking, which of course was ludicrous. Vampires couldn't die of cancer, only of broken hearts.

It was just Rurik, ever-present, obliging, handsome Rurik. And he had a human with him, a young man of Royal descent from the Russian tribe. The boy trembled with a mix of fear and excitement, because he would die on this night.

Since arriving, to keep peace between the tribes and to replenish their ranks as a hedge against reluctant factions of the Reptiles, she agreed to turn one Royal each night. The tribes sent their candidates, she obligingly killed them and activated their dormant gene, and more vampires were born. Tonight was a Russian night.

The boy, or rather, the young man, was handsome in a brutal way, with a shaved head and tattoos on his arms and neck.

"It's time, my queen," Rurik said. "If it pleases you."

"It doesn't." The process was draining, but her mastery was complete, forged in rage at the airfield. She gestured. "The bathroom," she said. "Take your shirt off and stand in the tub."

The young man obliged, and she ran her hand over his thickly muscled chest, felt him shake under her touch and enjoyed the power she had over him. When the blood began to flow, she knew her desires would surge, desires that would remain unsatisfied. And she knew Rurik would once again press himself against her, testing her, and once again she would rebuff him, for now at least.

Was this to be her life? Her undead life?

With a snarl, she sank her teeth into the young man's neck and ripped the skin and flesh apart, and felt his blood squirt into her mouth. His death began to blossom in the Meta, and she reached for Tucker's folding knife to open herself up once again.

The End

If you enjoyed *The Cowboy and the Vampire: Rough Trails and Shallow Graves*, please take a few minutes to review it on Amazon or Goodreads. Or both. Or anywhere you like.

And check out *The Cowboy and the Vampire: A Very Unusual Romance* and *The Cowboy and the Vampire: Blood and Whiskey* for more of the continuing adventures of Tucker, Lizzie, Rex and the rest of the gang.

For updates, fun stuff and to connect with the authors:
www.cowboyandvampire.com
www.facebook.com/cowboyandvampire
@cowboyvamp (Twitter)
@cowboyvampire (Instagram)